Truth Will Prevail

Truth

Why I Have Been Condemned

Will

Translated by
Jamille Pinheiro Dias
Breno Longhi
Eduardo W. Portela e Silva

Luiz Inácio
Lula da Silva

Prevail

LeftWord

Offset edition first published in November 2018
Digital print edition, January 2020

LeftWord Books
2254/2A Shadi Khampur
New Ranjit Nagar
New Delhi 110008
INDIA

LeftWord Books is the publishing division of
Naya Rasta Publishers Pvt. Ltd.

leftword.com

ISBN 978-93-80118-75-8

Original title: *A verdade vencerá: o povo sabe por que me condenam*,
by Luiz Inácio Lula da Silva
Translated by Jamille Pinheiro Dias, Breno Longhi,
and Eduardo W. Portela e Silva

The publisher would like to thank Denise Tarud for her expertise and work on the manuscript.

TABLE OF CONTENTS

Luiz Inácio Lula da Silva:
A Life in Pictures

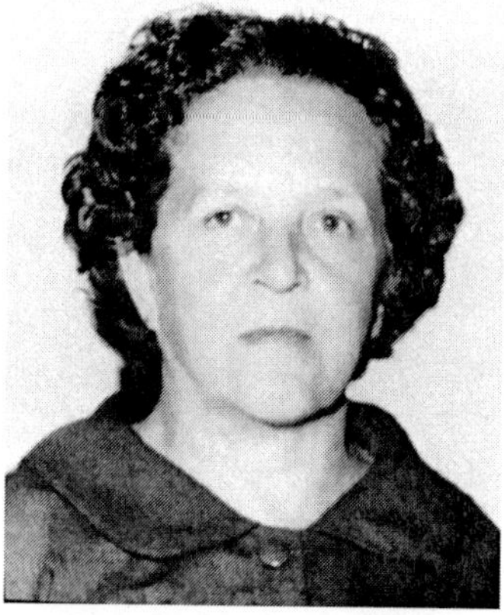

Eurídice Ferreira de Melo, Dona Lindu, Lula's mother. (Courtesy of the Silva family.)

Lula at the age of three, with his sister Maria. Taken in Garanhuns, this is their first portrait. Their clothes and shoes were borrowed from the photographer. (Courtesy of the Silva family.)

Lula's father, Aristides Inácio da Silva. (Courtesy of the Silva family.)

Lula, crouching, third from left, and Frei Chico, standing to the right with their soccer team the Náutico Futebol Clube, 1950s. (Courtesy of the Silva family.)

Lula on his graduation day at Senai, 1962. (Courtesy of the Silva family.)

Lula on the right, and his brother Frei Chico, 1960s. (Courtesy of the Silva family.)

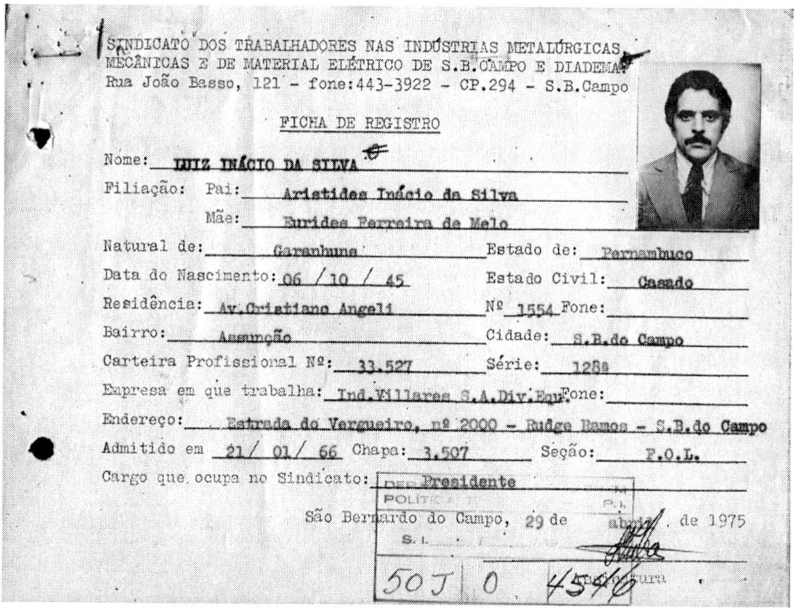

SINDICATO DOS TRABALHADORES NAS INDÚSTRIAS METALÚRGICAS MECÂNICAS E DE MATERIAL ELÉTRICO DE S.B.CAMPO E DIADEMA
Rua João Basso, 121 - fone:443-3922 - CP.294 - S.B.Campo

FICHA DE REGISTRO

Nome: LUIZ INÁCIO DA SILVA
Filiação: Pai: Aristides Inácio da Silva
Mãe: Eurides Ferreira de Melo
Natural de: Garanhuns Estado de: Pernambuco
Data do Nascimento: 06 / 10 / 45 Estado Civil: Casado
Residência: Av.Cristiano Angeli Nº 1554 Fone:
Bairro: Assunção Cidade: S.B.do Campo
Carteira Profissional Nº: 33.527 Série: 128a
Empresa em que trabalha: Ind.Villares S.A.Div.Equ. Fone:
Endereço: Estrada do Vergueiro, nº 2000 - Rudge Ramos - S.B.do Campo
Admitido em 21/ 01/ 66 Chapa: 3.507 Seção: F.O.L.
Cargo que ocupa no Sindicato: Presidente
São Bernardo do Campo, 29 de abril de 1975

50 J 0 4546

Lula's registration form as president of the ABC Metalworkers Union, April 1975. (Deops Fund/Public Archive of the State of São Paulo [Apesp])

Lula's inaugural speech as president of the ABC Metalworkers Union, 1975. (*Jornal Movimento*/Apesp)

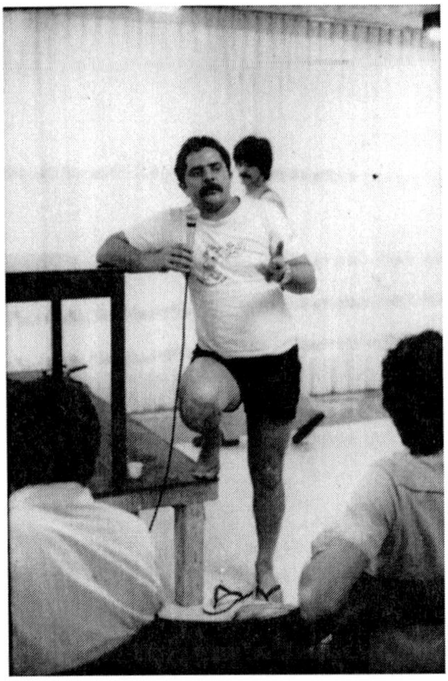

Lula speaking at the Third Congress of Metalworkers, October 1979. (Collection of the Documentation and Memory Center of the State University of São Paulo [UNESP])

Lula's departure after the federal intervention was declared. ABC Metalworkers Union, February 23, 1979. (*Jornal Movimento*/Apesp/ Collection of the Documentation and Memory Center of the State University of São Paulo [UNESP])

ABC metalworkers strike assembly in Vila Euclides Stadium, 1979. (*Jornal Movimento*/Apesp)

Speech at the general assembly of the metalworkers strike at Vila Euclides Stadium, 1980. (Collection of the Documentation and Memory Center of the State University of São Paulo [UNESP])

Workers' assembly at the gates of the Volkswagen factory in São Bernardo, May 1979. (Collection of the Documentation and Memory Center of the State University of São Paulo [UNESP])

The founding of the PT at the Sion School, 1980. Lula (left) was elected president of the party with 93 percent of the votes. (Ennio Brauns/Photo & Graphic/*Jornal Movimento*/Apesp)

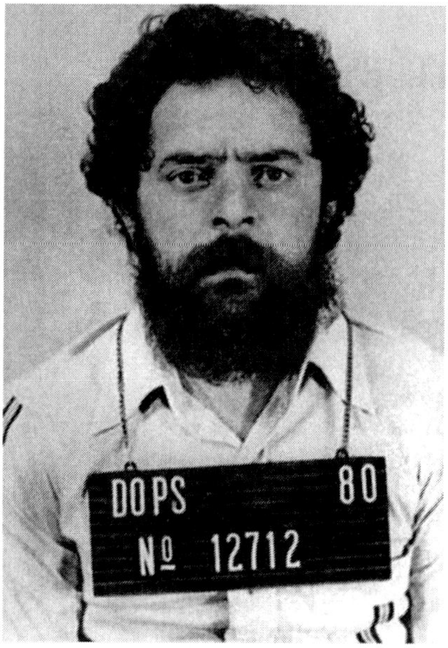

Lula was arrested in Dops, April 19, 1980, the seventeenth day of the strike. (Deops/Apesp Fund)

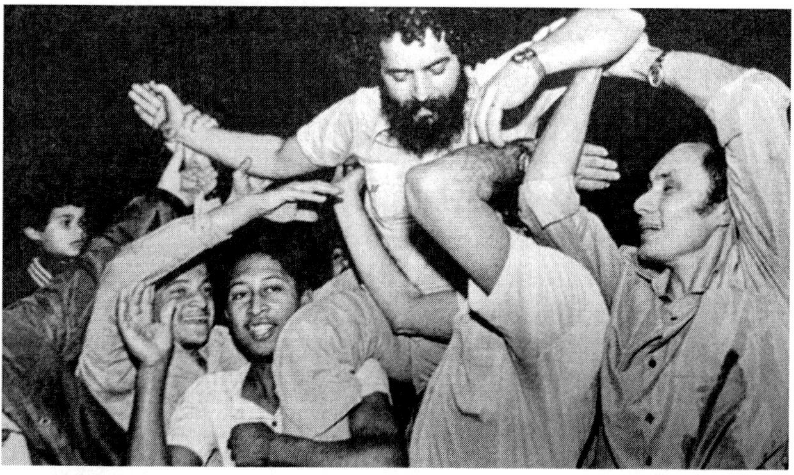
Lula celebrates the end of his imprisonment after thirty-one days, 1980. (Archive of the Lula Institute.)

A Note from Brazil

Ivana Jinkings, publisher of the Brazilian edition of this book

The appeal against Luiz Inácio Lula da Silva's conviction for passive corruption and money laundering, handed down by federal judge Sérgio Moro, was tried on January 24, 2018, in Porto Alegre. The game was already fixed when the three judges of the Federal Court of Appeal for the Fourth Region (TRF-4) confirmed the sentence and extended its duration. No proof was presented. Outside, tens of thousands of people, mostly workers and students, expressed support for the most popular political leader the Brazilian working class has ever produced. Faced with the undergoing destruction of Brazilian political and legal institutions, as well as with threats to our democracy, we decided to publish this book, which, in a way, synthesizes our reason to be.

Boitempo is an independent publishing house—it is not part of any large business group and is not linked to political parties, social movements, or religious institutions. Its sole source of income are the books it publishes. In two decades of existence, we have sought to balance our economic needs and an editorial line committed to critical thinking. We do not publish self-help books, textbooks, or literary fast food. We do not seek to comfort people with illusions. We are recognized for offering readers well-edited editions of high-quality works written by progressive authors of the most diverse trends—many of them with consistent criticisms of the Workers' Party positioning and political decisions. We do not support—as a company—this or that candidate. But we are aware that Brazil is experiencing an escalation of intolerance and prejudice, fueled by the April 2016 coup. The institutional rupture now has a cornerstone, the possible arrest of former president Lula. Regardless of whether or not we agree with his political personality or his conduct in government, we understand that the persecution against him transcends an individual or partisan matter. Confronted with one of the rare Brazilian leaders of global prominence, the Brazilian justice system has belittled its own role as guardian of the rule of law and of the Constitution, contributing to the narrowing of the democratic space. Now that Lula has been sent to jail, the country has launched into an authoritarian adventure that involves loss of rights—especially for the poorest—income concentration, economic regression, and degradation of national sovereignty.

With a profoundly democratic conviction, we have also published this book to insist that we do not want Brazil to be led by the obscurantist forces that took over the government by assault. This book represents our desire for change and an act of cultural resistance.

• • •

On Wednesday, January 31 of this year, I went to meet Lula in his office, in the neighborhood of Ipiranga, in São Paulo. He received me punctually for a scheduled thirty-minute conversation, but our talk lasted for two and a half hours. We talked about everything: the lawsuit against him, life, books, and of course about my proposal to take his testimony for what would become this book. He asked me for some time to think and to talk to his lawyers. Two days later he phoned me and said, "Let's do it!"

From then on, we created a task force to put this book together, bringing in the authors of the complementary texts and the team of interviewers. In the meetings that followed, former president Lula was open and did not hesitate to answer our questions—perhaps there had never been an interview in which he was so revealing.

Thanks are due the interviewers—Gilberto Maringoni, Juca Kfouri, and Maria Inês Nassif—supportive partners in this brief and intense journey; to Instituto Lula's José Chrispiniano, Marco Aurélio Ribeiro, Ricardo Stuckert, Paulo Okamotto, and Claudia Troiano, who did everything they could to facilitate the meetings and recordings; to the authors of the other texts that make up this volume—Luis Fernando Verissimo, Luis Felipe Miguel, Eric Nepomuceno, Rafael Valim, and Luiz Felipe de Alencastro—essential collaborations made in record time; to Mauro Lopes, responsible for the herculean task of transcribing (alongside Murilo Machado) and editing the interview; to Frei Chico and Larissa da Silva, who provided us with archival family photos; and finally, to the Boitempo team. Were it not for the dedication of this unique team, this book would not be ready at this dramatic moment of national life, which demands more than ever the unity of progressive forces.

—São Paulo, March 8, 2018

Prologue:
Birth Control

Luis Fernando Verissimo

The most unequal country in the world was not created that way in a couple of days. It was a long process, beginning when the first Portuguese, in the opening scene of our history, plundered the first native. And it continues to this day—more than five hundred years of submission to dominant and closed castes: first our colonizers, then a national oligarchy committed to keeping itself closed and dominant. The official political and economic histories of Brazil do not always acknowledge this deliberate commitment to protect the privilege and power of the Brazilian patriciate, preferring to attribute our social tragedy to some kind of damnation, to a fault of character, to the legacy of our Portuguese "discoverers," or even to the size of our territory and our climate. But Brazilian inequality is not a misfortune; it has identifiable authors, known parents. Throughout history, it has been maintained by the birth control of any left-wing option, forbidden to be born or to be raised. We have already seen how far the ruling caste is willing to go to prevent the left from flourishing. The cries of pain of those tortured by the 1964 dictatorship still echo in abandoned basements. And 1964 is just one example of a historical constant.

To this day, people still discuss whether Getúlio Vargas's government was "progressive" by conviction or by political expediency. In any case, it was one of the few times, before the PT (the Workers' Party) years, when the Brazilian "leftists" were able to approach power, even while making countless concessions not to be aborted. The first PT administration showed that it was possible to make consistent social policy without having to give in to dictatorial temptations of the Vargas era. There was income distribution—and inequality in the country began to decrease—hence the ferocious reaction of the ruling caste to the perspective of the PT's return to power, as shown in this book. The patriciate, in eternal vigilance against the birth of a viable left, has become aware of its distraction and now hurries to correct it—even with the repeated sacrifice of legal conventions and ethics.

—Porto Alegre, February 2018

Foreword: Democracy Stares Into an Abyss

Luis Felipe Miguel

When the ballot boxes for the second round of the 2014 presidential election were closed, a cycle of Brazilian political life also came to an end. The reelection of President Dilma Rousseff meant that—despite the most aggressive media campaign of demoralization against a ruler in Brazilian history, intense and uninterrupted for more than a year—conservative forces could not get the majority of the popular vote in the presidential election. At that moment, the portion of the political elite not happy sharing their power with the PT (the Workers' Party) began to study a new alternative, which included turning the tables and removing the reelected president. A broad alliance was forged, bringing together national business groups that could not tolerate the moderate measures of income distribution implemented by the government, as well as international conglomerates attracted by the prospect of denationalization of key sectors of the economy. The resentment of the middle class (including those sectors of the state bureaucracy, which paradoxically had gained much during the PT administrations) was also mobilized against what this part of the population saw as a reduction in their difference from the poor. The media had played its usual role, demonizing left-wing political groups and advocating for moralistic and authoritarian measures. The vice president's moral weakness was the final ingredient; to occupy a chair that did not belong to him, he was prepared to carry out the program laid out by the plotters of the coup. The set of events that led to the fall of Dilma Rousseff is well known. The lack of constitutional basis for impeachment and the flaws of the lawsuit have already been extensively demonstrated by the most competent jurists in Brazil and also by many of their foreign colleagues. However, the coup's agenda was never only to remove an unwanted ruler from office. Just as in 1964, but now through other methods, sacking the president was just a necessary and symbolic step to implement a program of accelerated social retrogression. This program is already underway, including the freezing of public investment in social policies (approved at the end of 2016), the suppression of labor rights (approved at the beginning of 2017), different measures of denationalization of the economy, and a severe restriction in access to retirement, a proposal that generates such a repulsion in the working class that even the parliamentarians aligned to the coup were not able to approve it.

Yet, there is a paradox in the midst of the coup's agenda. On one hand, it intends to severely limit the concessions made to subaltern groups, imposing without any negotiation a series of measures that were defeated whenever submitted to the popular vote. In the words of political scientist Wanderley Guilherme de Santos, they seek "an order of domination with no conciliatory purposes regarding the dominated segments of society." On the other hand, the designers of the coup are not willing to give up a facade of respect for the rules of liberal democracy. The memory of the 1964 dictatorship is still fresh in the collective consciousness and the distinct international conjuncture makes it costlier to opt for an authoritarian swerve without a veneer of respectability. This would also alienate part of the coalition behind the coup, whether because of the survival of a democratic impetus, or because of the fresh memory of the recent past—many politicians who supported the overthrow of Jango imagined that the military would hold presidential elections the following year and that they would be able to run (without leftist candidates, all prisoners, exiled and with their rights revoked), but soon their intentions were frustrated.

However, it is difficult to prevent the liberal democracy (with its civil liberties and popular authorization to rule) from being used to inhibit the adoption of such unpopular measures. A good example is the welfare reform: it was not approved, not because of a parliamentary majority committed to social justice, but because of the fact that, for better or worse, every politician must go through the next election if they intend to serve another term. Thus, the very dynamics of the coup forces the political class to reduce the democratic loopholes maintained as a way of legitimizing those in power. For this reason, Brazil is also experiencing an attack on civil and political rights. Freedom of expression is curtailed, with attacks against alternative media outlets, schools, universities, and research centers, as well as against artists. There is also an escalation of police repression against social movements and increasing violence against demonstrations and protests. In February 2018, under the pretext of guaranteeing public safety, the federal government promoted an intervention in the state of Rio de Janeiro, putting the army out on the streets.

There is, in general, what is being called the criminalization of the left, in which progressive political positions are no longer accepted as legitimate and are subject to persecution. The selectivity of the media and the state's repressive forces show corruption scandals as something exclusive to left-wing parties, which are then treated as "criminal organizations." More and more, civil rights are considered exclusively individual, in opposition to the collective; in this context, strikes, occupations, or even marches must be contained because they threaten the enforcement of private contracts and the exercise of the right to attend work and school. Moral conservatism sees the struggle for the rights of women and of the LGBT population as threats to the "traditional family," a social institution presented as natural and immutable, as the "basis of civilization," which, in turn, justifies any abuse in its defense.

RIGHTS AND THE RIGHT

It is in this context that the persecution of former president Luiz Inácio Lula da Silva becomes a central element of the contemporary Brazilian political conjuncture. According to all polls, the favorite candidate for the October presidential election is Lula. Regardless of the actions he would take in an eventual new term, his victory would represent popular condemnation to the coup. The lawfare against Lula has all the characteristics of an exception procedure. Its starting point already marks a break with basic principles of the rule of law: equality before the law and the presumption of innocence. Lula did not become the target of an investigation following a suspicion of improbity; in reality, police, prosecutors, the judiciary, and also the mass media began to search for anything that could be used to accuse the former president. The sentence came before any kind of proof.

The corporate media coverage, especially since the end of 2014, deserves a study by itself. Any rumor against Lula, however unreasonable, earned headlines and reports for days on end. A kind of triangulation was occurring. First, information contrary to the former president was leaked by the police or by the Public Prosecutor's Office. Then all the media turned the subject into the main topic of the time. Sometimes it was the opposite: a newspaper, a magazine, or a TV station announced the "scoop" and then the repressive forces officially endorsed the information, initiating an investigation. Finally, the third tip of the triangle would intervene: fake news websites, focused on right-wing militancy, prepared even simpler and more aggressive versions of the news, taking advantage of the credibility of civil servants and "serious" journalists. The result was the production of an environment toxic for political debate, which provides an essential service in the persecution of the left, in general, and of Lula in particular. Overcoming this system is a challenge for the restoration of some degree of democratic civility in Brazil. It is a situation in which arguments and evidence have become irrelevant and only "convictions" are valid. It is possible to speculate that the original intention behind the persecution was to leave Lula on the defensive and, above all, to demoralize him, weakening his political standing with the discovery of some uncontested accusations. However, this goal was not achieved. If voting intention polls are correct, after an initial negative impact, his prestige returned unchanged. Many believe that the lack of objectivity in how the lawsuit has been handled, the partiality shown by judges and investigators, as well as how disproportionately Lula has been treated in comparison to other political leaders, have contributed to maintaining his popularity. For those who came to power with the coup, there is no doubt that an election with the former president as one of the candidates is a very risky operation.

Therefore, the only way out was the confirmation of Lula's sentence by the Federal Court of Appeal for the Fourth Region (TRF-4) in January 2018. The weaknesses of the case against Lula were widely denounced: lack of evidence, lack of right of defense, illegal confinement of witnesses, accusation of crimes that did not exist in the criminal code, abuse of process, and bias against the defendant. The fact that the votes of the three judges were so aligned and that the media already knew the result well before its announcement also caused astonishment. Additionally, in order for the court to align its calendar with the right-wing political strategy, there was an unusual anticipation of the trial.

The maintenance of the electoral process for the next presidential election is vital to give legitimacy to the coup of 2016 and, as a consequence, to all the setbacks that will come from this situation. However, the need to prevent the favorite candidate from running makes the whole electoral process irreparably illegitimate. Therefore, the presence or absence of Lula as a candidate in the 2018 elections is the thermometer that will indicate the possibility of a negotiated restoration of the order established by the Constitution of 1988. The decision of the TRF-4 was used to show from the beginning that the former president was out of the game, familiarizing voters and political leaders with a narrow electoral scenario. The only question, according to the news imposed by the media, was whether (or rather when) Lula would be arrested. The transformation of the political situation into a criminal one would fulfill the triple role of (once again) demoralizing Lula, normalizing the 2018 elections, and showing that Republican institutions worked to perfection.

What led to this situation was the punitive downward spiral that began during the PT administrations and deepened after the coup. Two moments were especially important: In 2010, Congress approved almost unanimously—and Lula himself, in the presidency, sanctioned—the Clean Record Act (Lei Ficha Limpa), based on a popular initiative, which effectively determines the predominance of the judiciary over the sovereignty of the people. Amid the hectic enthusiasm of the media and many civil society organizations, very few voices dared to rise up against the law. It states that citizens who have been convicted without chance of appeal by the judiciary may not run for public office. The act rests on two premises: that court decisions are immune to political manipulation and that people—eternally seen as poor judge on public issues—will always be manipulated by bad candidates. Today, the Clean Record Act is what gives a formal basis to the possible obstruction to Lula's candidacy, sentenced by a biased court, with a clear political motivation.

In 2016, the Brazilian Supreme Court ruled that it is possible to arrest defendants before the final conviction. Although it is in direct opposition to what the Constitution states, the decision was based on the idea that it is necessary to punish those who, generally having resources and good lawyers, postpone a trial almost indefinitely. The fight against the impunity of some would justify the withdrawal of guarantees that benefit all. The subtext—crucial for the discourse behind the coup and mobilized in various contexts to support different kinds of setbacks—is that rights must be viewed with suspicion, as they cover up injustices. If this unconstitutional decision had not been made, the arrest of former president Lula would be a real threat.

LULA, A VICTIM OF HIS OWN SUCCESS

The lawsuit against Lula represents an essential step in the political project that sparked the coup in 2016. It is about protecting the measures implemented since the deposition of Dilma Rousseff from being repealed. In itself, this process also symbolizes the current administration's willingness to go beyond any limit to hold on to power. It was not former president Lula and his right to run in the elections that were condemned in Curitiba and in Porto Alegre. The court put an end to what was left of the rule of law and of formal democracy in Brazil. After Lula's trial, we were closer to the establishment of an openly authoritarian order.

By doubling the stakes against the former president, the coup leaders also announced their willingness to burn bridges, avoiding the reestablishment of democracy in the country. Lula, sometimes labelled as a "radical," has become much more of a conciliator. His project, based on extreme prudence and a very disenchanted assessment of the correlation of forces in Brazil, represents a non-traumatic exit to the situation created by the coup, reducing tensions and avoiding the most direct conflicts.

The "negotiated restoration" of the pre-coup institutionalism is not free from controversy—as Lula is anything but an uncontroverted figure—for the Brazilian left. The PT (Workers' Party) was born in 1980, when the military dictatorship was in the process of "opening up" to a controlled political transition. Led by unionists from São Paulo's ABCD region, who were responsible for the strikes that had symbolized the rebirth of the workers' struggle in Brazil, the Workers' Party had leaders of other social movements among its founders, veterans of the communist left, engaged intellectuals, and progressive Christians linked to liberation theology and the grassroots communities that the Catholic Church sponsored in the country. This heterogeneous group had in common their belief in more participative forms of doing politics. In its initial years, the PT believed that allowing the expression of the popular movements should be its priority, while the electoral dispute was in the background. However, the party was the victim of its own success. It is hard not to subject the rest of the political strategy in order to participate in elections and in the parliamentary game. The government was returned to civilians in 1985, a democratic constitution was enacted in 1988, and direct presidential elections were held the following year. The Workers' Party gained more parliamentary seats, won municipal councils, and became an important player in Brazilian institutional policy. Lula qualified for the runoff of the 1989 presidential elections. At that time, the party was still very hesitant to receive the support of moderate or conservative politicians, who were unhappy with Fernando Collor, a young, authoritarian, and arrogant upstart. Many considered that this reluctance was responsible for Lula's defeat. From there, external incentives and internal pressure grew, leading the party to make greater concessions and, in return, have even greater chances of electoral success.

When he finally won the presidential election on his fourth attempt in 2002, Lula already headed a heterogeneous coalition. The vice-presidential candidate was a wealthy businessman, José Alencar, affiliated with a center-right party. The electoral campaign was adapted to the model of low politicization of speech, which prevails in Brazil and in much of the world. Lula had brought to the political scene an "imperfect word," as linguist Haquira Osakabe once said, not only for using the prosody and syntax of the popular classes in the political arena, but especially for transgressing the formulas and models used by the elites and the traditional left. The Workers' Party founding discourse was based on real experiences of the workers and on the everyday struggles of social movements. In the 2002 election, however, the word was already "perfected" and ready to play—and win—the political game, as it has always been played.

In the presidency, Lula built a broad base of parliamentary support, following the pattern of his predecessors: The executive branch is a place of business, passing projects in Congress in exchange for positions and advantages. Former president Lula also maintained an economic policy that was favorable to banks, while implementing the historical demands of the party, like agrarian reform, with extreme prudence. Initiatives on sensitive agendas, such as reproductive rights, sexual rights, or media democratization, were repealed whenever the cry of more conservative groups surpassed a certain threshold.

The party chose to give up everything in order to guarantee one point: the fight against extreme poverty, through policies of income distribution to the poorest people. The greatest symbol of this direction was the Bolsa Família program, which was criticized by the right for its paternalism ("the government should teach how to fish, instead of just giving the fish away") and by the left for its merely compensatory character. However, for tens of millions of people, the program represented the difference between remaining in a situation of starvation or not. This sense of urgency—that political action must find immediate solutions to the most pressing problems of the majority of the population—led the Lula administration to adopt principles opposite to those of the early PT. It was a way of postponing the resolution of social conflicts and, in the meantime, ensuring some improvement for the poorest without threatening the privileged. According to political scientist André Singer, who became the most sophisticated interpreter of the Workers' Party strategy, what at first glance appeared to be mere capitulation becomes part of a project—very moderate, it is true, but decidedly oriented towards the country's change. Singer's main thesis is that the "weak reformism" of Lulism was not a rejection, but the "dilution" of the "strong reformism" of the earlier PT. The diluted Lulist reformism avoided at all costs confrontation with the bourgeoisie, opting for policies that, in appearance, did not affect any established interests. Critics on the left point out that such a strategy had the immediate effect of deteriorating the conditions struggling for further advances. This line of criticism does not reveal a posture of "the worse, the better," but an understanding that the Lulist path had costs.

Some of these costs were particularly high at a time when the dominant groups opted for the unilateral revocation of the pact and for the imposition of their program. The masses could not be included in the economy through the institution of socialized services, but through mere consumption (which ensured that there would be no interruption in the cycle of private appropriation of public funds, despite the introduction of new links). The predatory model of development, with high human and environmental costs, was accepted as an inevitable shortcut to improve the material conditions of the population. The market ideology was not challenged, nor did the government try to construct a social logic different from the capitalist, consequently allowing the radical right's discourse to advance even among the poorest. The chronic precariousness of many state-provided services, which the PT administrations faced very poorly, also helped to distance government from its potential base, as the 2013 protests made clear.

Among all those concessions made along the path of least friction with the ruling classes, the highest price was popular demobilization. It was the only guarantee that transformations in the Brazilian society would not exceed a very restricted range. The presence of a leftist party in the federal administration would require incredible restraint in order not to generate any kind of destabilization. Unionists and leaders of various social movements were called to occupy positions in the PT governments. While this move asserted that the state understood the demands of these groups, it also served to put the government concerns in the first place, encouraging behind-the-scenes conversations instead of mobilization as a way to achieve gains. As a rule, the main concern of the popular movements during the PT administrations was to protect the government—which, in turn, meant that the pressures on the government came almost exclusively from the right.

Therefore, demobilization was seen as support for the government. But the famous advice given by François Andrieux to Napoleon still held true: "On ne s'appuie que sur ce qui résiste" (We can only rely on what resists). By hindering the resistance offered by social movements in Brazil, the Workers' Party weakened its own base, as was evident in the crisis that ended up overthrowing President Dilma Rousseff and in the insufficient reaction to the criminalization of the left and to the lawfare against Lula. This was not a side effect and it did not happen unexpectedly. The weakening of the social movements that helped the PT in its heroic phase served to assure the capital that the moderate, pragmatic, or conservative inflection (the most appropriate adjective is still in dispute)—expressed in documents such as Lula's "Letter to the Brazilian People," published during the 2002 presidential campaign—would not be dead letter. By reducing the possibility of effective action by the sectors that would support a more radical transformation project, the model of accumulation could be maintained, as promised.

The Lulist experiment relied heavily on the belief that the institutions of electoral democracy would not be challenged, and that voting was a sufficient instrument for the political expression of the population. Whenever the government bet on expanding popular political participation, it did so by creating councils that usually had no effective power and in which the interests of dominant groups were also strongly heard. Breaches thus opened were not irrelevant and caused discomfort among conservatives—when an attempt was made to institutionalize the National System of Social Participation in 2014, there was an apocalyptic reaction, part as a strategy of agitation, part as a way to restrict mechanisms for the verbalization of popular interests and perspectives. As usual, the government chose to retreat. Broadly speaking, the Workers' Party believed that compensatory policies would be enough to win the majority of votes in the elections, while access to the government would provide the resources for maintaining the desired policies. Despite tensions and missteps, the model worked for more than ten years. Everything changed after the reelection of Dilma Rousseff. The offensive against the government and the increasingly palpable possibility of overthrowing the president led to a rapid devaluation of executive positions, which have always been the bargaining chip used to secure congressional support. With Eduardo Cunha in charge of the lower house, the legislative branch was dedicated to preventing, in practice, the exercise of the presidency.

In turn, Dilma's unconstitutional impeachment meant the revoking of the popular vote as the final criterion for the attribution of power. But Lulist bases are largely unprepared to express themselves in other ways. They turn in great numbers to the protests promoted by the former president all over the country, reiterating their support at every voting intention poll. However, they are mostly unaware of the extensive repertoire of popular struggle.

It is important to reflect upon the criticism of Lulism, just as it is necessary to reflect upon the response to it: the argument that a radical transformation of Brazil was never more than a very distant and uncertain possibility, and that, concretely, the only palpable alternative for moderate and even insufficient reforms was the unchanged continuation of the injustice that has always prevailed in the country. The debate is complex and will not end any time soon. The coup of 2016 adds a new factor to the discussion, showing that, with dominant classes as intolerant of equality as ours, even the "safe" path of extreme moderation is subject to destabilization.

A NECESSARY CANDIDACY FOR DEMOCRACY

In his statements as a pre-candidate for the presidential election, Lula—and many leaders of his party—appears to be willing to talk to those who have participated in the coup of 2016. It seems that his objective is to recreate the conditions that made the Workers' Party administration possible in the early years of the century, returning to the policy of the least possible confrontation. Some analysts—myself included—believe that this agenda is illusory and that, even if it seems to be successful at first, it will lead to an even greater tolerance to injustices and will have an even narrower margin to promote any social transformation in Brazil. However, this has nothing to do with Lula's ability to run for president. Be it right or wrong, the alternative represented by Lula's candidacy has the right to be part of the debate and to be subject to the people in a democratic election.

Forcibly barring Lula's candidacy is a clear statement that political authority must be separated from any reference to popular will. This has already happened with the unconstitutional deposition of a president and with the imposition—without any significant effort of convincing the people—of measures rejected by the vast majority of citizens. This is not, however, a banal step. It represents the deepening of a fissure opened in the Brazilian democracy in 2016: an election unable to legitimize the government that will emerge from it. We have slipped from an insufficient democracy in which inequality in access to political resources severely impaired the capacity of action, to a less-than-democracy, in which it becomes obvious that the powerful are in control of decisions still nominally attributed to the people.

Consequently, the persecution of Lula concerns not only the former president and the Workers' Party—and, precisely for this reason, the defense of his right to run brings together a broad democratic field that surpasses all of his supporters. The veto imposed on him certainly applies to any other progressive political option with actual chances of winning an election. The symbolic component must not be forgotten: regardless of the how one judges the policies adopted by Lula, he is the greatest popular leader in our history and appears, in the imagination of Brazilian politics, as a living symbol that the working class can attain power. Just as the campaign against Dilma was tinged by misogyny, the persecution of Lula goes through the mobilization of class prejudice. A central component of the strategy of demoralization is to associate the former president with goods and properties that are commonplace to the middle class, but could never be legitimately obtained by a "laborer." The reinforcement of social hierarchies—which is the basis of the political agitation perpetrated by the right wing—is accompanied by the moral panic generated by the greater visibility of feminist and LGBT agendas and by the discourse of "meritocracy," which highlights inequalities and condemns any kind of solidarity with the most vulnerable. The rupture of democracy walks hand in hand with a severe setback in the parameters of public debate in Brazil.

When Dilma's impeachment process was underway, it is possible that not every political sector—including those that already opposed the coup at the time—was completely aware of what was happening. There is no possible doubt today. There is an attempt to silence the popular voice in Brazilian politics. Barring Lula from the election is a central step toward the consolidation of the retrocession. The uncompromising defense of his right to a fair trial and to run in the 2018 elections is a dividing line separating democrats from authoritarians.

—Brasília, March 2, 2018

The Case Against Lula: How Brazilian Courts Have Failed

Rafael Valim

I intend to demonstrate to the general public some of the more serious problems of the so-called "case of the three-story condo." Former president Luiz Inácio Lula da Silva stands accused of passive corruption and money laundering for allegedly favoring the construction company OAS in contracts with Petrobras, in exchange for the ownership, renovation, and decoration of an apartment in the city of Guarujá (SP).

I will do my best to avoid the dreaded technical jargon known as legalese, to facilitate the comprehension of this text by Brazilian and foreign citizens, who thus may understand the real dynamics of events and the way the Brazilian justice system is unfortunately destroying the federal Constitution of 1988, all under the pretext of fighting corruption.

First of all, the defense of the federal Constitution and the rights and guarantees enshrined in it do not reflect any ideological discussion between left and right, *coxinhas* or *mortadelas*.[1] It is a matter of preserving the fundamental rules for social coexistence. Outside the Constitution, all that is left is barbarism, brute force, the arbitrary and violent exercise of power against the "enemies" of the moment. History demonstrates that the Constitution and the laws must be enforced in an isonomic way, that the organs of the state cannot "decide" whether to protect the rights of a certain person. Exceptions, which may be convenient to some at first, end up becoming mainstream, affecting the whole of society. The pretense of an impersonal rule of law gives way to the personal rule of men.[2]

PRESUMPTION OF INNOCENCE: FROM THE POWERPOINT PRESENTATION TO THE IMPRISONMENT BEFORE A FINAL RULING

One of the most disrespected constitutional principles in the context of Operation Car Wash is certainly the principle of the presumption of innocence. The provision establishes the simple idea that no one may be considered guilty before the issuing of a final and unappealable penal sentence—in other words, a person is only guilty after all procedural appeals have been exhausted.[3]

If all agents of the state are subject to the presumption of innocence, how can we justify the show put up by the Public Prosecutor's Office almost every week through press conferences and interviews, defiling the reputation and dignity of countless people, many of whom, after a time, are acquitted? In the case of the three-story condo, one of the most notorious cases involved the crude PowerPoint presentation made by the Public Prosecutor's Office, in which the former president appeared as a great mob boss. There is no way to justify or admit such exhibitionism, which results in serious attacks on the presumption of innocence, with the creation of a summary and unappealable judgment by the media.[4] In a democratic rule of law, charges must be pressed in a responsible manner, with the necessary balance between the right to information and the protection of the honor and the image of the accused.

Task forces formed by the police and the Public Prosecutor's Office are not only unconstitutional, but also victims of the very expectation they generate in society, to the obvious detriment of the principle of presumption of innocence. As Eugênio Aragão observes, the creation of a task force takes place with so much flair that it is under constant pressure to present results. No one creates a task force to close the inquiry. The fuss alone mortally wounds the presumption of innocence, consolidating in the public opinion the certainty that the initial theory about the alleged involvement of the chosen actors is correct, as a predictable novel plot.[5]

Another consequence of the principle of the presumption of innocence is that a sentence cannot be executed before conviction: that is, a defendant cannot be arrested before all legal appeals have been exhausted. Nonetheless, on February 17, 2016, the Supreme Court allowed that a criminal conviction could be enforced after its confirmation by the first Court of Appeals—that is, before all appeals have been exhausted. There is a lively discussion at court on maintaining this regrettable precedent.[6]

In the case of the three-story condo and other cases in the country, the explicit text of the Constitution must prevail, with the affirmation of the rule of freedom not only in favor of former President Lula, but also of all Brazilian citizens.

IMPARTIALITY OF THE JUDGE: THE INFAMOUS "PARTNERSHIP" BETWEEN JUDGES AND MEMBERS OF THE PUBLIC PROSECUTOR'S OFFICE

Another very serious problem in the criminal proceedings against Lula is the infamous and unconstitutional relationship established in many cases between judges and prosecutors. Especially in task forces, there is an open and declared "partnership" between these bodies, defying the administration of justice provided for in the Constitution, since when the Public Prosecutor's Office denounces a crime, it must be treated as a party to the proceedings, thus deserving the same treatment as the defense lawyer.

Public displays of appreciation among judges and members of the Public Prosecutor's Office, reserved conversations, or shared meals in the trial intervals are not mere details or nitpicking, but rather the final proof that there is a deep flaw in the Brazilian justice system and a clear disparity between accusation and defense.

Instead of an equidistant relationship, the prosecution receives deference from the adjudicating body, while advocacy is diminished and, not infrequently, criminalized. The case of the three-story apartment is eloquent proof of what we are saying. In the trial and appellate courts, judges and members of the Public Prosecutor's Office acted as allies, while the defense was, on several occasions, disrespected with belligerence. Suffice it to mention the fact that, in the text of the sentence that condemned former President Lula, a third of the paragraphs were devoted to disqualifying defense lawyers.

Nor can we forget the illegal wiretap of the entire law firm defending the former president, which resulted in the violation of telephone confidentiality of twenty-five lawyers and at least three hundred clients. Other clear signs of bias in the case of the three-story condo are the direct attribution of crimes to defendants and individuals under investigation, under the pretext of informing the public; the illegal disclosure of the content of intercepted telephone conversations; the participation in launch events for books with content explicitly contrary to the defendant or individuals under investigation;[7] participation in events of political or commercial nature, with manifestations contrary to the defendant or individuals under investigation;[8] not to mention, of course, the statement by the president of the Federal Court of Appeal for the Fourth Region asserting that the verdict was "irreproachable" moments after it was issued. What many people do not realize is that the principle of impartiality of the judge is not only an indispensable guarantee to every person, but is also fundamental to the preservation of public confidence in the justice system. It is an instrument of preservation of the judiciary itself. The following excerpt from the *Bangalore Principles on Judicial Conduct* is relevant: "The perception of partiality devastates public confidence, for if a judge appears to be partial, public confidence in the judiciary is eroded. Therefore, a judge must avoid all activity that insinuates that their decision can be influenced by external factors, such as personal relations with one of the involved parties, or interest in the result of the process."[9]

The disturbing bias of Brazilian judges deserved the reproach of one of today's greatest jurists, the Italian Luigi Ferrajoli, who wrote: "As a matter of fact, the elementary principles of the fair process have been and continue to be disregarded. The behavior of Brazilian judges shown here is, in fact, a clear example of what Cesare Beccaria called, in paragraph XVII of the book *On Crimes and Punishments*, 'an offensive process,' in which the judge—contrary to what he called 'an informational process,' in which the judge is 'an indifferent investigator of the truth'—'becomes an enemy of the defendant' and 'does not seek the truth of the fact, but tries to involve the prisoner in the crime, insulting the defendant. The judge believes they are losing the case if the defendant is not punished, and that the infallibility they expect in all things is therefore impaired'; 'As if the laws and the judge,' adds Beccaria, in paragraph XXXI, 'have an interest not in seeking the truth, but in proving the crime.'"[10]

In general terms, we must return to the principle of impartiality by the judiciary and, in the case of the three-story condo, recognize the obvious bias in the judgment that condemned former President Lula, thus leading to the annulment of all procedural acts.

DEFINING THE CRIME: CORRUPTION WITHOUT EX OFFICIO ACTION AND WITHOUT DEMONSTRATION OF PROCURING AND OBTAINING ILLICIT BENEFITS

According to the Federal Constitution of 1988, Article 5, XXXIX, states a universal principle of criminal law, namely: "There is no crime without a prior law that defines it, nor penalty without prior legal commitment." This is what is called the principle of legality, according to which punitive state power can only be exercised if the behavior is in strict accordance with what is described in criminal law. It means that the organs of state charged with the investigation and punishment of crimes cannot "come up" with a thesis not established in the law.

Well, former President Lula was charged with two crimes in the case of the three-story condo: passive corruption and money laundering. The act of passive corruption is described in Article 317 of the Criminal Code: "To request or receive an improper advantage, or to accept a promise of such advantage, for oneself or for another party, directly or indirectly, even when not exercising public office or before taking office."

However, the sentence and the judgment that condemned Lula do not present the elements that make up the crime of passive corruption. They acknowledge that the former president did not directly claim advantages as a result of contracts signed with Petrobras; there are no indications of an official act—an act within the scope of the powers of the public agent—allegedly practiced or omitted in consideration of the advantage received; and, finally, the alleged illicit advantage is not proven, since the former president does not own the notorious apartment in the Solaris building in the city of Guarujá.

The judges abandoned the Constitution and the law of the land and, by their own volition, edited—as self-proclaimed sovereigns—juridical rules tailored to the condemnation that they intended to impose on the former president. This example, along with so many others, should draw attention to the fact that it is not only corruption that undermines contemporary democracies, but also the systematic non-compliance of laws, even with the best of intentions. May one day society understand that, in a democratic state of law, everyone, including the control bodies, must observe the ends and, above all, the means provided in the legal order.

• • •

Although there are countless other immoralities that irreversibly jeopardize the criminal proceedings against Luiz Inácio Lula da Silva, this brief presentation allows us to glimpse the very serious situation of the

Brazilian justice system, whose dysfunctions threaten the society as a whole. Whether you voted for former President Lula or not, whether you like him or not, his rights have been grossly violated by public officials who have vowed to respect the Federal Constitution, and this cannot be tolerated.

Like any Brazilian, regardless of ideology, the former president should be treated in accordance with the law. Neither more nor less; without bias or persecution. Without realizing it, those who defend the opposite weaken themselves, because it legitimizes arbitrary choices regarding who deserves legal protection and who does not.

The most devastating fact is that the brutality that we witness every day was brought up by the judiciary itself, guilty of immoral acts such as the decision of the Federal Court of Appeal for the Fourth Region, under the report of Judge Rômulo Pizzollatti: it is well known that the criminal proceedings and investigations resulting from the so-called Operation Car Wash, under Pizzollatti's direction, constitute an unprecedented (unique, exceptional) case in Brazilian law. In such conditions, there will be unprecedented situations, which will escape the generic rule intended for common cases. Thus, since the confidentiality of telephone communications investigated in Operation Car Wash was breached in order to preserve the investigation from successive and notorious attempts to obstruct it, the secrecy of telephone communications (Constitution, Article 5, XII) may, in exceptional cases, be superseded by the general interest in the administration of justice and in the application of criminal law. The permanent threat to the continuity of the Operation Car Wash investigations, including suggestions for changes in legislation, is an unprecedented situation, deserving exceptional treatment.[11]

To conclude the presentation of this gloomy scenario, it is regrettable to note, beyond any doubt, that all these clear transgressions of the legal order serve the purpose of taking from the people the right to elect their representatives freely. It is democracy—or what is left of it—that is at stake.

—São Paulo, March 5, 2018

Lula by Lula: An Interview

With Ivana Jinkings, Gilberto Maringoni, Juca Kfouri, and Maria Inês Nassif

Luiz Inácio Lula da Silva is one of the greatest politicians in Brazilian history, perhaps only comparable to Getúlio Vargas, due to the changes he effected in Brazil. This interview was held on the eve of yet another crucial moment in his history, between February and March 2018, while the country awaited the judiciary's decision concerning his arrest as a result of Operation Car Wash (*Lava Jato*).

What follows is the result of three rounds of conversation that took place at the Lula Institute (*Instituto Lula*) in São Paulo on February 7, 15, and 28. Lula was interviewed by journalists Juca Kfouri and Maria Inês Nassif, international relations professor Gilberto Maringoni, and Ivana Jinkings, founder and director of the Boitempo publishing house. Journalist Mauro Lopes edited the text and wrote the footnotes.

Lula: Well, guys, by method, I don't censor the things I say, which is why I don't watch myself, because I always criticize what I said. I want to make you feel completely at ease. I think we have to start talking about the past, then talk about today and about tomorrow. I'll start the game . . . I'm still thinking about yesterday's goal against Cássio . . . If he had kept his hand still, the ball would not have gone in.[12] For seventy years I paid the price of rooting for Corinthians, I can't take it anymore, I'm going to switch teams.

What the hell . . . I just finished reading Galeano's book on soccer and it's extraordinary.[13] Then you understand how soccer got rotten when it became an industry. The players have no value today; they are just an advertising tool. What matters is the brand that they carry on their jerseys. By the way, what Neymar did yesterday . . . He's got some balls, right . . .?

Juca Kfouri: The Portuguese guy, right? He was not doing a lot, but then . . . swoosh. Two goals.[14]

Lula: Yes, Cristiano Ronaldo has an advantage: he knows he's not as nimble as Neymar with the ball, he knows he's not as good as Messi . . . But that's why he became a professional . . . The guy does nothing, but then he scores two goals like that. Cristiano Ronaldo once scored four goals in the same match, and when I came here [to the Instituto Lula] on Monday, a guy said: "He didn't do anything, he just scored the goals." Well, let me tell you something, just so you know how my head works in a moment like this. In a hundred years, they will say: "Damn, how did that old man's head work?" When I left the presidency [January 1, 2011], I was perfectly aware of the kind of administration we'd had in Brazil. I knew that whenever you win an election, you don't necessarily win the government, as the government is something much more powerful, it's comprised of institutions like the Department of Federal Revenue, the Federal Police, the Public Prosecutor's Office that go beyond the administration itself. But I had done everything I thought was possible, the best anyone has ever done in this country from the standpoint of social inclusion. In fact, my administration put into practice a little of what I learned in my relationship with social movements, with sectors of the Brazilian left, and with our secular aspirations . . . I want to remind you that my victory speech on Paulista Avenue was very simple; and there were people who criticized me because it was not pretentious—because usually a populist says something like: "I will put this person in jail, I will reduce that person's salary, I will . . ."[15]

No, I said: "At the end of my term, if every Brazilian is able to have breakfast, lunch, and dinner, I will have fulfilled the goal of my life." Why? Because there was a lot of hungry people in this country, no less than fifty-four million people. It was equivalent to the population of what would be the tenth biggest country in the world and they had nothing to eat. People didn't eat. I thought that was a challenge. And I thought that it would only be possible to end hunger if the poor were included in politics, if we could get them into the national budget. Because people who are hungry don't have a union, they have no political party, sometimes they don't even have a church. They don't go to demonstrations, nor do they go to Brasilia, or to Paulista Avenue. They carry no flag. A poor man's only flag is the sound of his empty stomach—the certainty that his life is screwed up. How to include these people? We needed to reach out to these people somehow. And I knew I was not one of them. I was aware that I was one of those who had food on their plates and that we had to reach out to those who didn't. When we created the Zero Hunger [Fome Zero] program, followed by the other social programs, everything was the result of things we started at this institute [Instituto Lula].[16] It was here that we conceived the Fome Zero program, here we did the My Home My Life [Minha Casa Minha Vida] program, the inclusion policies for social movements, our public safety policy, and youth program.[17] All before the beginning of my term. So the administration was putting into practice a number of things that we had learned here and in the social movement.

Often, even some members of the PT and ideologically more refined comrades thought that we had a conciliation government. For me, a conciliation government happens when you are able to do more, but you are unwilling to. When all you can do is less, but you still manage to do more, it's like the start of a revolution—and this is exactly what we did in this country. The sheer number of people we were able to include in the economy, in politics, in the organized society without a single shot—on the contrary, being the target of shots at times—is almost a peaceful revolution that was made in this country. I was aware of it and I was also aware that a portion of the population understood what we had done. I was not thinking about running again in 2014. I never thought of going back to the presidency of the republic. I was afraid . . . You know that player who leaves the team, who comes out as the best, goes abroad, and when he comes back, he thinks: "What if people compare me to what I used to be? I'm going somewhere else; I'm not going back to my old team." A president of the republic that ends his term with an 87 percent approval rating . . . If you remember, even here in São Paulo and in Rio Grande do Sul, which theoretically are the states that are more conservative in relation to the PT, I had an 80 percent approval rating when I left the presidency.[18] My idea at the time was to take the experiences I had during my administration and travel the world, trying to show poorer societies that it's possible to take steps forward. And that's what I tried to do. I thought I was going to live in peace. And I planned to live off lectures, which I think is the most decent way I can earn my living. I didn't want to be dependent on the PT, because whenever the PT paid me a salary there was criticism: "He is a professional politician" [in a lowered, dramatic voice].

Because it's a fact that a lot of people never cared about the way others live, but with me it's a permanent concern, ever since I imagined creating a political party . . . I'm not sure if you know that one of the first criticisms I received by the MR8 in Guarujá was during the 1982 campaign, when I was running for governor.[19] They went to a house that belonged to Airton Soares, on the beach of Pernambuco, which he had loaned to me, Greenhalgh, and Olivio Dutra, and photographed it; they said it was "Lula's house."[20] They even got in touch with the woman my father married and brought to São Paulo, photographed her in a poor neighborhood in Santos and published that "Lula abandons his mother."[21] The left did it all. So I always endured it, I always knew I had no quiet life. Then, after I left the presidency, I thought: "Now I'm going to live a quiet life, I'm finally going to fulfill the promise I made to Marisa in 1978.[22] I've done what I had to do, I've been president of the republic, I've had a good administration, now I'm going to take care of the family." I decided to start a company and earn a living with lectures. What did I start to notice? There was, on the part of the media, an attempt to create a separation between Dilma and Lula. Almost every day they attempted to create disagreement.

I said two sentences. The first: "I'm grateful for Dilma's success, because her success will be my success, and her failure will be my failure." I also said, "If there's a disagreement between Dilma and me, she will be right, and I will be wrong." I could not say anything clearer to show my degree of commitment to Dilma. It was a total commitment, from someone who had appointed and fully trusted her. And I trusted her technically and politically. I just thought that, with the same intelligence she used to learn technical terms, economics terms, she would have to learn the human relationship, the relationship with politics. Well, look how close our relationship was, mine and Dilma. Before the 2010 campaign, João Santana wanted me to tell Dilma that she would be a substitute candidate, but I refused.[23] I always stated that she was a full-fledged candidate. Interestingly, the same João Santana who suggested that, worked all the time to create a separation between us.

An unusual fact: when Fernando Henrique Cardoso turned eighty years old [in 2011], there was a big party promoted by entrepreneurs—who took advantage of the opportunity and held a fundraiser for his institute [the FHC Foundation]—and Dilma sent him a letter so laudatory that not even Fernando Henrique Cardoso believed it.[24]

I called Dilma and said: "Dilma, let me understand something; if I knew you thought of Fernando Henrique Cardoso like that, you would not have been my candidate." And she said, "You know I didn't write it." In fact, they wrote the letter in her place, saying it was important, and she accepted. The press put a highlight on the birthday letter for a week... And they tried to instill a disagreement, until Dilma, in a position of great loyalty, said: "No, wait there, my world is with Lula, don't even try to separate us. No! There's no separation between us. I'm the president, I run the government; don't try to use me to create confusion for Lula. We won't have it." She did this with great loyalty. She made many mistakes in politics because she didn't really . . . perhaps because she didn't really want to deal with politics; many times she didn't do the simplest things. I'm going to talk about the impeachment, which is already in the past and is now part of history: politically, when you decide to face a war like the impeachment process, those in government need to have a sense of their own strength. It's not about meeting with one congressman from a party! You have to call every congressman from the party that supports you, alongside with the president of the party that supports you, all senators and the ministers of the party that supports you, sit with them and say: "We are here, what's the game?" This wasn't done at all, they found fictional numbers, said we would have 300 votes, 280, 270. But it didn't turn out that way . . . From a political point of view, it's almost unimaginable that the government, with such a large political base, wasn't able to get the vote of 170 congressmen.[25]

Juca Kfouri: Why didn't you do that in her place?

Lula: Because you only do it when you get summoned. And you have to respect the rules of the game of those currently in the administration. There was one very funny thing: Dilma set up a team of negotiators who were comrades with the highest qualifications. But for the game that was being played, they should have done as the Brazilian National Team did against Argentina in the 1978 World Cup, when it was necessary to substitute a more peaceful defender and put a guy like Chicão in his place, to make clear that "the game is heavy here."[26] Because they [the opponents] had an army of people with very dubious qualifications who know how to deal with that Congress like nobody else, ranging from Temer himself to Wellington Moreira Franco, Geddel, Jucá [27] . . . it's something . . . and we were there, with my friend Ricardo Berzoini, my friend Jaques Wagner,

Aloizio Mercadante—in every conversation I had, people would complain 100 percent about him and 101 percent about Dilma.[28] I have never seen so much unanimity among congressmen and senators; everybody was complaining. I even told comrade Dilma: "Look, history will know you as the only president who wasn't even defended by her own ministers." Because when the ministers came to talk to me, I used to ask: "Why is this not happening?" And instead of explaining, they'd say: "You know her, you know her." I told her: "Dilma, everyone says 'you know her, you know her.' I'm not your minister and I always talk to businessmen, union members, garbage collectors . . . I tell everyone that 'Dilma will improve, she will change. It's difficult.'" I need to find a way to explain and there was a simple explanation . . . I usually make a parallel between Dilma and Fernando Henrique Cardoso; in 1999, he was in the same situation as Dilma in 2015: with 8 percent approval in the polls, dead. What was the difference? Fernando Henrique Cardoso had Temer as the lower house speaker, trying to get things approved, and Maciel as vice president, completely loyal to him.[29] Dilma had Eduardo Cunha as the speaker of the lower house, antagonizing her in every step of the way, and a traitor as vice president [Michel Temer].[30]

Gilberto Maringoni: And what did she say when you told her that?

Lula: That everything was normal. It's a big mistake when governments come to believe that all is fine. It's difficult to change that. And the party had little influence there, because Dilma was very kind, she used to talk a lot to Rui Falcão, who had several meetings with me . . .[31] The truth is that the things we said didn't happen, because it was not what she wanted or what other people wanted in her government. So, after being president myself, what did I say? "Well, she won, she has to rule."

Gilberto Maringoni: Mr. President, let me ask you something about the relationship with a president of the republic. It must be very difficult for someone to come and say: "You're wrong—"

Lula: No one says that, and this is a big problem. At the first ministerial meeting, after I took office in 2003, I said something that marked my administration a lot: "This is not a government of ministers. This is an administration where all public policies have to come from the government. There will be no such thing as a minister planning a road, or a port on their own . . . This is government. It's one for all and all for one." We created a manual, a newsletter called *Destaque*, so that every minister could receive every two months all the information about what was going on in the government, so that the Ministry of Culture would know what was happening in the Ministry of Agrarian Development, to try to unify and standardize the administration. In the case of comrade Dilma, by the way, it was different. One day I said to Dilma: "Look, comrade, don't confuse respect with fear. When someone respects you, they will do things you expect; when they are afraid, they begin to avoid talking to you." There was even a joke, behind the scenes of the administration, about the two joys of the ministers: the first was when they got a hearing with her, and the second was when the meeting was cancelled [laughing]. I don't know how to explain it; when I was president, I liked Dilma's way, because she was tough enough; so, when people complained to me, I would take them into my arms, give affection, attention, and even tell them: "She has to be just like that. She is protecting me." Everybody agreed. But when she came into power . . . Do you remember something I said at the time: "Where's Dilma's Dilma?" What was my concern? Dilma had taken the staff into the presidency, the staff moved to the Alvorada Palace. Maybe she thought there was no one besides her capable of doing things. It's a difference in background, in training. For example, I was never the first to speak during a ministerial meeting; I would open the meeting by saying what the problem was and then listening to everyone at the table; only then would I give an opinion, saying what I thought. Because, if the president is the first to talk, nobody says anything else; or, when they do, they won't disagree. So, people end up confusing the political role of doing good things for Brazil with the role of a bootlicker, trying to please. This is too hard. I was the only person who talked frankly to Dilma, saying things as they were. She listened, but because she has a very strong personality, she probably thought: "This guy didn't understand anything." She even spoke to a congressman jokingly: "You don't understand politics." The guy's been in the House for forty-eight years . . . [laughing]. People warned me that Dilma would have difficulties with politics, but I found her so clever . . . If she had set up a team . . . For example, I say now with all the affection: I didn't want Padilha to be the minister of health, I wanted him to continue as the minister responsible for political organization, because he was all we needed, a nice, sympathetic figure who had good relationships with everyone.[32] Ideli Salvatti filled his position and, despite being a laudable person, she is very different from Padilha in the human relationship.[33] I didn't want Palocci to be chief of staff and I told her, but she didn't listen.[34]

Gilberto Maringoni: You told her that you wanted Trabuco as minister of finances?[35]

Lula: What I told her was that my recommendation was Meirelles.[36] And I would say to her: "Dilma, the question with Meirelles is how to deal with him."

Ivana Jinkings: Why Meirelles?

Lula: Because Meirelles would convey the serenity that worked for the previous administration. The fact that he had worked with me was important. But she had her reasons and the answer was: "I don't want to."

Juca Kfouri: But wouldn't Meirelles's policies be at odds with PT's ideology and the government program?

Lula: No, I never stopped doing my social policies because of Meirelles. It worked like this: Sometimes I had meetings with Guido and Meirelles, or with Palocci and Meirelles.[37] There were moments when I realized that they had a lot of disagreement and [then] I would meet them separately, go home and think about what to do. Every time Meirelles said, "We need to raise the interest rate by 0.5 percent," I would say, "Okay, you may increase by 0.5 percent, and I'll bring the TJLP down by 0.5 percent."[38] Because there's a lot of hypocrisy in this interest story. I would tell Paulinho da Força Sindical and the CUT's president: "You are bothered by the SELIC rate, but none of you are asking how much the poor pay for the refrigerators they buy at Casas Bahia, where interest rates go up to 300 percent per year, or with credit cards that charge 8 percent interest per minute.[39] Don't come and say that interest is high because of the base rate. It's not true." The payroll deductible loan, which was the cheapest credit in the country, led to a confrontation with Banco do Brasil, because interest on this kind of loan was of 1.7 percent per month, which was close to 18 percent per year, and the SELIC rate was at 13 percent.[40] Do you really think it's the SELIC rate that makes the money that people borrow so expensive?

I wish to God that people could borrow money and pay 13 percent a year. The state pays 13 percent, but the people pay 300 percent, 400 percent, and I see no congressman giving speeches, or people in the streets campaigning against the interest they have to pay. That's why we created payroll deductible loans, to get money into the hands of the poor.

Well, when Dilma won in 2014, I was with her, I felt that Dilma was sad on victory day [October 26, 2014]; I was with her and Franklin Martins, and we were talking to each other from her house to the hotel where she made her victory statement; I'm convinced that it was the first time I've seen such a sad and uneasy winner.[41] The feeling I had was that she didn't like to win. As I approached her, she said, "I never want to participate in a debate, never again." She was visibly irritated; I don't know if it was because of the tight victory; but tight victories are better than anything else!

Ivana Jinkings: It was a very aggressive campaign . . .

Lula: It was. But I used to say: "Come on, Dilma, nobody knows Brazil and the government better than you. You don't have to read anything for the debate; and during the debate, you don't have to answer whatever the other guy asks, you don't have to talk to the jerk who asks the question. You speak to the people. He will complain: 'The candidate didn't respond, blah blah blah.' And you say with a straight face that you are not there to answer him. 'I'm here to talk to the people.'" But she was so worried about studying that . . . Palocci would tell me: "Look, Mr. President, we'll have meetings with her, and she'll write everything down; after every debate she writes a book." It's a technical perfectionism she must have had since her student days. So, I came back to Dilma soon after the reelection in 2014, and I said: "Look, Dilma, of the people I see around, if you want to put a guy who is respected in the market for everything he's written, for everything he's been talking about in the media, for all he says to defend the government, I think it's a good idea to talk to Trabuco. He has shown great loyalty to this administration in all the articles he writes. The so-called market would be really surprised." She seemed to have agreed, she went to Australia, I believe he was in Qatar at that time. She said she was going to talk to him. To my surprise, she comes back with Levy under her arm and she didn't tell me anything. I learned from the media that she was choosing Levy.[42]

Maria Inês Nassif: And what is your assessment of Levy in the government? Was his presence relevant to the impeachment process?

Lula: No. But he was responsible for discrediting her with the left-leaning sectors that had supported her in the second round.

Gilberto Maringoni: And what did you think of the fiscal adjustment?

Lula: Very bad, very bad . . .

Gilberto Maringoni: Publicly, you supported it.

Lula: Not really. I neither supported nor discouraged it. Let me tell you one thing: the administration had a broad base, a very strong social base. So you could not take steps without talking to these people, because it's they who are on the streets, who are in the unions, who are holding assemblies, who are talking to the part of the society that's on your side. You have your side; even though you rule for everyone, you always have your side. Honestly, I would never present a negative budget. I would have announced: "This country has so many billions of reserve dollars, this country has so many billions of reserve requirement yielding nothing in the Central Bank, we will get that money . . ." I would do as I did during the "little wave" of 2008, when I got R$100 billion[43] and made them available through BNDES [National Bank for Economic and Social Development].[44] Now, if I'm in a crisis, if I don't have jobs, what do I have to do? Create employment. To generate employment, we need development; to have development, we need growth; to have growth, we need money! [Slams his fist on the table.] You don't need a college degree to know that. To announce that I will cut the budget and then present a negative budget?! I would have placed a bet on Brazil. If I trusted what I was doing, I would say: "There's an economic crisis, it comes from an international crisis, but also from mistakes [slams his fist on the table], I made mistakes . . ." Every once in a while, we have to say that we made mistakes.

Ivana Jinkings: Can you be specific about which mistakes were made?

Lula: There were mistakes in the economy. For example, I told Dilma several times that if she increased the price of gas a little, it would not have effects on the inflation rate. It would be irrelevant. The economic team was adamant that they didn't need to increase gasoline prices. Okay, but if you don't increase it, it will break the ethanol industry. Later, Dilma announced the PIL, the Investment Plan in Logistics, which could have been named the PAC 3, the PAC 4 . . .but they decided to create the PIL.[45] It was a marketer's thing to create a new name, so that she could be the mother: "Enough with the PAC, let's create the PIL." And so they did. You can go out and ask what the PAC is, everyone knows; ask what the PIL is, and the person says, "It's a fight chicken." But she was the mother of the PAC, and the mother can have one, two, three, four, five children, they are all her children! I don't know who instilled in her mind the idea that it was necessary to create another name. I guess someone thought that talking about PAC seemed like a Lula thing. That's probably what they used to convince her. If I remember it correctly, she ended up setting a rate of return of 5 percent. Conclusion: no one came. Comrade Guido had to redo everything. They needed a year and a half, which was almost half of her term. If you announce a program and nothing happens, the government is already seeing its own end up ahead. There's a lot to talk about during this period. I used to say to Dilma, "Dear, don't wait until January [2015] to change your administration; it will be born old. Change it now, change it now." For me, it's hard to give names, because I'll still have to live with these people, and they're alive. And although our interview is going to be valid twenty years from now, I'm going to have to live with these people tomorrow . . . But I pointed out to Dilma some names for key places, so that she could face the situation. I always left with the feeling that it would happen. I would arrive at the Institute, and everyone, Paulo Okamotto, Clara Ant, Luiz Dulci, everyone was anxious: "So, how was Dilma?" And every time I said, "I think she's changed, I think it's going to happen now . . ."[46]

Gilberto Maringoni: You spoke of Meirelles. He is the brain of the reforms undertaken by Temer. What do you think of him now?

Lula: I don't want a genius to be responsible for the economy. The decision for the economy has to be political. I want a guy who implements the administration's political decision for the economy. Because, when you don't have a boss, if the boss is not giving any orders, if the boss has no objective and strategy, everyone is doing whatever he or she thinks is right, the Central Bank does as it pleases, Meirelles does whatever he wants, and then he ends up like so many ministers and technicians of the bureaucracy: doing everything nonchalantly and, when it doesn't work, they just shrug their shoulders: "Fuck it, I'll go to Harvard, I'll go to Sorbonne, fuck Brazil." No, none of it! What did I say? "I came from São Bernardo and I will go back to São Bernardo. [Slams his fist on the table.] I live six-hundred meters away from the union and I'll go back and stay six-hundred meters away from the union. I won't go to Paris and live there for two years, until everybody forgets about me . . ." This position always made me more responsible about things. All kinds of trade union movements want to have a discussion about the future of Social Security? Let's do it! But how? Let's get everyone together for a meeting. What you can't do is implement a pension reform in which the losing party will be the poor. Instead, I want to see them change the retirement programs of the Public Prosecutor's Office. I want to see them mess with the state elite's retirement. I want them to bring it all down to R$5,000 a month. Because, if you want to moralize the state, that's where you have to start things. Nobody will receive more than this. And that's it. End of story! But, if nobody is allowed to receive more than the president of the republic, which represents the salary cap, how come Temer's retirement paycheck amounts to R$45,000, according to the media, which is almost twice that cap. This represents a complete demoralization. That's the art of ruling a country, the way you handle things. I might have a privilege: I didn't know everything. It may seem like a flaw, but it's a privilege. Because when you don't know everything, you ask. I was never ashamed of asking, of taking a speech prepared by the press office and asking a minister, of going to three or four people and asking: "Do you think it's okay?" Many times I asked Dilma to read my speeches. In my time as a unionist, I never made a decision without first calling Barelli, of the DIEESE.[47] I talked to other people, too. It's very good to have three or four opinions before you say: "I'm going in this direction."

Juca Kfouri: What about your improvisations?

Lula: Improvising was the heart of the issue. I would first follow the ceremonial rite and read my standard speech in order to comply with the formalities because, after all, there were people from Itamaraty working on it. Marco Aurelio worked on those speeches and I would not simply throw them away [laughing].[48] Reading a speech with the sole purpose of complying with formalities is the worst thing in the world. It's like eating unsalted beans. Where is the spark in the eye? So I would think to myself: "I'm here with all of these people, I must talk to them with my soul, I have to be the man they elected as their president."

Juca Kfouri: But Mr. President, you were never someone who rigorously complied with the liturgy of the position such as José Sarney. You always kept the spontaneity which guaranteed your proximity to the voters, to the Brazilian people. On the other hand, you also brought about the proximity of people who, in a certain manner, took advantage of this informality. This is a burden you carry nowadays. From Léo Pinheiro and others, what about that?[49]

Lula: It's possible that I might have disappointed some people. It's possible. For instance, in the diplomatic community, comrades with whom I interacted, such as Celso Amorim, never cared about this.[50] On the contrary, Celso is actually pretty much like me. Maybe it's the court's structure . . . Well, when you win an election, there's someone responsible for letting you know where you will walk, where you will sit . . . This so-called liturgy is annoying as hell! As a matter of fact, I tried to break this. For instance, when Bush went to Torto to have lunch, the liturgy of both sides and the security detail would say no to this, no to that.[51] And there was this famous barbecue from *Guinness Book of Records,* from Figueiredo, twelve meters long. You could put an entire farm to roast in there [laughing] and everyone who visited it, Fidel, Chávez, was offered barbecue, which is our food, it's delicious.[52] So Bush got there with his huge security detail. When we went to Guarulhos, Marginal Tietê Expressway was shut down. Nonsense, everything is done in order to support the security detail. It's understandable if someone had tried to kill him in Iraq, but here in Brazil it's unlikely that someone would recognize him if he went to a bar to drink *cachaça*. This is the way Brazilian media sucks up with its inferiority complex. He gets more airtime time than other presidents of the region so maybe someone might recognize him . . . come on. Getting back to the barbecue: the security detail came to say we could not use knives. Now you tell me: how is it possible to make a barbecue with no knives? [Laughing.] The first thing Bush did when he got there with his wife (I was waiting there with Marisa) was to say: "Hand me that knife, I want a piece of this steak."[53] He grabbed the knife, cut the meat, and gave it back to the barbecue cook, making everyone look like fools. [Laughing].

Hu Jintao's wife came to have dinner at our home.[54] You're supposed to show some deference and kindness and Hu Jintao is a very formal man, he would read even a "good morning." [Laughing.] And Celso Amorim was troubled because I can't talk to people without touching them, I don't know any other way of having a conversation without touching people, this is my way. So, Hu Jintao's wife is a picky eater, she was sick and is very careful about food . . . We had tropeiro beans, a huge steak: she ate so much that by the end of the meal, she was healed! [Laughing.] We were rewarded when I went to China [in 2009] as he hosted me in a house located inside a park . . . You would never picture such a wonderful house, not even in a Disney movie. Both couples went together for dinner. So, there are rewards. And this is how I treat people, make friends. I am not judgmental if the person is right wing or left wing. As far as I'm concerned, that person is the head of state of another country who is in Brazil and I have to treat them decently. I want to treat them with great care in order to be treated in the same manner when we meet in their home country. I worked on this with a lot of passion. Sometimes I would treat them as if they were my own son. I was president and Evo Morales was running for president, he was called the "cocalero."[55] He said [faking a Spanish accent]: "President Lula, hermano mayor—he used to call me older brother—how should I treat my opponents?" I told him: "Treat them the way you would like to be treated. Do you want to be respected? So, be respectful." Politics do not imply rudeness. You have to be tough, but with *finesse.* You don't have to call your opponent a scumbag, a thief, a crook.

Gilberto Maringoni: This is very good for your image with the people, but the Brazilian elite seems to disagree . . . In the Supreme Court, Gilmar Mendes got to the point of saying he would "haul the president over coals."[56] Doesn't the elite take advantage of this informality?

Lula: These people were groomed in an exaggerated liturgy. A Supreme Court minister, a Superior Court minister . . . . The exercise of power by these people grows them apart from society. But I don't believe in this. You can be the same; you're only holding a different position. You can be a judge or the most important minister in the world and still treat the employee who works at your house as if they were your child, with great affection and respect. I always tell a story; there are people who behave in a certain way when they are behind a microphone and in a different way when greeting their maid; I'm the same person when I say good morning or good night. Sometimes Marisa would say I was exaggerating. "Marisa, this is who I am, this is how I learned how to do things." I used to do this at five o'clock in the morning at the gates of Volkswagen, I used to have a cachaça at 4:30 in the morning with the workers, sometimes I had to speak at four o'clock in the morning and my throat was a bit dry so I had to sip a cheap brandy in order to grab the microphone and have my voice heard loud and strong. This is my reality. I wasn't elected to become one of them. I was elected to be who I am. I'm proud to have lived on the other side without forgetting who I was. Sometimes I think to myself, "Why do people like me?" Because my vocabulary . . . .

Juca Kfouri: Allow me to interrupt you. People who like Lula think you ought to go to an embassy and not let yourself be arrested; people who like Lula think you should exploit politically the mobilization of the Brazilian people through your voice. This is not possible from jail, but it could happen from the embassy of a friend country. However, it seems that your decision is to go home and wait for the police to come.

Lula: Look, I know comrades who were exiled for fifteen years and didn't have a voice in Brazil. If I had made a mistake, if I had committed a crime—from among all of those that I'm being accused of—maybe I would do that. But since I'm fully aware of my innocence, they will pay the price. Everything has a price. I know there are many people who like me, but nobody likes me more than myself. I will fight here. I will make the Brazilian society discuss my case here.

Maria Inês Nassif: Do you believe the price they pay for your prison is higher than your exile?

Lula: Today's lie will be paid historically. I know it's hard for them to accept a metalworker—lathe operator—to tell them they are lying. But they are lying. The Federal Police lied during the inquiry, the Public Prosecutor's Office lied in the accusation, and Moro—who was aware this wasn't true—accepted those lies and built a case in which I was convicted [slams his fist on the table].[57] The Court of Appeals in Rio Grande do Sul also turned another lie into a conviction.[58] What is the last thing I have? My dignity. This is my greatest asset. They want to arrest me? Go ahead, pay the price.

Juca Kfouri: Are you going to suffer the humiliation of being jailed?

Lula: I don't know. This issue about humiliation in jail is not quite as people say. There were moments of a great deal of humiliation in jail, endured by many innocent people. Let's see. I don't have much experience because I was only thirty-one days in jail. Today I'm seventy-two years old; these guys know that what they are doing to me is a political obscenity. Because if they had solid evidence . . . If I had really committed the crime they said I committed, do you think I would be fighting the way I am? Do you think my lawyer—a good kid who was accused by many people of being no good—would be fighting the way he is fighting?[59] I tell my lawyers everyday: "I want you to know that you are defending an innocent man." [Hits table.] I don't need to lie to you. My children know. This is the chance I have to tell the Brazilian people to go on and fight. There's one thing I have to make clear: this should not be happening. They are not judging Lula, they are judging Lula's government and the PT terms in office. I have warned my comrades from the PT that our opponents have created the mothership, which is the PowerPoint presentation, to say that the PT is a criminal organization.[60] The next step is to label the PT a criminal organization. You just have to look at the legal briefs. They judge because I appointed Mr. So-and-so as minister. Then you have to explain: "Do you know how to win an election? With allies and with opponents. Once you are in office you have to bring your allies together in order to form a government. Every party that took part in the campaign is entitled to participate in the government, entitled to appoint a minister, and the minister is entitled to form their team." This is how things are done in the whole world; this is how it's done in France, in Germany. The exception is the United States because there are two parties. Even though once in a while the Republican Party needs a little backstabbing from the Democrats and vice versa. This is called politics, po-li-tics. I'm not allowed to open a public contest in order to choose a cabinet. Because according to their logic there should be a public contest. We will get back to this later on.

Gilberto Maringoni: Mr. President, you are being convicted by a law sanctioned by yourself, the Clean Record Act.[61] Do have any regrets?

Lula: No, I don't. The enacted legislation is supposed to be construed correctly and not politically. I didn't create this law for others, I created it for Brazil. I do want them to construe this law within due process. It's not possible for some people to assume that the president is not authorized to pick a cabinet or a company's director. Which is the role of a president then? [Hits table.] Is it to appoint the general attorney and the head of the Federal Police? And I have been seriously bothered because of my appointments . . . How did Temer appoint this group that is with him? How did Fernando Henrique Cardoso do it? What about Sarney, Getúlio, and Café Filho? Everyone appoints accordingly to their parliamentary political base.

"Well, but if so-and-so robbed, you knew about it." This tale of "you knew about it" is fantastic. You can picture a father whose son sniffs cocaine inside his bedroom and tells his neighbor: "Well, my son is studying, he loves to study, you can't imagine how much." And his son is actually sniffing coke in the bedroom. Is the father supposed to know? Is a father supposed to know if his daughter is pregnant? Is a father supposed to know whether his son went out to steal something? Come on, how am I supposed to know what a fellow did in Roraima? It's paramount to pay attention to one thing: they are judging twelve years of PT administrations. They want to demonstrate it's not possible to run the country the way we did. I have been warning it for a long time. And why is it that Lula is a victim? Because Lula is the most important person. If you look for the most important person in the history of the PT, it's me; if you look at the history of the government, I'm the most important person as well. Therefore, who is the unfortunate wretch that should be convicted? Lula.

Ivana Jinkings: Where does this hate come from? When you were first elected you wrote the "Letter to the Brazilian People," a very controversial document aimed at calming markets down.[62] You left office with almost 90 percent approval rates. After that there was Dilma's government, which also continued to calm markets down. Why do you think, despite all this effort, the elite won't accept you?

Lula: In that book by Galeano which I mentioned, about soccer, you realize that if the history of prejudice in society against the poorer is transposed to soccer, the exact same thing happens here. Imagine that the president of [Mexican soccer team] Puebla decides to pick up a fight against Televisa.[63] In a few months, he would be arrested, and his assets confiscated because he fought against Televisa, which owns [Mexican soccer team] América and the Azteca Stadium. When I left office, I doubt that in the history of humankind—I'm very presumptuous—there was ever a president who received that many requests from businessmen for him to run again. If we had a poll in 2013, 2014, I was a unanimous choice among the business community.

Gilberto Maringoni: And why has this changed?

Lula: Well, this is something I would like to find out.

Ivana Jinkings: Why did these businessmen bang pots and pans?

Lula: Let me tell you a story. The PSDB—if not the whole of the PSDB, at least our unforgettable Sérgio Motta and Fernando Henrique Cardoso—had a twenty-year project.[64] I'm a candidate in 2018, and if I win the election and make a good government, Dilma (if she hadn't been impeached) and I would have been twenty-four years in office. With twenty-four years in office one could double the life quality of the poorest and this could be a country with less poverty, less misery, and with more people ascending to the middle class. If we were able, in a little more than twelve years, to place four million youngsters in universities, in ten more years—the two years left of Dilma's term, and in theory two more terms of mine—we could have placed another four million or even more, turning Brazil into a civilized country. It's necessary to increase the education budget by a factor of five, like we did during my government, which would have implied a budget decrease in other areas. Take a look at the communications sector: we had a country where the communications budget was distributed among three hundred outlets and increased this number to over four thousand. All of this creates problems. We started to create a series of problems to the elite that never accepted it . . .

Gilberto Maringoni: Mr. President, Dilma cut down interest rates in 2012, which by the way was a demand from FIESP [Federation of Industries of the State of São Paulo], and granted several tax cuts to companies; even so, the business community was against her. I can't understand this.

Lula: You won't understand this because it's not a matter of interest rates. Those who were strongly against interest rates in Brazil were Antônio Ermírio de Moraes and José de Alencar.[65] Everyone has a different theory. I told Dilma several times: "Don't turn interest rates into an ideological issue. Don't lead the way." I think an economy needs several ingredients in order to function properly: first of all, the president must have credibility; you can't lose it because people have to believe that when you say something, it's going to happen. If people start to realize you don't have credibility, things are going to get ugly. But—and this is a lesson we must learn—the National Congress doesn't like a strong president, they prefer a weak president. The weaker a president is, the more they can enforce the rules of the game. The president must be strong. If you have a strong president, my dear . . .

Juca Kfouri: You said you were presumptuous. Do you intend on becoming the Brazilian Nelson Mandela?[66]

Lula: No, I don't. I intend on being Little Lula Peace and Love, which I always was, and to make history honorably, a benchmark in my life. What really offends me in this whole situation—this might sound a little too personal, but I can't acknowledge, can't acknowledge—is that a guy whose sole accomplishment is to have been approved in a competitive examination after studying for three years, to call a thief a man who has struggled for this country for seventy. If anyone stole something and wants to swallow their pride, go ahead. I didn't steal, and I won't swallow this. This is my greatest battle. Secondly, this whole process is their last resource in order to prevent my return. I have a successful career. If I were a soccer player I would have made it to the national team . . . I would be a backup [laughing], but there were good backups in my time. I have a long history. I was a common reader of *Diario da Noite,* of the Guzman column, the "Twenty News Items" of Guzman.[67] I used to catch the bus in Moinho Velho, in São Paulo, to head to work in Villares, reading this column. My brother Frei Chico was already affiliated with the Big Party [Partidão], but no one knew about it; he was a union leader and would drive me crazy to take me to the union.[68] I used to tell him, "Stop bugging me into going to the union; there are only thieves and doormats in the union." Frei Chico had a good relationship with Joaquinzão, who used to call me every time for nighttime meetings: "Let's go together and listen to a lecture."[69] My only reply was: "Frei Chico, I won't attend your clandestine meetings." He would take Emílio Bonfante, whose codename was Ivo, he would take him to São Bernardo and tell me: "A very important fellow will come here tomorrow, Emílio was responsible for the Merchant Navy strike."[70] So Frei Chico would get to the Matriz Church Square in Sao Bernardo (this was in 1974) and I would sit on a bench at the square reading the newspaper while Ivo sat on the back. I would then go home and tell Frei Chico: "What the hell, Chico, why can't he go to the union? I'm the president of the union, he can come to my office, and I'll offer him some coffee. He can ask as many questions as he wants. Why does it have to be clandestine? Why can't this be a healthy thing? Whatever it is that you talk about locked up in a house at eight o'clock at night, I shout out loud at the factory gates at five o'clock in the morning. You have to stop with this madness of everything being clandestine . . ."

Well, I joined the union [in 1968] because Frei Chico asked me to do it, since he was the one who was supposed to join it. So I did it. I never imagined being the president of the union. I never imagined becoming the leader of the first strike after the military coup [in 1978], but I became that. Not only had I created a party, which as of today consumes every one of my days, but I was also the most popular constituent federal congressman and became president of the republic.[71]

What is it that I want the most in my life? Everything is a collective construction; nothing would have been possible individually. I always had thousands and thousands of comrades who believed in me; so these are the people I work for. I won't say to Moro that I'm honest. I owe what I was and what I am to the comrades who believed in me. So when someone tells my story, I want them to say: "These guys have condemned Lula because he is a metalworker who only had elementary education and a course at Senai; he wasn't supposed to become president. But he did. He wasn't supposed to be a good president, he was supposed to finish his life like Walesa— destroyed, finished, with 0.5 percent of the votes— but he worked out fine.[72] This guy leaves office well-established, elects a woman as his successor, a fighter, a prisoner, tortured, and this woman is reelected. Then this guy places Fernando Haddad as candidate in São Paulo at the height of the Mensalão trial.[73] We must stop this guy. What can we do to catch him? Is he a communist? No. Is he a fascist? No. He is a democrat with some political awareness. We must finish him. What can we use to finish him?"

The subject that they always worked with: corruption. I read a lot about Roosevelt and the New Deal. I keep looking at the things they said about Roosevelt. The amount of insults, he was called a thief and all. Democrats won't use Roosevelt as an example for anything up to this date. He is a character who almost doesn't exist anymore in their debates. But he was extremely important. And that's why they want to finish me, I can't find another explanation. "Well, but when Lula was president farmers went bankrupt, the same way they did in [19]29 during the coffee crisis . . ." But no, not at all, they made a lot of money. "Well, but sugar mill owners were doomed." No, I was the king of ethanol. "Well, but he did break Petrobras or whatever." No, I was king of investments in research in Petrobras. "Well, but the car industry was very angry." Nope, we went from 1.7 million to almost 4 million vehicles sold in this country. "Oh, but hunger was on the rise." But hunger was not on the rise, banks made loads of money as well as micro entrepreneurs . . . I can't find a reason . . .

Juca Kfouri: President, is it true you own a helicopter? [Laughing.]

Maria Inês Nassif: What is the square area of your apartment in meters?

Lula: I believe it's 190. But let me tell you something about the helicopter. This is something they have always tried to use in order to play me off against the poor. It was during the 1982 campaign for governor. I was still a metalworker in São Bernardo do Campo. And there was this story that I lived in Morumbi [an upscale neighborhood in São Paulo]. It was pointless to deny this because someone who wants to screw you over won't stop repeating this story. So we made a film for the campaign and my leg was broken, I had broken my ankle . . . Chico Malfitani had this idea of shooting the video for the PT program in front of my house, with the cast over my ankle, refereeing a soccer match for my children and the kids in the street . . . And the camera would close in: Maria Azevedo Street, 273, which was my house's address. Pointless. There were people who said: "Yes, he lives here, but there's a tunnel which takes him to his real house in Morumbi." [Laughing.]

I am not an asset-oriented person. I had the obligation of providing a minimum of safeguards to the people I brought into this world. So, I had this dream that each one of my children would have a home to live in. I could even have bought one apartment for each of them but I didn't. I gave a down payment for each one but didn't pay it off, they must have felt outraged but I thought to myself: "They must feel what it's like to pay, they must have responsibility." So I keep track of them: "Are you paying? Because if you can't pay for one, paying for two is harder; if you can't pay for two, three will be even harder . . . So make a sacrifice and pay it." I managed to guarantee for them a small house, that's what I wanted. The story behind the Guarujá apartment is the most fantastic of them . . .

Juca Kfouri: It was priced at R$2 million . . .

Lula: What?

Gilberto Maringoni It was published today that it was priced at R$2.2 million.

Lula: Well, tell Moro to purchase it for R$2 million! I think they do all of this because they think: "This is what will touch people's souls." But I will face it. They won't catch me because of corruption.

They didn't catch me during my time in the union movement. I don't know if you know when Murilo Macedo intervened in the union . . . (you see Ivana, I said "intervened") [laughing] Good for me . . . Once I was with Brizola and he tried to correct me, and I told him: "Brizola, 'intervened' is correct" . . . [laughing]). Anyways, Murilo went to the union, he went to the Itaú Bank, and found nothing . . . It's all very nasty . . .

If I am the leader of a gang as they say, how come my "thugs" stole so much; R$100, 200 million and this sucker here only kept an apartment of a few hundred square meters. What a lousy gang leader! I get extremely angry about this, extremely angry.

Well, in 1989 there was another accusation; the famous Lubeca project, do you remember? Caiado made this accusation. It was a project of US$600 million in investments in São Paulo, in which someone from PT had allegedly taken US$200,000. So this comrade came to me and asked about it, and I replied: "Comrade, let me tell you something. If there's a business deal of US$600 million and someone sold himself for US$200,000, this motherfucker demoralized corruption here in São Paulo." [Laughing.]

I strongly doubt any president was treated the way I was after leaving office. I was hosted as a friend by all presidents of the countries I visited. I was received by Sarkozy, by the president of the Party of the Congress in India, Sonia Gandhi, who is the real authority there; in South America, I was hosted many times by everyone; in Africa . . .

Juca Kfouri: Do you feel resentful that Obama did not come forward to support you, given that he even had said that you are "his man?"[74]

Ivana Jinkings: Are the United States directly intervening in what is happening?

Lula: Obama did not intervene directly. We must distinguish between the American government and the American state. As to Obama, I don't know if those people know what Brazil is. Americans suffer from a delusion of grandeur and assume that no one else exists. If there is a war in Cambodia, Cambodia is important; if there is a war in Korea, Korea is important; but they don't care about Latin America and they never learned how to deal with Latin America. I believe the situation that you mention could have something to do with the fact that Brazil became a protagonist in Latin America.

It's not a small thing that Brazil got to lead the World Trade Organization.[75] And why did we get it? Because of Africa and Latin America. Do you think it was easy to win the bid to host the Olympics?[76] We got it because of Africa and Latin America. Do you think it was easy for a Brazilian to become the director-general of FAO?[77] Once again, that happened thanks to Africa and Latin America.

Gilberto Maringoni: Mr. President, Minister Celso Amorim says that he started to believe in a conspiracy theory. He thinks that everything is somehow connected. Do you think there is a big conspiracy behind this?

Lula: It's always hard to say, but if we consider what the interests are today, especially because of the pre-salt reservoirs[78] . . . Well, Brazil is huge. The United States re-established the Fourth Fleet in the Atlantic soon after we discovered the pre-salt reserves [in 2008]. Why is the Fourth Fleet necessary? Our continent is at peace. Our relations with Africa are peaceful. We have maritime boundaries with all African countries on the Atlantic coast, from Cape Verde to South Africa, and we don't have problems with anyone. Pre-salt reserves are the only thing to be considered in this context. Oil companies refused to accept the pre-salt production-sharing bill—the so-called "Lei da Partilha"—and the idea that the oil belongs to Brazil.[79] They refused to accept that 75 percent of oil royalties will go to investments in education.

Brazil is not fully aware of its potential. People from abroad are more aware of our potential as a country than we are. I find it sad that people who should be thinking big in this country, after having studied a lot . . . For example, the clever brains of the University of São Paulo [USP] shouldn't be right-wingers. They should at least be Brazilians. They should be nationalists. They should care about this country. They should start thinking about a strategy for building the country that we want. Why can't our car manufacturing industry be competitive? Brazil is the only large country that doesn't have a car of its own. We still lack a Brazilian car. We could have a Brazilian car.

With global warming, Brazil needs to be great enough to take care of issues related to biodiversity, forest reserves, agricultural production, ethanol . . . Our country can produce a fuel that sequesters carbon while it's growing and that doesn't emit carbon when it's being used.[80] That's really something! Then the Europeans come and say: "Yeah, but ethanol is taking up space that belongs to food." That's a lie. Thanks to new developments in technology, much less space is now required to grow food. Think about our production capacity in relation to how large the country is. Proportionally, you will see that Brazil is growing without taking up too much land. This has to do with genetic improvements made in this country. We used to send cows for slaughter at an average of five years of age. Now it only takes fifteen months. Broilers reach slaughter-weight in thirty-five days nowadays. In the past, they used to do that in ninety days. Brazilian coffee was considered of poor quality. We now sell sophisticated, high-quality coffee. It wasn't like this ten years ago. When Brazil realizes the strengths it has, that will make us unbeatable. We need to map this out and make our decision clear: this will be a great nation.

Ivana Jinkings: Do you see any similarities between the way you are being persecuted and what happened to Getúlio Vargas?[81]

Lula: There are some similarities when it comes to upward social mobility. I criticized Getúlio at the beginning of my political career because the trade union structure in Brazil is indeed fascist. My point was to attack Mussolini's Carta del Lavoro. What did we do in Brazil? We didn't change it in the law itself, but we did it in practice. If you start reading the Consolidation of Labor Laws (CLT) today, you will see what it meant for the business sector in São Paulo. Businessmen thought that vacations were a luxury, that being idle led to drinking problems . . . The idea of workers going on vacation made no sense for them. This was the mindset in the business sector in the 1940s. The CLT was a revolution. That's why those people couldn't stand Getúlio. So they disseminated slander and lies. It always happens the same way. I am still critical of the trade union structure in Brazil nowadays, but I think that Getúlio is among the most remarkable heads of state of the twentieth century.

Gilberto Maringoni: That's why oil is so symbolic . . .

Lula: Exactly. Look, we only discovered the pre-salt reserves at the cost of big investments. We invested billions in research. Back then we used to debate whether we were going to use it or not, as well as what specialists said about it . . . Some of them said that it would be too expensive to drill there, at depths of seven-thousand meters. They said it wouldn't be competitive. "With the development of the shale gas industry in the United States, Brazil will soon be lagging behind." They soon came up with this shale gas thing to undermine our pre-salt and our ethanol. How are our pre-salt and our ethanol doing after all this time? We can extract a barrel of crude oil at US$8.50. In Saudi Arabia, where the oil-bearing strata lies much closer to the ground level, they are extracting it at US$6.50. To compare, the cost per barrel of shale oil is at least 15 percent more expensive.

What we did was to believe. We dreamed about getting the naval industry back on its feet. It makes no sense for a country with a coastline measuring about eight thousand kilometers to have cargo trucks traveling four thousand kilometers, since cargo ships could be used instead. But our merchant navy was shattered during the Fernando Collor and Fernando Henrique Cardoso administrations. Trucks are now responsible for 85 percent of our cargo transportation. Should a country with such a robust production potential be paying for freight transport? No!

Let's build a powerful naval industry of our own—with a small base in Brazil, a small base in Argentina, a small base in Venezuela. Contrary to what the "inferiority complex" might suggest, if we have a regional bloc in Latin America, we will stand out as a global economic power. We must think big. We shouldn't be thinking only in terms of one or two terms. What are we planting today? This is what we should focus on. Otherwise we will never plant a tree. We will just hold a seed in our hands complaining about how small it is. Plant the seed. Plant the seed and believe in it. Fertilize this country. What does that mean? It means to create conditions for people to participate. And things do work out when people participate.

Maria Inês Nassif: What political strategy should be followed at this moment to avoid losing what has been achieved? You have already considered all the possibilities in terms of what may happen to you. What about Brazil? What may happen to Brazil from now on?

Lula: Brazil has no right to self-mutilate as it's doing now, in this political scenario in which the only way to please the so-called market—be it internal or external—is to wipe out its own wealth. We have used people's money to build important things, that are now being sold for nothing! This just can't be. The PT and the other left-wing parties need to decide about how we want to go down in history. You go down in history if you're bold enough to introduce new possibilities for society, awaken the dreams of the people, and show that things can be done. It's not enough to stick to the ethical debate only. It will solve nothing. Some of the problems still to be solved in Brazil are hunger, unemployment, the lack of treated water for everyone.

As we manage the country's budget, we should be thinking of what we already have, and of what we want from now on. We should be thinking of what an actual priority is. When Gushiken was at the Strategic Affairs Center, he presented a study that showed that the only unanimous thing Brazilians agree upon is the need for good schools; at the same time, 70 percent of the population doesn't believe that the country can offer that one day.[82] People want it, but they don't believe it's possible. I said: "Let's take that into account and show that this can be done." If we were to discuss this issue in economic terms, we would not have PROUNI, FIES, technical schools, a minimum wage for teachers, and a five-fold increase in the education budget.[83] Because someone will always come around and say: "It can't be done." Well, why can't it be done? Money owners are the ones who say it can't be done. And who are the money owners? Those who have lifetime funds in public budgets.

Maria Inês Nassif: You must be in power for that, but the government is gradually being closed off to the left. What is the path to regain democracy?

Juca Kfouri: There is parliamentarianism . . .

Lula: Every time there is a crisis here in Brazil, there's always a wise guy who comes and talks about parliamentarianism. Brazilian people have rejected that idea twice [in 1963 and 1993]. But there are always those who think that "if we have parliamentarianism and if we can keep control of Congress, we will always be ones who choose the prime minister." That's how they think. In order to introduce parliamentarianism, you need parties that actually represent society, not business-oriented parties—not parties created because of money received from party funding.[84] Politics can't be serious if a congressman gets money to run for office after becoming the president of a party in their state. You need ideologically well-formed parties—maybe two, three, or four of them. You shouldn't have thirty-two political parties. This is an outrageous amount. This is not synonymous with democracy. You need strong parties for which society can vote ideologically. Then you will be able to make political agreements over government programs, instead of agreements motivated by interests. This is a serious problem that Brazil needs to address. We need a political reform, and it's not for the president to carry out a political reform. Political reforms are carried out by parties at the National Congress. The president rules the country. Party leaders run parties.

Juca Kfouri: Looking back, if you had to change something—I'm not talking about regrets, but if you had to change something—what would it be?

Lula: I would have studied economics. I think economists are the best. I make jokes with them and say, "Hey, economist, it's fucking great when you're a member of the opposition, because you think you know it all." They are like "Mr. Know-it-all." But once you are in government . . . The difference is that when you're in the opposition, you live based on what you *think*. When you're in government, you begin to live based on what you can actually *do* depending on the political and economic circumstances. If I could go back in time, I would like to graduate with an economics degree. I like economics because I had to deal with it since my union days.

Ivana Jinkings: Mr. President, during some of our recent meetings you made lots of comments about the books you have read or are reading. Why do people say that you don't like to read?

Lula: People who say that have perhaps not read half of what I've read, and they are way more ignorant than me. When Sarney, Collor, Fernando Henrique Cardoso, Dilma, and I went to Mandela's funeral [on December 15, 2013], we got off at the airport and went to the wake. We all stayed together, and Fernando Henrique Cardoso said: "You know, I thought that old age would never come; I can't read any books these days, because they keep falling from my hands." But since he is known as an intellectual, people think that at eighty-two, eighty-six years old, he can read a thousand-page book like when he was forty . . .

Gilberto Maringoni: Mr. President, in December it will be twenty years since the first election of Chávez. And then we had the rise of the so-called "pink tide" or "red tide" of presidents in Latin America. Twenty years later, many things have changed, while others are still quite similar. Cristina Kirchner is under pressure by the judicial system.[85] Fernando Lugo was ousted by a coup.[86] Rafael Correa is experiencing difficulties in Ecuador.[87] Venezuela is heavily affected . . . Do you see a pattern in how the right-wing is gaining momentum?

Lula: Yes, I do. The same thing is happening in El Salvador. The Farabundo Martí Front is facing challenges to govern.[88] But let me add that the judiciary has a role to play, which is to do justice. If people involved in the judiciary want to play politics, they should leave their role as judges, join a political party, and run for elections. When the judiciary does justice, people believe in justice. The problem with Car Wash is that at the same time they thought they were fighting corruption, they made an agreement to achieve the support of the Brazilian media. "No matter how big a lie is, I turn it into the truth. We have to have an enemy." Let's be frank: what they tried to do with Temer . . . There were many people among us saying, "Temer will fall tomorrow." I would say, "The reason why Globo wants to overthrow Temer is not the reason why I want it. That's not funny." Why? That was a sordid thing to do, fabricating a lie to get another term for Janot.[89] And to make the current speaker of the lower house the president of the republic was a sordid thing to do.[90] For that matter, I must historically acknowledge that Temer knew how to stand his ground. He demoralized Janot, Joesley, and Globo.[91] The subject simply vanished, and now he's able to govern. But look at Brazil today. No president should be prevented from picking a minister.

Gilberto Maringoni: Are you referring to Cristiane Brasil[92]?

Lula: This could apply to anyone. Even to me! If I want to appoint you as my minister tomorrow, that's my problem. I will be held responsible for the political consequences of having done so, but no one can stop it by saying things like: "He broke the neighbor's window when he was a kid."

Ivana Jinkings: Do you think that Cristiane Brasil should have been allowed to take office as minister?

Lula: I don't know her case and I don't defend it. I just think that preventing the president of the republic from choosing a minister is a serious thing. What if this becomes a trend? She failed to pay employees and she was sued. How many thousands of entrepreneurs fail to pay employees, and nothing happens to them? Temer will have to pay politically for his choice, because the opposition parties will crush him, the press will crush him. But it's not up to the judiciary to decide who will be a minister and who won't.

Gilberto Maringoni: That's why I asked you about the Clean Record Act, because it prevents candidates from running for office if they have been convicted by a second instance court.

Lula: But that was an interpretation. The Supreme Court's decision is that it's possible. It doesn't say it's final. It's just that people at the second instance level now seem to hold divine power.

Maria Inês Nassif: Do you believe in the legal system?

Lula: If I didn't, I wouldn't have proposed founding a political party. I would have proposed a revolution. I did it democratically, believing that every institution has a role and that the judiciary has the role of doing justice, of giving people the right to defend themselves, the right to the presumption of innocence and, when proven guilty, of making people pay for their crimes. I don't want someone who's being treated unjustly to be convicted, or someone who's guilty to be acquitted.

Ivana Jinkings: That's not what happened in your case.

Lula: We always learn from history. Look at what's happening nowadays... I left my house today and saw a sign reading: "No to Lula's imprisonment." I don't like this poster. I don't even know who created it. I would rather have them make a poster saying: "Lula is innocent." Because if I were guilty, I would have to be arrested. The same line of reasoning applies to my candidacy. I never liked the expression "elections without Lula are a fraud." Because it would have been better to focus on a more positive message: "We will prove Lula's innocence so that he can run for president." Of course, when you are receiving solidarity, you don't have a say in the matter. Anyway, I'd rather talk about how sordid what they're doing to me is. Because there's a part of the population that doesn't like me. They didn't like me in 1978, they didn't like me in 1982, they didn't like me in 1994 . . .and they still don't like me. There will always be people who don't like us. The same thing happens all over the world. So you work to persuade people. People can be persuaded. This is what politics is about. It's the art of persuasion.

Maria Inês Nassif: What if you do run for the presidency and win in 2018? What would your priority be?

Lula: In order to lead the country, someone who is elected president of the republic today should be committed to goals that go beyond economics. First, we need to restore the credibility of institutions and stabilize democracy. The National Congress has to re-establish credibility, and that can only be done with the quality of its members and their behavior; you need to make people believe again that the judiciary will ensure the Brazilian Constitution is properly enforced, and that the reason why the government exists is to benefit Brazilian society. But first, credibility needs to be re-established, because if you win the election and say, "I'm going to create a tax reform bill," it won't be approved. I did that twice . . . The tax policy process I carried out in 2007 was supported by all the twenty-seven governors, party leaders, all industry CEOs in this country, and the entire union movement. I had so much support that when I sent it to the National Congress, I said: "We are going to implement a tax policy for the first time." What happened then? I said we needed to put the project in the hands of someone who really wanted to approve it. I told Arlindo Chinaglia to ask Palocci to prepare the report.[93] But he sent the process to Sandro Mabel.[94] The following week, Serra started traveling around the country and speaking badly of Mabel, that he was this and that, that he was a racketeer . . .[95] That was the end of the tax reform. These things don't happen by magic. As far as tax reform in Brazil is concerned, we must consider that the people who pay more income tax proportionately are the working class, the ones whose taxes are deducted at source. It should actually be the other way around: the rich should be the ones to pay more. This means we should start discussing how inheritance taxes work, for example. The income tax that rentiers pay is a shame.[96] But in order to address that, you have to win the election by opposing it, knowing that you will have lots of people against you. Also, you need to elect Congress members that agree with you, or you won't succeed in changing the policy.

Gilberto Maringoni: Mr. President, will recall referendums regarding the reforms be possible?[97]

Lula: Yes, we need to talk about what we really want. Do we want a recall referendum or a new constituent assembly? Because our Citizens' Constitution—so well led by the late Ulysses Guimarães—no longer exists.[98] Altogether, 105 articles have been modified. A new Constitution has been formulated. Let me tell you something that sometimes bothers me. I keep thinking, "What if I was on the other side?" I always try to put myself on the side of opponents. I imagine they must be thinking, "We came up with a fraud scheme that made the coup possible, then we managed to remove Dilma from office. And we did all this for Lula to return for another term? Running the risk of him bringing Dilma back to the government?" Because I would indeed bring her back, so that she could do the things like no one else knows how to do. Would they run the risk of me setting up ministries even stronger than the first time? Fuck [slams his fist on the table]. People like to live well. No one is happy to earn little, no one is happy to eat poorly. The fact that Moro asks for housing aid when he thinks he's not getting what he needs shows that people are fond of living well.[99] [Laughing.] This is what we want to teach people: "Supplement your income by claiming housing assistance."

Juca Kfouri: Mr. President, don't you think that was the problem with the PT administrations, in the sense that it thought more about consumers than about citizens?

Lula: No, I was thinking about citizens. Because citizens that can't be consumers are considered nothing at all. Citizens that can't eat, can't get dressed, and can't drink are rejected. They are not viewed as citizens.

Gilberto Maringoni: The PT administrations have been accused of co-opting social movements and undermining their militant spirit.

Lula: That's not the truth. That's an unjust accusation, just as the allegation that the PT has appointed too many of our staff members for positions of trust. But when you think about the history of Brazil, it's clear that the PT was the party that least created positions of trust. The right is smart: they accuse us of doing that to make sure they keep their positions there. And we didn't co-opt social movements. During my administration, we put in place social policies that responded to decades-long demands. Just think about it. In twelve years, lands made available for the agrarian reform in Brazil represented a total of 52 percent of all the lands destined for that purpose in five hundred years. We have passed a bill that guaranteed a minimum wage adjustment according to GDP growth and inflation. For twelve years, there were wage increases in all the organized professional sectors in the country. There was no co-opting.

Look at what I told the union movement. One day they brought me a document aimed at reducing work hours, and I said, "I won't do it. It's your job. You take it, you sign it, go to the gates of factories, talk to the workers, then come to Congress. Don't come ask me to do it from top-down. I won't do it. This will only work if the workers want it." So I think that social movements have grown complacent with the policies we created. I have held seventy-four national conferences to discuss public policies; there were municipal and state conferences, and then the national one.[100] This gave the impression that I was being heard and participating. But especially during Dilma's administration, and particularly from 2013, 2014 onwards, we limited our discussion to economics. We started talking less and less about politics at the gates of factories and among social movements.

Ivana Jinkings: How do you feel today about the prosecutions and all the persecution against you?

Lula: I feel this is really unfair to me. I would never have imagined I would be going through what I'm going through in 2018. I don't deserve this campaign of lies disseminated against me. Think about my political history and my day-to-day life. Think about everything I've done and everything I am. Think about how appropriate my attitude was and will always be in relation to this country. However, from a politician's point of view, I believe that all of us who take sides pay a price for it. I'm willing to pay mine. Sometimes I'm in a bad mood, sometimes I'm in a good mood. The only thing that gives me peace of mind is that I know I didn't commit any crime, and that I know what they want. I think we were able to foster political sensitivity among the population. The Carnival showed that.[101] There were no bands supporting Moro or Temer. We have witnessed Globo growing ashamed of doing an interview. We have witnessed a lot of things . . .

Gilberto Maringoni: Do you feel that in the streets? Don't people harass you?

Lula: I've never been harassed. I'm very careful. Since before I was president of the republic, I have a great sense of self-preservation and I avoid going to bars and restaurants. Never before in Brazilian history was a president so rarely seen in restaurants. When I was president of the republic, I went to two restaurants in my travels: once in the United States, because they invited me saying that I would eat fantastic meat (and I didn't like the meat I ate there); the other one was in Norway . . . I was with the prime minister and really wanted to eat cod . . . Then I got there and discovered that there is no cod in Norway, they don't even know what cod is. I remember that my mother used to cook cod for the week of Easter, cod with coconut milk, which we eat a lot in the north-east. I was like: "Wow, Norwegian cod, that's what I want to eat." I went there, but there is nothing of the kind [laughing]. Cod is something that the Portuguese and we like to eat; and the fish that the Portuguese cook and sell is not even called cod. It was such a disappointment.

But what I really mean to say is that I have not left the house for a long time. If I have to drink, I drink at home. I must take precautions. That's why I was angry with that guy from the *New York Times* when he wrote that story about Lula's tippling, because I doubt that a journalist ever saw me drunk.[102] The last time I got really drunk was when we bought drinks to watch the Brazil vs. Netherlands match for the 1974 World Cup.[103] A union doctor brought his seventeen-inch television—the first color TV I had ever seen—and we were waiting to drink after the victory. But then we lost 2-0; we cursed the players and drank. I was in a pitiful state when I came home, and Marisa, who had guests, said: "And now, how are you going to do it?" And I, with that drunk talk . . . She said, "You're going to have dinner"—I'm talking about 1974—"you eat your dinner here to get a little better, and I'll go to the living room." She served me a nice dish of rice and beans, and I fell face first into it [laughing]. What a scene! To die in my own house, drowned in bowl of beans. Then I strode through the room and said: "Good night!" The worst thing in the world is when a drunk person pretends not to be drunk [laughing a lot]. It's better to just accept it. All I remember is that I walked straight to the door, but I tripped on the coffee table and fell on the sofa [laughing even more] . . . And I never got drunk again. So it pisses me off when people say they saw something that didn't happen. I've never been ashamed to say that I drink. I don't hide that I like to drink, or that I'm a Corinthians fan. My team is Corinthians and I don't hide it. I like to drink. I love to have a little whiskey and a bit of cold cachaça from time to time. But at my age, I take care of myself. I have to take care of myself. Something happened this week. I have a bottle of 1961 Romanée-Conti that I have kept for twenty years. Because being poor sucks. Marisa and I used to be given alcohol as a gift and say: "Oh, let's save, let's not drink it" [laughing]. Just to tell other people: "I have a bottle of Romanée-Conti." But I learned my lesson. If somebody gives me a nice bottle, I won't say, "I have it." I'll say, "I drank it."

So, this week I opened the box to finally drink the Romanée-Conti. It looked like it had a pharaoh buried in it. The box came with all the necessary equipment, the corkscrew, that thing to cut the seal, and all the things to serve the wine. When I put in the opener, the cork just fell into the bottle. It was pure vinegar. The other day I went to open a bottle of rum that Fidel gave me. It was one hundred years old. He gave it to me in 1985 and it was like a jewel for me, I showed it to everyone; One day I said to Marisa: "Let's drink it?" . . . When I opened the bottle, there was only water inside. Now I have at home a liter of rum that Raúl gave me.[104] It came in a huge box, it looked like a table; when I opened it, there was this really tiny bottle in honor of the five hundred years of Santiago de Cuba, and soon, I'll drink it. I've been criticized too much because, during the 2002 campaign in Rio de Janeiro, Duda Mendonça bought a bottle of Romanée-Conti . . . But it was for eight people![105] They gave me a dose the size of this little coffee cup, and I had to explain myself for a long time. It's always been the same. That's why I'm so cool-headed, because I know how it is.

Ivana Jinkings: Mr. President, let's talk a little more about Car Wash.

Lula: I never imagined that the processes would have the progress and the treatment that they had during the entire proceeding. Let me give you an example of the former. When the first problem with the apartment came up, I went to talk to some lawyers, and they said, "No, Lula, this isn't going to work. This is so insignificant, it's so . . . You know? You need to have a title deed. No one can say that the apartment is yours, if the apartment is not yours." I remember when a very important comrade, Nilo Batista, who was part of the first process, said: "Lula, there is no chance that this process is going to work. This will stop. This is so ridiculous!"[106] Do you remember that, during the first hearing, I said: "Hey, Moro, have you ever gone to a store to buy shoes with your wife? The seller brings her lots of boxes, she tries on a couple of shoes and, then, she puts them all back into the boxes, right? Did she buy any of them? No, so she has no shoes. Now, imagine that the storeowner would sue her for trying on the shoes. Does she have to pay for them now? I was willing and able to buy an apartment . . . Did I buy the apartment?"

This was the most elementary process ever, and everybody said that it was not going to work . . . They had to take me to Curitiba [where the headquarters of Operation Car Wash are located], because it only made sense to sue me to take make it part of Car Wash. They invented a terrible story. They showed up with an offshore company that had bought an apartment in the same block, saying that, therefore, this company was related to [contractor] OAS, and that, therefore, Petrobras had something to do with the building. That was the explanation for taking the process to Curitiba. Five days later, someone discovered that the same offshore company owned an apartment that belonged to the Globo organization in Paraty, and that it also owned Globo's helicopter. A woman was arrested and then released, the offshore disappeared, the subject disappeared, but Lula ended in Curitiba.[107] With all the complaints we made, they never paid attention to any arguments of the defense. It was at this moment that I began to realize that Lula was not being personally judged. The government was on trial. The way we carried out our government was on trial.

I've already told you about it, but it's worth going back to it. They begin to ask, "How do you choose a minister?" Instead, they could ask Temer how he chooses a minister. Or they could ask Fernando Henrique Cardoso how he used to choose his ministers, how he was able to approve the reelection law. Anything! But the problem was the Lula administration. Why did you pick someone from the PP? Why did you pick someone from the PMDB? Come on, comrade! Any democratic regime, any government that runs an election—especially in a presidential regime—but doesn't have the majority in the Congress will have to establish political alliances. And it's normal for parties in the coalition to pick names for the government, you know? It's the same thing all over the world. The thing was so serious that one day I called the director general of the Federal Police and Jose Eduardo Cardozo and I said: "Guys, a person can't become a police prosecutor without political training!"[108] Then, I started to realize that the government itself was on trial. They were judging the way we made our government. How does someone pick a person for a position? How do we appoint a director for Petrobras? Let's think about Paulo Roberto and Duque, who had a career of thirty years in the company.[109] When someone picks the name of a guy like that, he passes through the GSI [Institutional Security Office]. The GSI researches to find out if they have any problems. It's odd that, after they were chosen—and we are talking about people who had a thirty-year career—the Petrobras Council, which is actually responsible for picking the names, said nothing about it. The workers' union didn't question it, the engineers' union didn't say a thing, nor did the Public Prosecutor's Office.

Nobody contested it. When such a name arrives without contest, and the guy is professionally capable, what happens? He gets appointed. And that works for everyone. But they didn't want Lula. In 2015, I told PT, during an event in Brasilia, that the party should be careful, because they were working to criminalize the PT; we had the example of what happened with the PCB [Brazilian Communist Party].[110] Later, everything was confirmed with Dallagnol's PowerPoint presentation, as I already told you. If this were a serious country, he would have been laid off for the sake of the public service, when he made that PowerPoint presentation. A guy builds such a blatant lie and, after an hour and a half, says: "Do not ask me for evidence. I have conviction." This can't be serious. He must have agreed with someone to turn those lies into truth, it's the only way he could have done such a thing. It was the media, led by Rede Globo de Televisão. I think Globo made it for him, the people who build PowerPoint presentations for *Fantástico*.[111] After that, they started to follow all the lectures I gave, asking for the transcripts, which I had no obligation to have. In all my lectures, I read the speech that was written, and what I say adlib was recorded, photographed, and I still gave interviews in many places. Yet, their first suspicion was that the lectures were secret! So we have the speeches, the recordings, and the photos, but none of this matters to them. It was necessary to continue lying. And then there's the trip to Africa, the port of Mariel in Cuba, and the money that went to BNDES.[112] For them, everything turned into ammunition, so they could say that the PT is a criminal organization and therefore everything the PT did was wrong.

I even joke with the lawyers. If in the simplest process the guys gave me twelve years in jail, think about what will happen with the most difficult ones.

Ivana Jinkings: Which ones are the most difficult?

Lula: From now on, all of them, dear . . . A good example is the case involving Frei Chico, for which I testified on Monday [February 26, 2018]. Odebrecht had a guy linked to the old Communist Party, and he hired Frei Chico to advise Odebrecht on its conflicts with the trade union movement. Suddenly, they say that I was responsible for getting Frei Chico a R$3,000 job. Since I had done Odebrecht a favor, Odebrecht was going to give R$3,000 to Frei Chico! Hey, I must be a pretty useless thief! A guy like that should be arrested for demoralizing corruption! And if someone was to hire Chico, he deserves at least ten [thousand reals], because Frei Chico is a good unionist, he has political history, he has a good head on his shoulders, you know. I was with Frei Chico yesterday, and I said, "Frei Chico, what can I do?" Frei Chico, who is a personality in the trade union movement, shouldn't have to go through this. If, at some point, Odebrecht needed to hire Frei Chico, the company was hiring a guy who had a trade union background. He was vice president of the São Caetano do Sul Metalworkers Union. He left only because he was arrested along with Vladimir Herzog in 1975.[113]

I told the police deputy: "The guy you accuse of selling himself for R$3,000, actually spent seventy-five days being tortured by the police." Seventy-five days. Do you think a guy with his track record would sell himself for R$3,000? And do you believe this guy would need his brother, who is the damn president of the republic, to talk a company into giving him three thousand? Oh, fuck off! [Slams his fist on the table.] Other ludicrous things will be cleared up with time. In this moment that I am living, my only satisfaction is to be able to say: "I am making history." I don't know when it will be told properly, but I'm trying to contribute, I'm trying to make history. That's why people say: "Oh, Lula, you could go to an embassy, you could ask for political asylum." But I will stay in Brazil, in my home. If they want to make history by sending me to jail, so be it. What impresses me the most is the absurdity of the method, of how this lie has been told. And what is the most serious thing about this process? It's how it is based on a huge lie, the one told with a PowerPoint presentation, the one that's called mothership, and that they have to maintain at any cost. Magazines like *Veja* and *IstoÉ* serve as the basis for almost every investigation. Take the condo for example: it's all based on deceitful news articles published by *O Globo*. Moro quotes *O Globo* five hundred times. So, since everything is based on lies, and they've been lying for the past four years, it's impossible for them to stop now. That's why I told him during my statement: "Come on, Moro. Your only option is to convict me. You're *Globo*'s hostage." And *Globo* is his hostage. One feeds the other.

Juca Kfouri: What makes you more outraged? Is it the feeling of injustice or of impotence?

Lula: It is the feeling of injustice. The feeling of injustice, the dirt behind the most blatant lie ever told in this country, and all the harm it has caused to my kids. It harms my kids and my grandkids. Four of my children are unemployed. And who is going to give a job to someone from the Lula family? My son Fabio, who owned PlayTV . . . In 2006, when *Veja* decided to make a cover, what was it for? It was to harass him, because PlayTV was getting better ratings than MTV.[114] So, "let's destroy this damned Lulinha." Since 2006! I'm talking about twelve years ago. So it is not just the feeling of innocence, but of persecution.

Gilberto Maringoni: As far as the press was concerned, you had a cordial relationship with Globo's high command, with Roberto Marinho and his children. How is it now?

Lula: I had a cordial relationship with everyone. Although it doesn't seem like it, I'm a very cordial guy in my relationships with people. It was just like that with Bandeirantes, Globo, Record, with Silvio Santos, and Folha.

Juca Kfouri: Where did the relationship go wrong?

Lula: They can't stand social mobility in this country. Specially among the oppressed.

Gilberto Maringoni: But they profit from it, don't they?

Lula: In reality, all the money they make won't make them less annoyed on the airplane, or in public spaces, you know? Guys, the Brazilian elite are so perverse that, during the Battle of Guararapes, the colonels let neither the blacks nor the Indians participate and said, "If we win with them, they will come after us."[115] It's just like that. I've always treated everyone well. Always.

Maria Inês Nassif: When did you realize that they were plotting against you? During the Mensalão scandal?

Lula: Actually, I never believed the Mensalão story. This was the greatest discovery of the twenty-first century: how to use the media to criminalize people before justice. The media has made the decision to turn some of the PT leaders into thugs, instead of waiting for the justice to catch up with them. If Zé Dirceu had not been arrested, I was afraid that a fanatic could have attacked and killed him on some street here in São Paulo, such was the hatred they spread against Zé Dirceu.[116]

Ivana Jinkings: How do you evaluate José Dirceu's behavior throughout the whole story, including when he was arrested?

Lula: I think José Dirceu is a warrior. Sometimes, I think he doesn't take care of his own image. But he is a man of great dignity and a comrade who was able to face the whole process he is going through with his head held up high.

Juca Kfouri: Do you believe he is innocent, and was persecuted like you?

Lula: I can't be categorical and say whether José Dirceu had contact with a businessman, if he asked for money, if he did something. He acknowledged having done some things. In my case, I continue to challenge Moro, the appeals court, the Federal Police, the Public Prosecutor's Office to prove that I received even a penny from a businessman in my life. I never needed favors. It's not just a question of honesty, it's a matter of political behavior. It was like this when I was in the workers' union, that's how I was in the PT, that's how I was during the presidency. No businessman ever had the courage to offer me a penny. It only happens when the receiving party has it written on their forehead: "I will accept it if you offer it."

Gilberto Maringoni: Mr. President, you often say that: "They never profited as much as during my administration." Do you think this an advantage or a problem?

Lula: The problem with the capitalist system is that you can't survive if you're not willing to make money. A guy like that will never start a business . . . If I want to start a business, I have to know whether my product is profitable. Then I do market research before I start my company. If the perspective is positive, I go ahead. If not, I just don't do it. I'll give you an example. Sometimes, left-leaning people have an ideological behavior, but this ideological behaviour doesn't fit reality. I start an acquisition process to build a table like this [knocks on the table]. If the guy realizes that the rate of return is small, he will simply not do it. If he doesn't do it, you'll have to create another acquisition process, or start a state-owned company to make the table.

Ivana Jinkings: Mr. President, how is your relationship with the business class right now? None of them came back? Despite the conviction, you are ahead in the polls . . .

Lula: Come on, guys. Everybody is afraid! Who will be crazy enough to have a meeting with Lula? Who is this foolish?

Ivana Jinkings: Not even discreet meetings, with no information given to the media?

Lula: It's difficult, Ivana. I know it's difficult. When you are under attack . . . I'm under attack by the Federal Police, by the Public Prosecutor's Office, by the judiciary and by the Federal Revenue Service. Do you know how much the revenue service has fined the [Lula] Institute? Almost R$18 million! This blockade is fiercer than the one being made against Cuba for the past sixty years. They want to prevent our survival. The strategy is to choke us economically and to kill us politically. This is how things are going in Brazil. No businessman would give even ten reals to the institute, because every real must be accounted for. Who would be willing to give? It won't work. So, the only thing that makes me happy is to know who my real friends are and who were circumstantial friends. Who's with me today? It's the people who were always by my side. The circumstantial friends are gone.

To me, that's a life lesson. I had been through this in 1982, when I lost the workers' union, I lost the elections for governor, and I was a nobody. I discovered that I was nothing. I got up in the morning at home, Marisa and I tried to find money lying around, we went through the boys' little piggy banks to find a coin and buy a cigarette. We drank coffee with bread without butter, because we could not afford it. And no one came to see us and ask: "Hey, Lula, do you have butter? Lula, do you have a cigarette?" Never. So, I already had a bit of that life experience. These things don't hurt me because I know how things are. I know how it is. I don't do things expecting favors. I just don't. That's why I want to go back. I'll be much more mature when I come back. I won't come back harder, because my heart is all peace and love . . .

Juca Kfouri: That's the question. So, the way you will treat the people who were able to do everything they're doing is going to be the same again, because of your big heart . . .

Lula: Let me tell you something. Whoever takes over the presidency of the republic shouldn't treat an entire sector as their enemy. All the friends that have disappeared will come back. They will ask for meetings; they will want to talk. I know how it works. Now, If I'm coming back to be angry, I'd better not come back at all. If I'm coming back to hate someone, I'd better not come back at all. I want to go back to rule and to prove that I have the competence to recover this country; after four years, I want to make this country smile again; I want to make people happy and to make sure they are able to work. That's why I want to go back. Not to fulfil my revenge against anyone.

Maria Inês Nassif: Mr. President, how do you classify the plea bargain informers?

Lula: I'm going to tell you a story. In 1989, Paulo [Okamotto] was my campaign treasurer. He asked a businessman for money, and the guy simply said, "I do not have money, I can't give any money, I'm screwed." And he didn't give any money. It's alright. After the elections, the same businessman came to my house with R$60,000 in banknotes, and said: "Lula, I couldn't give you the money because I didn't have any at the time, but I know you owe a lot and I've come to help you." And I said to the guy: "Oh, thank you, thank you very much, but I needed the money during the campaign. The campaign is over; I don't need the money now. You can take your money back." The guy: "Oh, Lula, no! Lula, are you offended? The only reason I didn't give it to you before was because I didn't have it. Take the money." "I won't take your money. Thank you very much, my dear. I'm grateful, but if you gave it to me before, during the campaign, I would have taken it. Now I don't want it anymore." The guy couldn't believe it. And why did I have this behavior? It's because I like to respect people and I like to be respected too.

Ivana Jinkings: Did the 1989 campaign owe a lot of money?

Lula: Yes! And not even the family gives money to the defeated candidate, you know? So I did that, and I always do, because whoever wants to run for president in Brazil always has to walk with dignity. Always! I can't look at an entrepreneur, whatever their size, knowing that I'm stuck with them. So it's better not to be a candidate.

Ivana Jinkings: I would like you to talk about your plans for the future. What will you do if you are elected?

Lula: I have attended many meetings with economists recently. And I always say to them: "There's a component that you don't discuss in the economy, which is the central base of economic success—the presence of a leader with credibility in the eyes of society. A leader who uses this credibility to ensure that what he says is accepted by society. You can't forget that before I took office in 2003, every economist I met would say: "Brazil is bankrupt. Brazil won't work. Brazil went bankrupt twice in the

Fernando Henrique Cardoso administrations. Lula won't be able to rule. The IMF won't let him rule . . ."

I even told them: "Guys, If Brazil is how you're telling me, why do you want me to be elected president of the republic? It's better if they win. If the country goes bust, let it go bust in their hands." I was aware of that. But my obsession with not getting it wrong was too big. It was a commitment of faith. If I were to make a mistake, how would I go back to São Bernardo? I couldn't mess things up, because I wouldn't be able look all the workers in the eye. They don't know what it's like. None of the guys who got there know what it's like, because none of them made the commitment I made. See, I'm thankful to Fernando Henrique Cardoso for the smooth transition. Don't think that I forget. I don't. What makes me criticize Fernando Henrique Cardoso is that he expected my failure to return, and didn't know how to deal with my success. He could have been a winner, a partner of my success. But he didn't know how. Regrettably, that's exactly what happened. So I used all my political power to make a heavy adjustment. You certainly remember that I raised the economic surplus to 4.1 percent of the GDP, because I had to trade it for the things I wanted to do.

Gilberto Maringoni: The interest rate rose too . . .

Lula: The interest rate was already at 23 percent and it came to 26 percent. But it had already been at 49 percent in the past. The fact is that I started to gain credibility with this. Then, suddenly, Tony Blair began to speak well of me. Gordon Brown began to speak well of me.[117] Chirac began to speak well of me, Bush began to speak well of me. Schröder in Germany.[118] Angela Merkel too, and so did China. Suddenly I became the consensus. And I think that, because I was the only person from the working class to become president of Brazil, they said, "Damn, this guy is doing what needs to be done."

Gilberto Maringoni: The media is always saying "Lula is a radical." The left, that "he's a centrist." How would you define yourself today?

Lula: I don't like to put a label on my forehead, you know? You have to be a leftist when you need to be more of a leftist and you can be liberal when you have to deal with people who think differently. I can't deal with an entire country trying to make it just like me. I even make fun of it sometimes. Obviously, some comrades take offense. I used to say, "Any person who wants to be more leftist than me is going to be a moron, not a leftist." Being a leftist doesn't keep you from saying palatable things. A moron is a person who talks, and talks, and talks about something he knows—but he won't make any of it come true.

In 1980, I learned to avoid saying "80 percent or nothing" when I was bargaining during a strike. Because, in the end, we would be left with nothing. So I learned to always have in mind the goals that were attainable. I remember one time I went to a journalists' strike and ended it, upon comrade Davi de Morais's request.[119] We were picketing in front of Estadão and I saw some good-looking journalists flirting with the Federal Police officers. I also saw lots of employees going to work, with the newspaper in their hands. I said: "Fuck off, is this how you hold a strike? Some girls are flirting with the police, and there's more: the newspaper is circulating, the guys are coming to work and they are reading the newspaper! So you didn't stop the distribution, you didn't stop the printing. Is it supposed to be a strike, or what?" Some of my friends didn't want me to put an end to the strike. At that time, I was called a "neo-blackleg," "dictatorship's little helper." That's how it is. I learned a lot. One thing that really makes me proud is that my discourse was always coherent. If you look at a speech I gave in 1979 and compare it with a recent one, you'll see the same sequence. I learned some new words and expressions, nowadays I say "en passant"—something that I absolutely didn't say before [laughing]—I don't say "we was" anymore . . . But the structure and the coherence are the same. You know what? I'm not a scientific worker, as my friend Prestes would prefer.[120]

I'm a worker worker. I'm more than scientific: I'm a worker. Once I went to a debate with Prestes in Cajamar and, afterwards, he said: "I really like Luiz Inácio, but he is not a scientific worker." I replied: "What the hell, Prestes, I'm already a worker, and you want me to be scientific too? Be damned!" [Laughing.]

Maria Inês Nassif: In an eventual new administration, your support base will be very defined, very polarized. Would it be different from the 2002 elections?

Lula: If we don't change the Brazilian political model, if we don't accomplish a political reform in which the political parties are more ideologically defined, whoever the next president is—be it comrade Manuela, comrade Guilherme Boulos, comrade Ciro Gomes, Bolsonaro or whoever the most popular candidate is—by the end of the vote count, the winner will have to see how big is their base in Congress and in the Senate.[121] They will know that, to have anything relevant approved in the National Congress, they will need at least 247 votes. Without it, they will need to negotiate. And these negotiations usually involve talking to people who voted for other candidates. That's how the Second World War came to an end. Somebody had to negotiate. What did Stalin want? What did Truman want? And what about Churchill? You have to negotiate. That's how it is. If it is not so, you can't rule. In Brazil, there is an issue that many people don't see: the problem is not the PMDB, the PMDB has a face, you know who is part of the PMDB; the real problem is the amount of medium size parties with twenty congressmen, eighteen congressmen. Together, they become the absolute majority. Look at the crime that has been just approved: the Electoral Party Fund. If the PT has a candidate for president, a percentage of the fund is specifically destined to the presidential campaign. I'm telling you to look closely at this issue, because almost no party will want a presidential candidate. So, the parties that have a presidential candidate will have to use thirty percent of the fund's money for the presidential campaign. On the other hand, parties that choose to have no presidential candidate will be able to get all the fund's money and distribute it among the candidates for Congress. So, a party with a presidential candidate will give five hundred reals to each of their candidates to Congress, while parties without a presidential candidate will be able to give two or three million reals. This is the dictatorship of the minority against the majority, son! And the National Congress has just approved that.

Gilberto Maringoni: But isn't it good that they banned the private funding of electoral campaigns?

Lula: Private funding wasn't banned. It's over for us. Even before the law, the PT decided no longer to accept private funding and this is what the PT is going to do. The PT will have to learn how to sell t-shirts again. I'm a good product. If the party wants to sell me, the PT will make a lot of money. Before giving a speech, I used to say: "Dear comrades, we're selling balls, shirts, overalls. If you buy it, I'll have money to go to the next city." People bought it. It's harder, but it's more enjoyable. And you are able to sleep with a clear conscience. The PT will do just that. I want to know who's going to do the same. There will still be private funding of campaigns and I doubt candidates will finance their campaigns with money from their own pockets.

Show me a congressperson from any political party that has sold their car to fund their campaign. They usually borrow it from other people. It will take a long time to moralize this country. If I'm a candidate, I'll use my campaign to discuss the importance of proportional representation. It's no good to vote for a decent left-wing president, and then vote for a right-wing congressperson. It doesn't matter if you sympathize with the landless, if you are voting for large landowners. So let's take some time and try to politicize the campaign a little. Make the voter more demanding. When the guy votes for a right-wing bastard who attacks the PT all the time, he doesn't have the courage to say who he voted for. He may even forget two hours after voting. So we'll try to politicize the campaign a bit and build a stronger Congress during the campaign process. The best Congress I ever had was the Constituent Assembly. There was a guy who was not a leftist, but was a good man, like Mario Covas.[122] There was Ulysses Guimarães, who was no leftist, but was a man who had credibility and didn't give in to everything the left wanted, but neither did he give in to everything the right wanted.

Gilberto Maringoni: Mr. President, let me ask you something that popped into my mind several times during our conversation: do you tell the PT what to do?

Lula: No, I don't. And I don't want to.

Juca Kfouri: But, if you don't direct the party, what is it that you direct? Corinthians?

Lula: The PT is a different thing. You'll understand. The PT is different from the so-called "traditional left." In the traditional, historical left, the general secretary of the party was almost an emperor. When the general secretary spoke, the Central Committee obeyed, and he often spoke on behalf of the Central Committee. When a congress opened, the general secretary read his speech, and the congress was decided. In the PT, thanks to our background in the union movement, in the grassroots communities, in the social movements, a leader is not respected for his position. He is respected for the work he does. With the PT, if you are not careful, you go to Roraima and, once there, if you talk some nonsense during a meeting with the local party leadership, they won't hesitate to raise their voices and tell you: "No! Here things are not like that! No way!" So you have to talk to them. This kind of culture doesn't exist in other political parties. It just doesn't exist. Obviously, I know that I'm an important figure for the PT. I know that my opinion carries weight. I know that. But, for example, I was outvoted in the discussion about the punishment of Airton Soares, in 1985, before he voted [for Tancredo Neves in the Electoral College].[123] I thought that we should wait for the crime, and that he should only be punished after the fact. But the party base, including my comrade Djalma and other metallurgists, decided to expel Airton Soares, Bete Mendes, and José Eudes, against my will.[124] "You know what, Lula, you are good, but the decision is made by the majority!" You see? That's how things are done in the party. And I find it wonderful. Wonderful.

I once went to a congress of the Cuban Communist Party with Cervantes.[125] There were three thousand delegates, I was sitting there, and in every polling, the guy talked like that [speaking with Spanish accent]: "We are going to discuss now the thesis about industrialization. The committee has prepared a proposal; we sent it to Commander in Chief Fidel Castro today, and he agrees with it. Let's vote!" [Laughing.] Every decision was unanimous. So I said: "Hey, Cervantes, let me tell you something, damn it! In PT, if eleven members of the party executive committee meet and we come to an agreement, from the room where we made the agreement to the plenary, there's already dissension. It's impossible." Then he told me: "You'll see that there will be a lot of debate around the foreign policy issue, because it was not taken to the base to discuss." The next day I went there. Rafael, a great old Communist, spoke to the plenary: "Compañeros y compañeras, we will now vote the last thesis. Foreign policy. We didn't take this issue to the base, but yesterday we met with Commander in Chief Fidel Castro Ruz. We wrote a text and he agrees with it" [laughing]. Unanimous! I found it awesome! But that's how it is. When João Amazonas led the PCdoB, it was just like that.[126]

Before João Amazonas, it must have been even worse. It was like that in the old PCB. In other left-wing organizations . . . Everybody wants the PT to be democratic, but, when they met with small groups of Trotskyists and Maoists, there was nothing democratic about it. So, the most sacred thing is that the PT is a great political innovation in the world. The other day, in a plane coming from Cuba, I was talking with Guilherme Boulos.[127] Guilherme was really happy for talking with Podemos and who knows who.[128] I said: "Guilherme, let me tell you something, dear. Do you know the difference between the PT and Podemos? The PT is a thirty-eight-year-old human being. Podemos still wears diapers; it had no time to make a mistake, because it didn't even take office . . ." Now Guilherme wants to start the Avante, Vamos, Começamos . . . I have no idea. He will figure it out.

The PT made members of the left feel like citizens. The left was marginalized. A lot of small groups hidden everywhere. And suddenly, the PT appeared, opened a big umbrella. Each one of them has a place within the party, a chance to speak. The PT was against the occupation of Afghanistan when almost the whole left was favorable, even the Trotskyists.[129] I was against the Russian occupation; I was against the American occupation. I thought they should mind their own businesses. So the PT was able to establish the democratic coexistence even in adversity. Ivana doesn't have to think like me, or have the same religion as me. She doesn't have to be a Corinthians fan. She does whatever she wants to. But we can build together a project for this country. I think this is what makes the PT so ground-breaking. Its doctrine doesn't exclude those who think differently. Do you know what a soccer hooligan is? The PT is not that guy. The hooligan—as our Uruguayan comrade Galeano says—is not the guy who goes to the field to watch the game; he goes to the game and stares at the opponent, wanting to fight.[130] The game is the least important thing to him. The PT is not the hooligan. The PT wants to watch the game. And, if you pay attention, the more progressive things that happened in this country from the point of view of the public administration began with the city halls led by the PT in the 1980s.

Gilberto Maringoni: You mentioned several characters: Covas, Prestes, Ulysses. I was always very curious about one character that the PT had an eternal love-hate relationship with and that is Brizola. There was this episode in the runoff in the 1989 election in which Brizola transferred almost all of his votes directly to you. How was your relationship with Brizola?

Lula: Brizola was an extraordinary character. The issue with Brizola was that he had a very strong personality. He wasn't so fond of listening. You know that kind of leader who doesn't like to listen to other people? That kind of leader will come to a meeting and only talk. But there was a very funny situation with Brizola, which was in the runoff of the 1989 election. We had established a dialogue with him and we went to his house on Atlântica Avenue, in Copacabana. When we got there, his house was packed with PDT leaders, everyone was very agitated. Brandão Monteiro was there next to him, Vivaldo Barbosa was also there.[131] Brizola was there and I think there was another person. So José Dirceu, Gushiken, and I got there and started to talk. And Brizola says: "Look, Lula, I want to tell you something about the election, it was a virtual tie. Five hundred thousand votes are not much of a difference. So I think you and I should withdraw the candidacy and support Mário Covas." And I replied to him: "Hey, Brizola, this is not a poll! This is an electoral result. If people wanted Covas, they would have voted for him. Why the hell didn't they vote for him? I won the election and I want to talk to you about your support, man!" And so we talked about union issues, labor issues, the Getúlio issue . . . and they had prepared me for the following: "If Brizola grabs your hand and takes you to the window, this means you've won him over!" We kept on talking and talking, and when Brizola decided to change his stance he started to change his arguments and said: "You know, Lula, Australia had a prime minister who was a union leader and was responsible for the country's development!"

So I thought to myself: "I've won him over." So he gets up, grabs my hand, goes to the window . . .[laughing]. He worked very hard in the runoff. And why were his votes transferred to me? Well, you must be very careful with what you say . . . Brizola was dead sure he would make it to the runoff, dead sure. So his whole narrative was the following: "If I win, I will have Lula's support in the runoff. And if Lula wins, I want to give him all of my votes." And he said this with the conviction that he would win. So, it was really something, a landslide. When I went to talk to Brizola, there were polls indicating that his voting transference to me was of 75 percent for the runoff.[132]

Ivana Jinkings: There is an episode in front of Getúlio's tomb that Juca describes in his book . . .[133]

Lula: Brizola was resentful that I never visited Getúlio's grave [in São Borja, RS], especially because the PT was a severe critic of the Brazilian union structure and the Estado Novo [New State]. There are articles and books by many PT intellectuals criticizing him. Today I recognize Getúlio's mistakes but also his successes. But this was the reason Brizola complained. He wanted to be my vice president in 1998.[134] I really didn't want him to be my vice president. I wanted him to be a senator of the republic. I went to Rio to try to convince him and he said: "No, Lula, I want to be your VP." And he started to lecture me: "We will win and we will nationalize all private enterprises." And I told him: "What the fuck, Brizola, if you say this we won't even make it to the runoff. This is the kind of thing we can only accomplish if we don't talk about it. If we mention this, we will never succeed in doing it."

Brizola was so impetuous. He would board an airplane—I think he was a licensed pilot or had a pilot license for a while—and it didn't matter if the pilot said it wasn't safe for landing. If there was an opening in the clouds he would tell the pilot to aim for it. Would I back him up? No! I would say to the pilot: "Man, you are the boss here." He managed to get to places during the campaign where I could not. I would never tell a pilot to land through a hole in the clouds. The pilot is the authority. If we can land there, great! If not, let's sleep over here which is fine as well. And Brizola would say, "Let's visit Getúlio's grave." This was quite something . . . I was visibly emotional, and he would talk to Getúlio and introduced me to Getúlio, as if he was alive: "Look, Dr. Getúlio, we are here with Lula. He is a real laborer, he works in a factory, he is a comrade. Unlike both of us who were not laborers, he is a laborer and can accomplish quite a lot in this country, Dr. Getúlio. I will be his vice president." And he would keep talking and becoming emotional. Once he was done with the talking, people clapped and he said: "Lula, wouldn't you like to say something?" I answered: "No, Dr. Brizola, not really." [Laughing.] I had nothing to say. He gave me some flowers, so I could place them on his grave. I placed them on the grave, and that was it. But he was very thankful. And he wasn't my vice president. [135]

Brizola is badly missed. I think people with a personality like Brizola's are badly missed, like Miguel Arraes and Eduardo Campos.[136] If Eduardo Campos hadn't run over history, we wouldn't be discussing Lula's campaign today. We would be discussing . . . Eduardo Campos would be running for president of the republic with the support of PT.

Ivana Jinkings: Would he take part in the coup against President Dilma?

Lula: It depends. I had talked to Eduardo Campos in June 2011 in Bogota. A politician who is in his second term usually starts to worry about the future. I knew I didn't want to be a senator. I told him: "Eduardo, if Dilma is fine she has to run for reelection. How am I supposed to remove her? But if you want . . . ." We were having a Blue Label [Johnnie Walker whiskey],

Eduardo, his wife, Renata, and me.[137] He had just been to a debate about governance in Bogota and I was supposed to give a lecture there. I thought he had agreed with me. It was a nice talk. I said: "Eduardo, I think Dilma won't need the PMDB's support in 2014 because she won't need airtime anymore. When we are known to the people, there is no need for so much airtime. So I think we can work with you on the vice presidency." And time went by and he became a little bit resentful because Dilma wouldn't treat him the same I did.

I had a very strong bond with Eduardo. I had a strong bond with Arraes and then with Eduardo. I treated him very well and vice versa, to the point that some governors from the PT became jealous about our relationship. I don't know whether this was the reason. I know I was invited one day . . . this was in 2012 and I had a very sore throat . . . there was a meeting in Rio with Sérgio Cabral, Eduardo Campos, and Jaques Wagner.[138] A weird conversation took place over lunch. Eduardo said: "Dilma's term must be seen as a theater play consisting of two acts. There is the first act, the second act, and I think the first act is not good." From 2012 on, he believed Dilma's government was not succeeding. I told him: "Eduardo, let me tell you something: Wagner, Sérgio Cabral, and you didn't invite me here to speak bad of Dilma. I hope this is not what's happening here. If you want to complain about Dilma, you have access to her cabinet. Give her a call and tell her, not me, what you have to say. Let's switch subjects because . . ." And so we stopped talking about this and our friendship was not the same again, never again. It was a pity. I thing Brazil lost something with this.

Juca Kfouri: Do you think this lunch meeting was decisive for his isolation?

Lula: I think his mind was set regarding Dilma. He has already thinking that maybe it was his turn. So he began with that narrative: "I won't run for the presidency if Lula is the candidate." He would call me and say: "If you are a candidate, I won't run." And he ran. It was a pity. I think Brazil lost so much with this. If he hadn't run, he wouldn't have been on that plane. He would have been recording with me at the studio—I got the news about his plane crash when I was recording at the studio. So it was a pity. This is the way people are. People must be patient.

Another example: comrade Ciro Gomes.[139] I like him. I just think Ciro is part of a select group of people who understand so much about everything that sometimes they forget to ask people "how are you doing?" because they already know how we are doing. We don't ask this question because we don't know the answer. We ask this question out of humbleness, to make others feel well when they answer. So, what do I think about Ciro? I think Ciro must learn how to win the PT over. Nobody will be a candidate from the left without the support of the PT. It is unnecessary to offend the PT and Lula. Ciro is entitled to offend my person, but he could say: "I don't like Lula, but I love the PT." But he won't do that. He ridicules the PT.

Juca Kfouri: It seems to me that it's exactly the opposite. The feeling I get is he likes you, but he doesn't like the PT.

Lula: Oh, but he does speak ill of me. He doesn't miss one opportunity to do so. It's a pity because I like Ciro. I think he is very intelligent, to a certain extent. Because if he were really smart, he would be standing up for the PT right now, if he truly believed I won't be able to run for the presidency. A vast part of the political class doesn't want me to run. Alckmin will say the following: "Lula can't run because if he runs we would only have one spot left in the runoff.[140] One of the spots is his, since he will make it to the runoff. He might even win the election in the first round. So, if he doesn't run, things will be pretty much the same. It's like a watermelon truck: there is room for everyone, except Bolsonaro."[141]

Temer is trying to launch his candidacy with this military intervention in Rio de Janeiro.[142] You see, he switched between a project [Social

Security Reform] rejected by 80 percent of the population to a proposal which has the support of 80 percent of the population, which is the public safety issue. The PMDB has expertise on this matter. The Cruzado Plan was inaugurated on September 26, 1986 and ended in October 1986.[143] It lasted until the elections: twenty-three governors and 306 constituent federal congresspersons. And Temer was already in the PMDB. So he is just making another move. Since nobody wants to stand up for his government, I think he is playing with the hypothesis that, if I am not a candidate, the only one kind of "consolidated" is Bolsonaro with his public safety approach. "If I carry out an intervention and militarize this issue, I can finish with Bolsonaro, taking his place as the candidate of public safety. Given that everyone has about 6, 7, 8 percent in the polls," he must think to himself: "I can recover my public image and make history as the man who tackled—at least momentarily—the issue of violence and criminality. That's why he made this decision. And do not be surprised if he reproduces this intervention in other states.

Gilberto Maringoni: Do you think this intervention represents this government's closure?

Lula: This is a complicated process for those whose dream is democracy. It is a delicate issue. I don't believe it will work.

Juca Kfouri: But is this a regression?

Lula: It is a regression for democracy, firstly because civil society is discredited and secondly because the army is not prepared for urban criminality. The army exists in in order to defend Brazil's sovereignty against external threats. There is no dialogue with an external threat, there is shooting. And this is not what will happen in a favela. The Army occupied the Maré Favela for one year but the outcome was not as expected. Nobody can explain why the UPPs, which were a success case in the beginning, have now failed.[144] Not even Globo mentions UPPs anymore. How come UPPs didn't succeed? There were tanks in the favela, it was a TV show. Society believed it would succeed. Do you know why it didn't? I think it's because some things must be enacted. It is important to remember that, prior to the 1988 Constitution, the armed forces were responsible for the police. The states and we, Brazilian democrats, fought our whole lives in order to get the armed forces out of public security, so that it could be the responsibility of the states. The states never accepted intervention because the police are an important power sphere that they use very well. So much that nobody wants to give up police power. Pezão didn't ask for an intervention. They were the ones who decided to intervene.

The armed forces have an extraordinary role, of course. We have eight thousand kilometers of maritime boundary. Most products that get to the country get here by sea. You don't have to go to the Atlantic Ocean in order to see contraband, just go to Itaipu Lake. It's possible to prevent drug smuggling if you have certain police control in Brazil. We also have sixteen thousand kilometers of nearly uncontrolled land borders. I remember that during my government, we decided to grant the army police powers, so it could carry out arrests. It's pointless to just watch someone smuggling. "Hey, come back here, you are not supposed to smuggle!"

We must have a system that will take care of our borders. We considered purchasing those remote unmanned Israeli planes during my government. The Federal Police should be present at our borders; they are not supposed to be in those huge buildings in São Paulo and Brasília. They should be at our borders! This is something the armed forces could do in an extraordinary manner. If we don't walk this path, we will be lost, because once we really need it . . . When Paraguay decides to attack us [laughing], our army will be in the favelas. How would we handle that?

Temer could have called the ministries of public safety, the governors, the army, the air force, the navy and specialists to have a serious discussion about public safety. I suggested the creation of a national guard, a more prepared police organization, which—in case of an emergency, and when demanded by the governor—could intervene in the states in order to assist local police. They did not even mention the national guard. So I am afraid that when this is over . . .

Juca Kfouri: Cláudio Lembo said the following a few days ago during a lecture: "Once you get the army out of the barracks, it is very difficult to bring them back inside. This is the problem." He went even further: "I know from personal experience; I took part in this in 1964."[145]

Lula: Speaking of which, Cláudio Lembo is a guy from the right-wing who I actually like. A person of great dignity . . . So I think that, in Brazil, people need to understand that pyrotechnics won't always work. This is not an issue for pyrotechnics. The problem remains and is of a political nature. And in my view, it is connected to the socioeconomic situation of our country. I went to the gym today; I got there at 5:30 in the morning. The girl who works there lives in Montanhão [a neighborhood on the outskirts of São Bernardo] and is married to a young fellow who works at TVT [a TV network belonging to the union of metalworkers of the ABC region and the union of bank workers of São Paulo, Osasco, and the surrounding area]. She leaves her house at 4:30 in the morning and gets to the gym by bus. She was going down Marechal Deodoro Street [downtown] and a guy grabbed her by the arm and said: "Hand me your cell phone and your money." This guy hurt her arm. He also grabbed her by the neck and said: "I'm carrying a gun. I just want your cell phone." This happens every day.

In a country where people mug and kill for a cell phone, a jacket, a pair of sneakers . . . This has less to do with criminality than with the socioeconomic issue. We are talking about poor people stealing from poor people. My sister-in-law, Joana, who works at my place, was coming to work when this guy places his hand on her shoulder and says: "Listen, cell phone." "But I don't have a cell phone," she says. "Yes, you do," he replies. She did actually own a cell phone, but she had hidden it somewhere in her shoes, trousers, or purse, I don't know. And then he says: "Money." "But I only have money for the bus ticket," she answers. And he says: "Give it to me. But next time I want your cell phone, you hear me?" She got home very scared, you know?

In a country where people are mugging for things like these, do you think the army will solve the problem? People must be treated with respect because they are also scared. Now, let's see. How do TV shows like *Datena* work?[146] These TV shows are actually fostering criminality. There is nothing educational about them. They are just about beating, killing, shooting.

I don't know if I told you. Who shot that Globo journalist who went to that funk party? Tim.[147] Globo killed him! Globo sent him undercover to the favela, when he could have said: "Look, I'm going there to write a story." How do you send someone like that? And then when he dies, you blame others?

So I think the debate on public safety is deeper than simply intervening with the army and saying: "It's over! I won." Public opinion will certainly be happy. They will see an army tank in the street. Everything will be wonderful!" This is irresponsible. This is irresponsible with the army, irresponsible with the people, and it shows the government is not approaching the issue of public safety in a serious manner.

If only these people had jobs... What is the issue with these types of crimes? A fourteen-year-old is not a criminal; he is not a murderer. He can get by. What happens if the state is unable to provide him with means of livelihood? Crime rates are higher where the state doesn't exist. The inexistence of public policies by the state is greatly responsible for these youngsters who get lost, who die.

I don't have the numbers here. But anyways, fighting crime is a responsibility of state governments and it is a complex subject. We created the PRONASCI, which had the objective of creating quality schools for these kids, and then it stopped.[148] I remember a criminal called Nem who was interviewed by Época's magazine: "Lula is my idol. I love Lula. He was the one who fought crime the most efficiently. Because of Rocinha's PAC. Fifty of my men quit drug trafficking to work in construction sites. Do you know how many went back to criminality after this? None, because they realized they had a job and a future in civil construction."[149]

Fighting crime is connected to smart police work and jobs, opportunities, education, leisure, and culture in the favelas. People need to see their mayors taking care of them, that public policies are there. But they are born abandoned. We need to tackle this issue: who will take care of public safety? Is it the federal government? Let's discuss it. What is the role of the states? The situation can't continue like this. There is no longer a civil authority in Rio de Janeiro. The intervention is disrespectful to Pezão because this is not a problem that belongs only to him. If you go to Acre or you go to Ceará, everyone complains about public safety.

I remember that, within PRONASCI, there was a program called "Mother of Peace." I went to inaugurate this program in Pernambuco. These were women who were going to take care of young kids who were committing crimes. These youngsters must be able to realize: "Someone is giving me another chance, showing me a different path." If you don't offer this, nobody will. I even asked Fernando Haddad to help in the formulation of the government plan, had him call governors, specialists, and formulate a proposal.

It is pointless to just curse at the situation. It is pointless to say that police forces are murderers. It is pointless to say that no one is committing crimes. There is a bit of everything in it. We need to gather those who understand the subject in order to build a consistent plan.

Juca Kfouri: Do you still trust the Federal Brazilian Court?

Lula: It's paramount to trust them. If I lose confidence in the judiciary, I would have to quit being a politician and start to say that only a revolution would solve these kinds of problems. I don't believe in popular courts, I still believe in democracy and in the functioning of institutions. Let the judiciary fulfill its role, let the executive fulfill its role, let the legislative fulfill its role, let the unions fulfill . . . you know? Then, everything will work.

Juca Kfouri: There was a statesman (I'm not really sure whether he was quite a statesman, but anyways, he made history as if he was one) who said the following: "Those who make peaceful revolution impossible will make violent revolution inevitable." The statesman who said this was called John Fitzgerald Kennedy. It wasn't Fidel Castro, Che Guevara, or Mao Zedong who said this. Does it make sense?

Lula: Yes, it does. For that matter, comrade Mino Carta published a magazine cover of *Carta Capital* with the headline: "The Brazilian elite is pushing Lula to the left."[150] Learning the democratic way is a long process . . . Picture this: I gave an interview to *Folha de S. Paulo* in which I said I didn't see it as possible, for a metalworker, to make it to the presidency by means of at-large voting.

Less than five years later, in 1989, I had 47 percent of the votes in the runoff. I realized that it was possible. And I made the choice to build democracy in order to make it to power. And we made it. We lost three elections [1989, 1994, 1998], but we made it. And we were able to accomplish important things. What have I learned? That attaining the government is different than attaining power. It is paramount to bear in mind that this understanding of power attainment sometimes turns people—a little bit—into dictators. I don't wish to control the judiciary. I don't wish the judiciary to be kind to me. When I appointed judges to the Brazilian Supreme Court, I wasn't pondering whether they would do me any favors.[151]

My wish is that they were consistent with our Constitution and that they would abide by what is written in the Constitution. You can ask them if I have ever, for even one second, said anything like "I will need your help!" Never. That's not why I nominated them. I was trying to strengthen democratic institutions.

So when someone says that in order to attain power you have to be the boss of everything, I say: I don't want it. I think the richest thing in our passage in this life is the fraternal co-existence in diversity. Instead of having the landless and ruralists killing each other in the field, it is much more beautiful to see them discussing in Congress, making their cases, proving everything, voting . . . may the best contender win. This is what I believe. Sadly, democracy is an exception to the rule in Brazil. They civilized the coup; they modernized it, meaning that if we had a civil war in the past, now there is no need for one. There is no longer the need for a military coup. You can do it within the law: you build a majority; you conquer public opinion—the media is there for you. You create a majority in society against the government, you produce a majority in Congress against the government, and everything is done legally. This is what is happening in Brazil.

Ivana Jinkings: And the judiciary is a hostage of Brazilian media.

Lula: The most serious problem is the lack of outrage in society. But not only regarding democracy. It's the lack of outrage in society with people living in the streets. It's the lack of outrage when they cut investments in science and technology, when they want to put an end to FIES, when they want to put an end to PROUNI, when they think having graduate studies abroad is unnecessary spending. And I'm not referring to poor people. Why aren't scholars protesting against cuts in science and technology? This is what really pisses me off! Sometimes I think education and schooling would bring political awareness to people. Bullshit! What we see is a bunch of conservatives who don't have the guts to stand up for their interests. These people's children won't have the same things we had three years ago! The lack of vision . . . And if society isn't outraged by this, who's going to be?

I would like to get back to the presidency and say: "Education won't be considered spending. Education will be considered investment!" This country will never be competitive—whether industrially or technologically—unless we invest in education. We read about world history and we know what happens elsewhere. How did the US bring about development? What about South Korea? What about Germany? Education! But not in Brazil. We think things are good the way they are. We need millions of people saying: "We must invest in education again. Temer can spend money elsewhere, but education must be a priority." It's either this or we are not getting anywhere.

This is such a hypocritical country that prior to my government, the minister of education wouldn't have the guts to receive university chancellors. You can count with one hand the number of presidents who visited universities. Which president received university chancellors? Well, I held an annual meeting with university and IFSP chancellors for eight years.[152] Every year! As a matter of fact, we built our first university in 1920. Peru's first university dates back to 1550. It took us almost four hundred years! This is the Brazilian elite. This is the legacy of the Brazilian elite. Why do we need universities? What for? We don't want an educated population.

Take São Paulo for example, which is the most important municipality of the republic. São Paulo lost the war, right? It lost the battle of 1932.[153] What did they do next? They become aware of that and founded the University of São Paulo.[154] They lost the war but won the cultural and educational battle. They figured: "Let's be the brains of this country."

Ivana Jinkings: But the elite says you foster class struggle and that you are the leader of a gang.

Lula: I will tell you two different stories that I like telling in order to show a little bit about my life to those who think I'm a thief. I attended a school named Visconde de Itaúna, which is nearby, and I lived in Vila Carioca, which was quite far.[155] I used to get there by a street which had a street market. We didn't have apples back then, they were rather rare. So there were these little boxes that came with Argentinian apples. I remember the blue paper that wrapped each apple. So I used to walk by the street market and crave one of those apples. Picture a twelve-year-old longing for an apple . . . And at that time, I knew that if I stole one, I would have to run. If the vendor caught me, he wouldn't beat me; he would take me to my mother and tell her what I had done. Therefore, since I didn't want to embarrass my mother, I would just stare, with a watering mouth. I would then swallow it and head home without my apple. This happened for months and months while I was attending school. I tell this story to show them: if I didn't steal an apple when I was hungry, would I steal one or two reals when I became president?

The other story is about my craving for North American bubble gum. At that time—a long time ago—we used to call it American bubble gum or Ping Pong.[156] I knew some kids who used to buy that American gum and chew it and make bubbles the whole the day. I was never able to buy that fucking gum! And there was this kid called Boquita—who was the son of a guy from Sergipe, Aracaju—who kept the chewing gum in his mouth the whole day. And we were playing soccer. When he was about to dump his gum, I would ask him to give it to me. I would then wash it and put it in my mouth in order to make those bubbles. A motherfucker who went through all of this and who makes it to the presidency with the commitment I made, would really want his name tainted for stealing a penny in the country?

That's why I challenge the business sector. I challenge any business owner in Brazil, any governor who has interacted with me, any senator, any journalist, and anyone, to say that I have once, ever, asked them for anything, even for five bucks. And this is not bravado. Emilio Odebrecht might show up and say: "I gave Lula some money." Then tell me where did you make the deposit, or where did you deliver it, which is my bank account where you deposited it?

If someone took the money on my behalf, tell me, who did you give it to? Do not bring me into this. I say this because coming from where I came, walking with your head up is not something easy. If you lower your head, they will put an oxbow on it and you will never again be able to lift it.

I tell these stories so people can understand that not everyone comes with a price tag; "Serious women do not exist, what really exists are women who were not groomed properly." I don't accept this narrative. I don't come with a price tag. And even if I did, it would be unpayable, just like Messi in Barcelona: there is nobody willing to buy him, because they know they can't afford him.[157]

Juca Kfouri: This drive by the elite against the PT reached its peak in the elections of 2014, the runoff was insane . . .

Lula: The possibility of Dilma being reelected freaked them out because they had imagined that after that I could win again in 2018 and be reelected in 2022. We would be the party in power for the longest period of time, for at least twenty-three years. I took part in many campaigns and I have never seen such a radicalized dispute as this one. I thought that having a woman running for the presidency would make them more civilized and respectful, but the aggressiveness was the greatest I have ever seen. It wasn't like this when I ran against Collor, Serra, or Alckmin.[158] Poor Alckmin, since he doesn't have any aggressiveness in him, the more he yelled, the more votes he lost. Serra and I treated each other respectfully, Alckmin was civilized as well. But Aécio totally crossed the line.[159]

Juca Kfouri: Do you think machismo played a role in that sense?

Lula: No. I think it was a political and ideological dispute. And they firmly believed they could destroy the PT once and for all. The amount of lies, accusations, that *Veja* magazine published two days before saying that Lula and Dilma "knew about everything."[160] The fact that the magazine issue was brought forward three days before the elections . . . *Veja* was distributed throughout the country. It was quite an operation. For the first time, the elite had assembled a high command. It had found a candidate to play their game, and they went for it with full power.

We were lucky that a significant part of society, especially young people living on the outskirts, realized we could lose the election and Aécio could become president. So they came with very strong support for Dilma and managed to turn the tables. They were already celebrating in Minas Gerais.

I remember leaving here at five o'clock in the afternoon to go to Brasília and a pollster called me asking: "President, where are you?" "I am going to Brasília." "Let me tell you something, it is going to be by a narrow difference, but the PT won the elections." I got there and the atmosphere was heavy, very heavy, especially in the coordination, among the people who worked in the campaign, with that information that Aécio was ahead. The counting was coming to an end and Aécio was still ahead . . . When the results favorable to Dilma came in, I felt something I will never forget—I talked about this at the beginning of the interview—I was of the impression that she didn't like that she had won. She was there, looking toward infinity, looking ahead, and she told me: "I will never participate in a debate again." I found it awkward because she had just won the election and, the tighter the results, the more you get . . .You know when a team is losing 4 to 3, and scores a goal with two minutes to go? And then from a tie comes the victory.

Juca Kfouri: But if this was your feeling, how would you explain that she didn't let you be the candidate instead of herself?

Lula: I don't know. We, human beings, react to emotions. And the way one would have reacted today is not the same as yesterday. I was certain 2014 would be the year I would get back to the presidency, but I was also certain that I should respect the democratic rite established by my own party. When I nominated Dilma [for the 2010 election], people said she would be a replacement candidate, that we should meet with her and tell her that she would only be the candidate to save Lula's spot for his comeback. I refused this notion of a replacement candidate. She was a full candidate and, if her administration was successful, she was entitled to run for reelection. The only possible way I would run this time is if Dilma came to me and said: "Lula, I think you should be the candidate." Since she never came looking for me and the party started to suggest a "Lula, come back" campaign, I went to a rally in Anhembi and Dilma was about to arrive, and I decided to put an end to this "Lula, come back" idea. "We have to stop joking around, we have a candidate, which is Dilma. And let's fight."

Ivana Jinkings: But you never talked about this?

Lula: No, never. I never had the guts to talk about this issue. I had a very bad experience when Olívio Dutra was the governor of Rio Grande do Sul and Tarso Genro suggested a caucus which Olívio accepted.[161] I told Olívio: "You can't accept a caucus. If you accept it, it means that you agree with a group of comrades from the PT who are saying you were not a good governor. Even if you win the caucus, it will be difficult to win the election because you were questioned internally." And what was the outcome? We lost the election. So I would never bring this subject up with her. I remember a minister came to ask me, I'm not sure whether this was on her behalf: "Lula, the president is worried whether you want to come back or not." To which I replied: "No, I don't want to come back, she is the one who has to decide whether she is a candidate or not. If she wants to run for a second term, she is totally entitled to do that." So there were internal problems in the PT, some said we could have held a debate, others wanted me to be the candidate, but I kept telling them: "I can't come up to a comrade who is still in office and tell her: your time is up, please get out because I want to get back." I would never do that. My relationship with Dilma is one of honesty, fidelity, and lots of comradeship. She always treated me fairly. She always respected me.

Juca Kfouri: Don't you think your decision to nominate Dilma was a mistake?

Lula: No. Many people said that I shouldn't have nominated Dilma, because she had never been a city councillor or anything.[162] ... Why did I nominate Dilma? First, because the PT was shorn of its main cadres, and because when I brought Dilma to be my chief of staff, the way she worked gave me a whole lot of peace of mind. She was like my guardian in all good causes. She did everything I wanted faster and more effectively than I imagined. And she was always loyal and faithful, so that no minister would lie to me ... Just extraordinary, you know? So when it comes to nominating someone, you ask yourself, "Who am I going to choose to run for president?" She was by my side, I had appointed her as "mother" of the Growth Acceleration Program (PAC), she really worked hard ... Dilma, Graça Foster, Miriam Belchior, Tereza Campello ... These women were a golden quartet during my presidency, because if on a Saturday night I asked them to do something, it would be done on Monday.[163]

Juca Kfouri: But didn't you consider that she was not as used to talking to congresspeople as you are?

Lula: But my feeling was that Dilma would learn how to do it. I learned it, so she could also do it: an educated woman, with master's and doctoral degrees ... she knows much more than I do, so she could easily learn. You also have to consider that she's a member of an experienced political party, with experienced people. At the beginning of the interview, I told you about how Ideli Salvatti was appointed as the political coordinator of the government instead of Padilha. That was a mistake. But the president had the right to pick whoever she wanted. There were plenty of people who had experience with political militancy and political coordination to help her; what matters is whether she wanted it or not. Whether she accepted it or not.

Gilberto Maringoni: The beginning of that administration was quite troubled, right? Even before, during the reelection, things were already complicated. She was reelected with 54 million votes, but polls in May showed that her popularity rates had plunged. Which mistakes may have been made between the election and the beginning of the government?

Lula: When you begin your second term . . . Well, it's hard to give an interview without speaking badly of people [laughing]. But when the second term began, I talked to Dilma, showing that some things had to change. I wanted to talk to her about the Chief of Staff Office, the Ministry of Justice, the Ministry of Finance . . . I wanted to talk to her about the appropriate timing to do things. Because there's a time for everything. If you don't take care today, if you don't propose to the woman you love, someone can do it before you. So ask today! But Dilma had her own timing, there were things she believed in. There was someone in the government trying to show Dilma that her second term should reflect her identity. I honestly think that João Santana played an important role in trying to create an image of Dilma that was detached from Lula. I'm going to tell you something: in the 2010 campaign, I was in Belém and Dilma came to me. First, I got a call saying, "They took you off TV, and Dilma's popularity started falling. If you don't go back to television, she's going to lose the election." I went to meet Dilma in Belém, in a rally that we had with Ana Júlia, who was our candidate for governor.[164] When I reached the podium, Dilma told me, "President, you know they want to dissociate me from you, but I don't want to." Who were they? The coordination of the campaign was Zé Eduardo Dutra, Zé Eduardo Cardozo, and Palocci, plus João Santana, who was the publicist, and Gilberto Carvalho, who was a kind of link between Dilma and these people.[165] When Dilma told me that, I called Gilberto Carvalho immediately and said, "Gilberto, you tell João Santana, Palocci, and both Zé Eduardos that I want a meeting with them tomorrow morning when I arrive in Brasília." I was really angry when I arrived at the meeting. The question was: "I want to know who among you has a say here. I want to know which one of you has a say. If you don't have a say, I do. Which one of you decided that Dilma should dissociate from me? Think about how long it takes to wean a calf. Weaning can only be possible once the calf is ready. In this case, weaning can only start after we win the elections." Then I demanded to record a show, and things went back to normal.

I also noticed signs—and people talked about it—that there were several moments when they tried to dissociate Dilma's administration from Lula's administration. Let me give you an example. When I was president, Clara Ant produced an internal newsletter called *Destaque*, to make sure the actions of the government were understood by the leaders of the government themselves. So every minister, anywhere in Brazil, knew what was being done in the government. After Dilma was elected, it took some time for *Destaque* to be published again, so I asked her: "Did you notice that *Destaque* hasn't been coming out?" It was understandable that the newsletter hadn't yet been published because Dilma had been in office for one, two, three months, and perhaps there wasn't much to write about. And I said to her again: "Dilma, if our goal is to have continuity from the previous government, you can keep doing things that were already being done. There's no problem." But no, that's not what happened. The people who made the newsletter for Dilma tried to distinguish it from *Destaque*, maybe for technical reasons, I do not know. I felt they were trying to dissociate the two governments. And it didn't take long for it to happen. That was in 2011.

I remember that there was a coordination meeting in the 2014 campaign, and the prevailing idea among government personnel (not Dilma's idea)—including advertising—was that it would indeed be Dilma's first term, and that this was the message that should be conveyed to society. This was worked out by comrade João Santana, who felt that it was necessary to make Dilma's first term a "pure-blood" one. There was a serious argument, and statistical data showed that we needed to focus on the idea of continuity; otherwise, we would be doomed. "Muda Mais" [one of the buzzwords of the 2014 campaign] was created because of this discussion. Dilma's advertising management team wanted to convey the notion that her term wasn't based on continuity, which would have been a disaster.

Well, what happened after 2014? We won the election with a speech that Dilma gave. She said, "There's no way I'm going to mess with it, I won't do it." This inspired all kinds of people you can imagine to get involved and say that the right could not win, including the youth from the outskirts, from funk, rap, and punk movements, as well as our comrades from the PSOL.

The appointment of Joaquim Levy as minister of finances, however, was a disaster for our militancy. Then came the pension system reform proposal presented on December 29 [2014], and we lost a lot of credibility. Party militants know it. Dilma knows it. She does know that we lost credibility in that moment. People from social movements, from the union movement, said: "We have been betrayed." That was how militants felt. And then our opponents seized the opportunity. What did PSDB propaganda say? That Dilma's victory had been an embezzlement. That really affected us.

Gilberto Maringoni: Mr. President, the media is a recurring theme in our interview. And it's really a key issue in Brazil. When do you think the media started a war against you?

Lula: It has always been like that. Ever since I was born. The media never cut me any slack. When Itaboraí Martins used to work at the *Estadão*, he was delighted after talking to me one day and wrote a full page for the newspaper, with a title that said something like: "A new unionism arises."[166] That was a little before 1978. The approving tone of the article made me the fad of the day among many people. What was I? I was a worker, a unionist, someone who didn't like politics. It was all they needed. I was a full-blooded unionist [laughing]. I didn't know politics at all. This is so true that I coined a phrase that said, "I don't like politics, I don't like people who like politics." It was 1978, and I believed that thinking like that was great. I realized how foolish that was only when I was older. Some tension arose in 1979 and I started to notice that things were changing. The MDB began a big campaign calling for freedom of organization for parties. I remember that the first time I was booed was at a rally in São Bernardo, when I said that we needed to create the PT. It was a rally put together by Tito Costa, from the MDB.[167] I began to realize that they wanted freedom of organization only for themselves. Founding the PT was very difficult. It was not as easy as creating Rede, the PSOL, Democratas . . . At that time, we needed to legalize the party in fifteen states; if I am not mistaken, we needed to obtain signatures of at least 15 percent of the electorate in the states, and at least 3 percent of the votes in the first elections. On top of that, there was the Falcão Law.[168] After we created the PT, I started to notice that "Little Lula"—the king of new unionism, the king of the world—had become the devil. Then that "full-blooded" leader was no longer "full-blooded." I lost space in the media after I got involved with politics. I only get mentioned when I'm beaten up.

Juca Kfouri: What about your relationship with Fernando Henrique Cardoso?

Lula: Oh, he wanted me to win in 2002, but then he started to cheer against me. What was his rationale for doing so? His rationale was that if I won, I would fail, and people would welcome him back with open arms. That's why he didn't want José Serra. If Serra had won, he would have wanted to be reelected. He spoke to several interlocutors about this, and people told me about it. He was supportive of my candidacy. The transition between our governments happened smoothly. It was extraordinary, as I said before. This is so true that I presented a provisional measure to encourage smooth mayoral transitions. Nowadays, many mayors leave office and steal the ambulance, the ambulance engine, the computer, the key to City Hall . . . this was not the case with Fernando Henrique Cardoso. The transition was very civilized. When did he fail to show greatness? As he was waiting for me to fail and that didn't happen, he didn't know how to handle the fact that I succeeded. That was his dilemma. I'm not going to explain it; he's the one who has to explain it. Then he complained that I never invited him for a cup of coffee . . . Well . . .

Juca Kfouri: Do you think the honoris causa degrees that were awarded to you made him jealous?[169]

Lula: But that was from 2007 to now. But it's true, this may have caused a problem because I was awarded an honoris causa degree from Sciences Po, which is a degree he does not have [laughing].[170] But would he understand? I did things he couldn't do, and I did things that he didn't think he could do. A Fernando Henrique Cardoso administration wouldn't place the fight against hunger high on its agenda, as I did. And this is understandable, because the Brazilian elite never bothered with it. I've never seen Fernando Henrique Cardoso or any other president—except for Juscelino—interested in creating universities and expanding higher education to low-income students . . .[171] I was interested in that because it was a moral commitment I had made to myself. I didn't have the right to go to university, so I want workers to be able to put their children through college. I will go down in history as the president who founded the most universities and technical colleges until now, and who helped most young people have access to higher education. That's something I'm proud of, and that's why I was awarded a lot of honoris causa degrees. In addition to that, if you consider the fight against hunger, wage increases over twelve years, the minimum wage, and all the social achievements, the degrees I was awarded weren't only my merit, but also the merit of the evolution of Brazilian people. They show the evolution of a lot of people who helped. I couldn't have done it alone. I was able to do it because the people trusted me and helped me. I wouldn't have been able to do it. I don't think Fernando Henrique Cardoso understands that. There are those who say, "Lula, you should talk to Fernando Henrique Cardoso." And sometimes I think about talking to him, but then I read the newspaper and there he is, making a criticism, sometimes based on a prejudiced view. So I think, "Why should I do it?"

Maria Inês Nassif: Do you think he was actively involved with plotting the coup?

Lula: Sure. I know he was. He was one of the clever brains behind Aécio. The *tucanos* [leaders of the PSDB, dubbed *tucanos*—toucans—after their party's symbol] don't make any commitments before talking to Fernando Henrique Cardoso. I don't know how things are now. But he was very influential in Aécios's campaign, one of its mentors. If you want to know what I think, I believe they didn't try to impeach us in 2005 [at the time of the Mensalão] because they were afraid.

Ivana Jinkings: Afraid of what?

Lula: Afraid of the streets. What happened in 2005? The atmosphere was very tense. I went to a meeting of the Economic and Social Development Council and said, "You are following the press and you know the history of Brazil. The Brazilian elite has led a president to shoot himself through the heart because of accusations. The Brazilian elite didn't want Juscelino to run for president, it didn't want him to take office, and it tried to plot a coup against him three times; it plotted against him once again so that he could not run for reelection in 1965.[172] The Brazilian elite pressed João Goulart to adopt parliamentarism, and yet they didn't let him have full powers to lead the government."[173] I said all of that during the meeting. Then I continued: "Let me tell you something: it's not my vocation to kill myself, it's not my vocation to leave Brazil, and it's not my vocation to be overthrown. So there's only one way to do it, which is winning on the streets." And what did I do? Soon after, I went to Garanhuns to launch the Safra Plan [for family farming]. From that moment, I didn't leave the streets. If they wanted to fight, they would fight with people on the streets. What were they thinking? "He's already bleeding, there's no need to impeach him, he won't even . . . ." I remember meeting some people from Globo in early 2006 at Carlinhos Drummond's house, when he was a representative of Globo in Brasília. After I left, João Roberto said: "Wow, the president is doing well, he is excited." I know that because a journalist who was there told me later. Then Merval said: "He's putting on airs, but he's dead. He's not a candidate for reelection. I can tell you that he won't be a candidate for reelection." They assumed that I was going to lose the election . . .

Juca Kfouri: Mr. President, are you rich?

Lula: Compared to when I came from Garanhuns, I'm rich.

Juca Kfouri: What is your estate?

Lula: The apartment I have lived in since 1998, two 645-square-foot apartments in Vila Baeta, in São Bernardo do Campo, and a piece of land I bought in 1992, also in São Bernardo, that cost me two reals per ten square feet. What else? After I left the presidency, I realized that the best way to live my life, without relying on the PT and without relying on consulting, was to give lectures. This is a good question, because it gives me a chance to better explain that.

I talked to my colleagues here at the institute about what kind of lecture I could give. We did some research about what was being done around the world—for instance, by Kofi Annan, Tony Blair, and Clinton—and our conclusion was that I was going to prepare my lectures by using the same structure that Clinton adopted.[174] Basically, the argument was that Clinton had been the best president of the late twentieth century, and I had been the best president of the early twenty-first century. The kids who work with me decided to think big, and I started to charge US $200,000 per talk. A deluge of invitations for lectures began to arrive, 80 percent from outside Brazil.

Every time someone wanted to hire me to give a talk, I would send people to figure out what they wanted me to say. Because, when I saw Obama's talk here, he didn't say anything relevant. I saw one of Clinton's talks here, and what prevails is the inferiority complex. People applaud any bullshit he says. But what did the guys who hired me want? They wanted me to tell what we have done in this country to make Brazil an international geopolitical protagonist; they wanted to know how Brazil managed to grow for eight consecutive years, what I have done to earn the respect of Bush, Obama, Chirac. They wanted to know how famine ended and what the payroll deductible loan is . . . I would ask: "Don't you want anything different this time?" "No, that's what we want." So if you listen to my speeches, you'll see that they show the narrative of the things that were done in this country. Nothing more, nothing less, no inventions.

There's a funny story. I remember I was invited to go to London by Santander, for one of my last talks, and I felt some gastrointestinal discomfort . . . When I walked up to the tribune I was cold sweating. [Laughing.] I looked everywhere, but I couldn't see a bathroom. . . And I was sweating and thinking: "Damn it, I won't even be able to talk excitedly." [Laughing harder.] My advisers are a bunch of assholes, because every time I need an adviser . . . and usually they should stay where I could see and call them . . . No, mine just disappear . . . [Laughing harder.] And I was looking for the damned bastard, but I couldn't find him, and there I was sweating, and my stomach was roaring, roaring . . . [Laughing even harder.] All those pretty girls were standing in front of the Formula One cars, because there was an exhibition there. And I thought, "Fuck, that's the last thing I need right now . . ." It wasn't easy, but everything worked out in the end.

After I finished my talk, I told them: "Now I want to say something to you. Every time I come here to give a talk, someone asks, 'What about China?' But then I ask: would you like Brazil to follow the Chinese political model? You certainly like China because of the volume of reserves it has in the United States and because of everything they buy and import from you. But if you want democracy in Brazil, I challenge some of you to come here and tell me which country, with the exception of China, offers more opportunity to make money and make investments than Brazil." Then I would mention how many kilometers of highways, how many kilometers of transmission lines, the world's three largest hydro-electric power plants, the World Cup, the Olympics, agriculture, ethanol, Brazil as the only country in the world to really produce clean fuel, with carbon sequestration and zero emissions . . . The guys were baffled, and I was like, "See if any country is doing it, investments of so many billions (I can't even remember how much it was at that time). What country offers this with political freedom, democracy, and legal certainty?" It happened in the first Dilma administration. If I had not had cancer, I would have made a lot of money.[175] I knew that, like a soccer player, my performance would not last forever. If the player knew he had ten or twelve years to make money, he would be more professional. I created a company that's now going bankrupt, the institute doesn't receive a penny from anyone today, because the IRS fined us R$18 million after targeting us in an operation. I took some of the money I earned and put it into the private pension of each of my five children, who can't find work.

Juca Kfouri: Mr. President, I already asked you about imprisonment and exile. Still, I would like to return to that topic, since it is one of the most urgent issues at the moment, next to your candidacy. Are you considering the possibility of being arrested?

Lula: I am. What I'm not considering right now is armed resistance. I'm too old for that. I'm a democrat and, besides, I have never learned how to shoot. So that's out of the question. The PT was not born to be a revolutionary party. It was born to be a democratic party and to lead democracy to its final consequences.

[Interview interrupted so Lula can talk to former Uruguayan president Pepe Mujica on the telephone.]

Lula: The PT was not conceived for that. It was created to ensure—within a democratic regime—the transformation that Brazil needs, and we proved this is a possibility. I am not leaving Brazil, I'm not going to hide in an embassy and I am not running away. "Running away" is an expression that doesn't exist in my dictionary. I will be at my home, getting there between eight and nine o'clock at night, going to bed at ten o'clock, waking up at five in the morning to work out. There are two higher instances to which we can appeal [STJ and STF], and we will appeal. They will make the decision. I am ready to be arrested. It will be their decision.

Ivana Jinkings: How do you prepare your heart for this?

Lula: I don't. I'm a lighthearted man. Everything is part of history. We are going through an important historical moment for me. I'm sure of that, because I'm the one being judged. My conscience is clear, but they can't say the same. I doubt that the judges who condemned me have the guts to look into the face of an eight- or ten-year-old child and tell them the truth about why they are condemning me. In the future, they will be indicted by history. But this is not something that will happen overnight; history is not defined in a day.

Gilberto Maringoni: When you say that you know why you are being judged, we can imagine what you mean, but could you clarify this for the reader?

Lula: The reader also knows. If they didn't, I would not have the support shown in the polls.[176] Let's think about this: Brazilian society is historically divided; 30 to 35 percent of voters, more or less, are waiting to be convinced. This is the differential that helps us gain votes. I ran in 1989, 1994, 1998, 2000, and 2006. The exception was in 1994 and 1998, when they formed a big block against me, as never before in Brazilian history, and there were no televised presidential debates. People don't talk about that, but in 1994 and 1998 there were no televised debates, because they didn't want to expose Fernando Henrique Cardoso . . .[177]

I'm really proud because, even with all the tempests I'm going through, whenever there's a poll about who was the best president in Brazilian history, I appear with 50 percent, while the next name has 11 percent.[178] When it comes to popularity polls, even Moro is starting to lose. He used to have almost 90 percent, but when people started to see his political connections, they noticed that something was wrong.

Gilberto Maringoni: You said to the press that you are wiser now. What do you mean?

Lula: Look, at my age [seventy-two], I have been through everything I could have imagined. I've been through a lot.

Juca Kfouri: But what did you want to be when you grew up? You said you wanted to be an economist, but I bet that was not your dream as a child . . .

Lula: My dream was to be a truck driver, but I became the president of the republic and that was the "little truck" I got to drive. When you reach my age, nothing scares you. I've survived cancer; I've been very close to disgrace. I wouldn't wish the chemotherapy I went through on my worst enemy. I was told radiotherapy was healthier. It may be healthier when you have cancer in your big toe, but when it's in your throat or anus, then you'll know what radiotherapy is really like . . . So I've been there, I've been president of the republic, I've done so much . . . What else can they do to me that I'm afraid of?

Juca Kfouri: Do you imagine yourself leading a civil disobedience movement?

Lula: No. I'm too old for that. But I imagine [such a movement] may happen.

Maria Inês Nassif: Mr. President, in this whole discussion on the judiciary, you agree that there has been a process of politicization that happened in all instances. How do you explain this process of politicization?

Lula: I've been saying this for the past two years. I told everyone at the institute: "Look, the coup won't be effective until they come after me." Now, if the coup was orchestrated to prevent the progression of the poor of this country, they can't take Dilma down and let Lula return two years later. I've talked about it twice and I'll talk again, because it's important. I am warning the PT: they will try to force the PT into illegality.

Maria Inês Nassif: At what point did this politicization start?

Lula: It was set up, they needed to find a way of avoiding another military coup and take power by legal means. They made the mistake of coming after me too. It was a mistake, because it's a matter of honor for me now. I don't know if it's going to take ten years, I don't know when, but I'll prove they're liars.

Ivana Jinkings: Then the final blow would come with you being arrested and prevented from running for the presidency?

Lula: There's a price to pay for everything. After the Federal Court of Appeal for the Fourth Region decision, it will be very difficult for them to forbid me from running for president. A lot of people say: "Oh, Lula, it will be okay if they simply take you out of the election, without sending you to jail." It's not okay, because for me it's a question of personal pride and honor, of life behavior. They shouldn't have messed with me. I'm not bigger than the law, but they shouldn't have messed with me and I'm not going to die being thought of as a thief. [Slams his fist on the table.]

Gilberto Maringoni: Today, it's possible to see that the coup began inside the government, with Temer and all the PMDB ministers. With the way the lower house of Congress is currently set up, I honestly don't know if it would be possible to rule without the PMDB. But do you think this kind of agreement will be repeated?

Lula: I don't think it will. But the coup was orchestrated from the outside in, and not from the inside of the administration. It came from a part of the Brazilian elite and the Brazilian economic power, in cahoots with the financial system and multinational interests, with the desire of dismantling the Brazilian financial system, especially the public banks, and giving Petrobras to foreign capitals. It also came from the media, which was mainly responsible. None of this would have happened without an agreement with the media. Nobody is talking about something called Millennium.[179] Many times I tried to start a conversation about the Millennium Institute, and we came to a point in history where all the magazine covers were pretty much the same.

Juca Kfouri: And the Millennium Institute has something to do with magazine covers?

Lula: The Millennium Institute is the main coordinating agent among conservatives in the media, shaping people's minds, discussing headlines, guidelines. Formerly, *Veja* was competing with *Época*, and the headline was kept in a safe. *Folha* and *Estadão* headlines were secrets of state.

Ivana Jinkings: Now it looks like they are aligned and make collective agenda meetings . . .

Lula: It's not just an impression. They really do that. And it's a cycle. In the time of the Mensalão, I discovered that the cycle necessary to paralyze a government is like this: on Thursday, the rumors begin; on Friday, things start to appear on the Internet; on Saturday, they talk about that on *Jornal Nacional*; on Sunday, it goes to the print press and, at night, it's on *Fantástico*. Then, after this genocide, it lasts until the following Thursday, when the cycle starts again. It was like that every time. I couldn't stand my advisers entering my office to say: "The cover will come out like this, the cover will come out like that." What did I decide? "From now on, you either give me good news, or I do not want to hear the news anymore. [Slams his fist on the table.] I will prove that it is possible to rule this country without reading *Folha*, without reading *Estadão*, without reading *Veja*, without reading *O Globo*.

Gilberto Maringoni: Why wasn't it possible to create a communication apparatus able to oppose them?

Lula: Because it's not easy to do that. I created something incredible; I created a TV channel, TV Brasil.[180] It passed in the Senate with a budget of R$350 million, the same budget of [TV] Bandeirantes. It was supposed to be a communications company that spoke to all of South America. Why didn't it happen? Because we're too Republican; you start to tinker with their things and then you hear, "You can't interfere here." We set up a council that tried to fit everyone; we put people without television experience to do television. Instead of doing something new, we put together two old things and doubled the number of employees . . . You know, it was not a nice thing. In fact, we should have finished what existed and created something new.

Ivana Jinkings: Temer had no problem finishing what existed.

Lula: He didn't. I would never fire the guy who brewed our coffee. I kept with me the woman who used to iron Fernando Henrique Cardoso's clothes. I didn't want to know whether she was close to Fernando Henrique Cardoso. What mattered to me was that she was a poor woman doing a job. There was this amazing dude who was a [Brazilian soccer team] Flamengo fan, but Temer came and simply fired the guy. When Temer was vice president, this was the guy who used to serve him coffee every day![181] Did the media criticize him for that? No. He got rid of everyone . . . even the elevator operator was fired. No criticism. How does Temer pick a minister? Have you ever seen someone criticize him for that? No. How did he get the votes at Congress? Everyone knows how it was done. But nobody criticized him! Without awareness, people won't be able to climb the social ladder . . . if we are not willing to engage in more serious fights. They accept the leftist intellectual; they accept a progressive intellectual, but they don't accept a worker with awareness.

Juca Kfouri: Is Little Lula Peace and Love dead?

Lula: No. I'm still very peaceful and very respectful. But today I'm aware of who my friends are and who are the double-crossers, who likes Brazil and who doesn't. So, I won't come back in a vengeful way, because my heart has no place for hatred. I pardoned Marcelinho when he lost that penalty against Palmeiras and took Corinthians out of Libertadores.[182] [Laughing.] That night I thought I was going to have a heart attack. If I had seen Marcelinho that night, I would have punched his neck. [Laughing.] I forgave him! I hold no grudges.

Gilberto Maringoni: Did you forgive everyone, even those who accused you unjustly?

Lula: I'm not an instance of condemnation. I'm a human being. If I get mad at you, I'm going to suffer because it's going to give me heartburn. I obviously don't want to marry them. So why would I have to like or hate them? No, people should do as they please. When someone writes an article against me, do you know what my revenge is? I simply don't read it. Because the person who wrote it wanted me to read it, and get angry; so, I don't read it, I don't get angry. The only people who are going to be angry are the authors, because I simply don't read those articles. I am so aware of the role I can play in this country, that I have no room for vendettas.

Gilberto Maringoni: What about Palocci? He wasn't kind in his deposition.

Lula: I feel sorry for Palocci. Why should I be angry with him? I have an old thesis. The informant only snitches because he stole. People snitch because they want to do business. Think about poor Léo. How many years has he been in jail? Almost three years. And what is the great theory? Tell him Lula knew it. Then Léo changes his lawyer. When Léo said under oath that Lula knew it, Zanin asked: "Why did you change your statement?" And he says: "Because my lawyer told me to."[183] Do you think I should believe it? Palocci's testimony, his letter . . . do you realize that they [the members of Operation Car Wash] may have plotted this?[184] Because Palocci was talking about money in a slush fund, and they said: "No, no, no, bribery, bribery." They were the ones who created the bribery thesis! So, everybody has to say that. Why did they coerce me in my own house?[185] Is this why they got me, why they got Paulo Okamotto, my five children, and everybody who's close to me? It's simple: when they didn't find anything after lifting the bank secrecy of my accounts—they went to Switzerland, to Taiwan, and who knows where, but they didn't find anything—they thought: "This guy must have something at home, he must be just like Nuzman, piling gold bars at home."[186] They invaded my home. At six in the morning, every Federal Police officer with a camera in hand, to be able to show anything they could find: "Look at this, we found it, it's here, a gold bar, Marisa's jewels, a bundle of dollars." [Slams his fist on the table.] After they didn't find anything, why didn't they apologize? No, they didn't say anything.

Maria Inês Nassif: Does it make you uncomfortable talking about Palocci?

Lula: No. It is just that I can't say more than necessary. You are a journalist, you know this. You can't write everything you would like to write. Sometimes you write with the words you are allowed to use. I think Brazil owes Palocci for gaining the necessary confidence in order to get the economy to grow . . . I think Palocci had a very important role; due to his style, to the tranquillity in which he took care of problems, to the reliability he conveyed. Palocci is the kind of person who would give you a "no" and people would say: "He is so good, he gave me a 'no,' but I liked it." He left my government because of foolishness. I told him: "Palocci, a minister of finances can't beat a housekeeper. Either you find an explanation, or you'll have to get out."[187]

Nowadays I can only think about the following: I don't know the psychological structure of this guy once he is in jail. I don't want to make assumptions—and have never made them—about people who were imprisoned. I never wished to judge anyone on the basis of "John Doe accused Richard Doe . . ." Never . . . Each person knows his or her pains. I never thought Neymar would cry over a little toe.[188] A flattening machine crushed my little finger at two o'clock in the morning and it got squashed, it was hanging from my hand, and I didn't cry, for fuck's sake![189] So, when I saw Neymar crying, I said: "A grown man like this, crying in a stadium, in front of one hundred thousand people?" But it's my duty to respect him, because each person knows where it hurts.

Palocci has diminished himself for doing what he did. I firmly believe Palocci started to appreciate money. In my understanding, the plea bargainer might be doing his plea bargain for two different reasons: either he couldn't bear it and wanted to be freed, or, he has money and is bargaining some of it, like other plea bargainers did. I am sorry for I was a friend of his mother ever since the founding of PT, this is not a small thing. Therefore, I lament this. It makes me sad. I am not angry, I am sad.

Ivana Jinkings: This kind of accusation and attitude, such as Palocci's, has yet another terrible consequence, which is the fostering of the disillusionment with political institutions. It's like: "You see? They are all the same!"

Lula: Exactly. And it's also because . . . let me tell you something. Nobody forgets Tiradentes. The same way nobody forgets Silvério dos Reis. The traitor also makes history. Palocci could have made history with a positive impact on his image. It was a negative one. It is sad but this is the way history goes.

Gilberto Maringoni: Do you picture them doing the exact same thing with Fernando Henrique: breaking into his house?

Lula: No. Let me tell you something. There was a campaign during which they asked me whether I wanted to look at some private life stuff of a given candidate. And I said: "Listen, don't come to me with private life stuff. If the guy smokes weed, if he snorts cocaine, if he has a mistress, it's none of my business." There was this time a journalist from Globo gave me his card because he wanted to show me where Fernando Henrique Cardoso's flat in Higienópolis was, so I could denounce it in my campaign in 2002. I said: "Don't give me a card. I won't denounce anything. You do it. And if this guy bought his flat in an honest manner, why should I denounce him?" And I didn't. This is not part of . . .When someone came to ask me whether a candidate had an out-of-wedlock child, I replied: "Listen, I won't do the same atrocity they did to me. Lurian was my legitimate daughter, she was accounted for, had a birth registration, and despite this they announced her as being a clandestine daughter in 1989." This is why I say there is no such thing as a person with bad character; either a person has character or he or she doesn't. I'm not into this kind of scam.

If these guys have something on me that they can prove, then prove it. They will now break into the cottage, it will be the same saga, then they will get into the Institute, and it will be the same thing, then they will break into my apartment.[190] You see, I pay the rent of the flat next to mine since 2003. I have been paying the rent for almost fifteen years. They now made up that I didn't pay for it. So they took the receipts and it was proven we'd paid. But they didn't believe in the authenticity of the receipts. So, we asked for an expert report and they also went after another expert report . . . It would be so much better if Dallagnol went to the TV and apologized: "I would like to say I'm sorry, Brazil. We do good things, we arrested people who robbed, but as for Lula: hey Lula, I am sorry." He won't do that because the disgrace of someone who tells the first lie is that they will go to the grave lying in order to justify the first lie.

Gilberto Maringoni: This whole campaign affected Dona Marisa?

Lula: It did. Marisa had an aneurysm issue for seven years. She had a checkup every year and the doctor used to say: "It is normal; it hasn't developed any further." But sometimes when he suggested operating she would say: "If there is nothing wrong, why should I have an operation?" Well, with all of that going on she became tense, her mood, and didn't want to leave the house. Every time something happened against one of our sons she was deeply hurt. When they coercively took me, that violence, I think this was the final straw. [Cries.][191]

Ivana Jinkings: Mr. President, looking at things from a distance now, is it fair to say that if Dilma had talked more, she could have prevented the coup?

Lula: It's hard to say after all that happened. Tension was building up between Dilma and Temer. It's like a marriage. Let's say you are married, things are fine with your partner, and suddenly you start an argument, and then another, and another. Soon you no longer want to be home early, and neither does your partner. And then comes the day you say: "Well, let's get a divorce."

It's a little more complicated in politics, because it might end in a coup. Dilma knows there were profound differences with Temer. I went to Temer's house when he wrote that letter.[192] I told him: "Temer, this is not the role of a vice president. Your role is to get there, talk to the president and make a deal. And afterwards, Temer, you must be aware of your dimensions, you were a congressman for many years, you were a prosecutor, you are a lawyer, you shouldn't go down in history as the guy who carried out the coup, the guy who tore the Constitution apart." I went there with Sigmaringa, we had whiskey together.[193] I even thought I had convinced him. Not at all. I think he pondered: "I don't like Dilma, I have three years in office ahead of me, I wouldn't make it even for congressman in the future . . ." And he did it. They tried to do the same thing with Zé Alencar, they tried to convince him to take office. First of all, he didn't accept it. Secondly, he was more to the left than I was [smiling]. So, they were afraid of him because of his standing on interest policies. I was able to choose the best vice anyone could have on earth.[194]

Juca Kfouri: Fernando Henrique says the best vice is Marco Maciel . . .

Lula: What about Zé Alencar? He was extremely loyal and had a powerful speech. He went as far as to say: "I am condemning interest rates because Lula can't do that." And "bang" on the interest rates [laughing].

Maria Inês Nassif: Mr. President, let me suggest an exercise here. There was a severe radicalization during this period of the coup. Would it be possible in this election? Even if there were the most favorable conditions; with the judiciary stepping back, with you being a candidate . . . Would there be conditions to govern with the political center and right-wing like you did before?

Lula: Yes, there would.

Maria Inês Nassif: Secondly, the judiciary has proven to have quite remarkable veto power . . .

Lula: But it was the politicians who brought about the judicialization of politics. Everybody knows that when a candidate loses something, they would make legal claim. And the judiciary began to like this and started to do politics. This is what happened. We need a restructuring of our institutions. Someone has to win the elections, bring society together, all sectors, and say: "Is everything all right or is everything wrong? When will we be a serious nation again? A country where the executive, the legislative, the judiciary, and the audit court will exert their prerogatives. With no disputes over who is the greater power." This is feasible. When Dilma was president, I once told her: If I were in your shoes, I would call the president of the Supreme Court, the president of the Congress, the president of the Senate, the presidents of other superior instances, you could even call some representatives of social movements for a very open conversation and say: "Look, the situation in Brazil is this. The responsibility is not only mine. I want to know whether we are willing to find a solution for this country." I imagine Dilma did not want to hear the name "Eduardo Cunha." And it is very difficult to do politics when you turn political differences into personal ones . . . It is very difficult. My advice is not to get into politics. Because politics is the art of talking to opponents. I joked the other day in Rio de Janeiro, and said I really wished to see Freixo becoming mayor.[195] I would like to see him dealing with the city council, social movements, everyone wanting something different, with all city councillors, aspiring for a job position. When you are opposition you are entitled to be a person of principles. Once you are elected, you have to put your principles on the table in order to achieve them. And that's where many people don't want to win. The Italian Communist Party spent almost half a century not wanting to win the elections.

You guys think you are radicals [laughing]. I was so stupid that I thought the owner of a boozer was a capitalist. I didn't want him to become a member of the PT [laughing]. My mother-in-law, the mother of . . .You see, I'm such a nice guy that I treated as mother-in-law the mother of Marisa's ex-husband, and she lived with me. I had three mothers-in-law: my first wife's, Marisa's mother, and Dona Marília . . . Well, she was retired, and her husband left her a 1970 Volkswagen Beetle; she earned around R$1,000 from her retirement. But she was that kind of old lady who liked to dress up, she was very elegant, very well dressed, she was chubby and all. She would come to PT board meetings and I used to think to myself: "here comes Lula's bourgeois." [Laughing].

So, when you start a political career you have to think: "I don't like Juca, but what is the difference between Juca and me? Because Juca could help me . . .Why can't I be close to Juca? What about that other guy?" Once you get elected, you find out substitutes don't vote and do not make deals. You make deals with the people who are there, in Congress. If the person who is there is a thief but has a vote, you either have the guts to ask for it or you will lose. If you think you can succeed by saying, "I will bring people to the streets, I will win . . . ," you won't.

I already said that after holding rallies with millions and millions of people, with all leaders—from Ulysses Guimarães, to Lula, Brizola, Tancredo, Mário Covas, and everybody in the streets—we got our asses kicked at National Congress during the *Diretas*. We headed home with our tails between our legs and waited for the Electoral College. And when Tancredo passed away, we said: "Well, Sarney it is" [laughing]. And let's be honest here: despite all criticism towards Sarney, he played a paramount role in order to secure the democratic process in this country at the time.[196] The Brazil of 1985–1989 was not easy at all.

Gilberto Maringoni: Let me ask you something else related to this. You have skyrocketed in recent polls and at the same time there is a culture of hatred in society. Our society is divided; "I hate Lula," and those who hate Lula, want to kill him. Do you think society has become more conservative? What could the government have done? Was there anything that could have been done?

Lula: But those who won't vote for Fernando Henrique Cardoso or Serra are also full of hate. Let me tell you; I think this is a by-product of the Internet on human interaction. Because the Internet allows hate to go viral very quickly. In the old times, you had to find someone in order to speak your mind about whatever you thought of me. You had to speak badly of me over the telephone or go out for a beer with a group of friends. Not anymore. Nowadays, you pick up your mobile [drums fingers], get into WhatsApp, and you can do it. It's much easier. This facilitates the spreading of hate. When I was the president, there was a blog called "Death to Lula," you know?[197] Of course, I know one-third of the population doesn't want to hear the initials "PT," as well as another third can't hear the initials "PSDB" . . . Only politics can change that.

Gilberto Maringoni: But the government could have done something, like a campaign . . .

Lula: I don't know . . . I think sectarian groups such as MBL are something new.[198] Many people now feel ashamed . . . They can't mobilize anymore, because they are such cretins and imbeciles that nobody can take them seriously. I believe there is radicalism, but people are getting tired of it. I have often told people: "Don't be wrathful or you will die young. You'll make death come earlier than it otherwise would. Say hello to people in the elevator. Greet your neighbors when you meet them." Why are people so angry? Why? People use their smartphones to order food, to call a cab, to pay their bills, to listen to a joke, to watch a movie. When they leave home and see someone waiting for the elevator, they think this person is standing in their way . . . "I was doing fine in my virtual world and now this guy is annoying me." Humankind will have to address this issue.

Juca Kfouri: Do you think anyone will bang pots and pans again?

Lula: I think it's possible, but now they are ashamed. Some of those who banged pots and pans [in demonstrations against Dilma Rousseff] are thinking whether they should bang their heads, they are ashamed of saying they banged pots and pans. We can't live in the past, though, and everybody needs to realize that. Let me tell you a story so you can understand what I'm saying.

I spent thirty years of my life carrying banners against the IMF. Suddenly I am elected president and have to deal with a German fellow named Köhler, the head of the IMF.[199] I met this guy in Paris. We started to talk and after a while he hugs me and starts crying. He had never heard about the story of a laborer who made his way to the presidency. So, I can say that the guy from the IMF respected me. He started to say good things about Brazil in several places. Well, he left the office and became president of Germany. And then Rato took office, the Spanish guy.[200] So, I called Rato to invite him to come to Brazil and told him: "Look, son, I want to get this issue of Brazil's debt with the IMF over with. I don't want to be a debtor." And he [with a Spanish accent] said: "No, President Lula, the IMF likes Brazil, the IMF has no problem with Brazil . . ." And I replied: "No, Rato, I'm not talking about whether you like us or not. I don't want to be a debtor. I want to pay everything off." It took a while before he accepted it because it was important for the IMF to have Brazil as a debtor. So, I paid it off and Brazil got rid of the IMF.

I went to Germany after some time, and guess who honored me? Köhler. As I said, he had been elected president of Germany. He cried during the tribute speech. I thought to myself: "I just made a German man cry, for fuck's sake." [Laughing.] And we became friends. Because I used to tell him: "I do not accept anyone telling me what to do. I do not accept that. Because I know I ought to be fiscally responsible, I know I must pay my bills, I know I can only acquire debts I can afford, so I don't want any advice. I didn't learn this at university like you did. I learned this from an illiterate mother. She used to say: 'Don't go spending what you don't have. If you are in debt, make sure you can pay it off.' So, this is the way I want to run the country; and I don't need any advice."

Juca Kfouri: You'll be a danger in prison . . . You'll start an uprising . . .

Lula: Do you know what happened when I was arrested in 1980, when Tuma detained me?[201] It was really funny. Tuma would come to prison to get my statements . . . He would bring the questions in writing, I would answer them, he would take them away, then he would bring more questions, I would answer them once again, and so on . . . I would also talk to some investigators there, and one of them had a Rolex. And I asked him, "How much do you make, comrade?" He replied, and I said, "Don't you think that someone who looks at you and sees that Rolex will know that you've been receiving money illegally? Why don't you organize, go on a strike and ask for a pay raise?" [Laughing]. Then Tuma arrived. He got fucking nervous [laughing].

Gilberto Maringoni: Mr. President, lots has happened all these years . . . You've served two terms as president, you've helped Dilma get elected and, when everything seemed to be going well, the coup took place . . .

Lula: Let me tell you something. Only a few people who were on our side believed that there would be an impeachment. I remember that I had a conversation with Dilma at the end of December 2015, and I told her, "We had a fever of 39°C and we have 37°C now. You have to decide whether you want to lower it to 36°C or make it reach 40°C. You have the month of January to make a decision before Congress goes back to work." The fact is that a lot of people didn't believe that there would be an impeachment, that they would have the courage to do it, that the climate was not favorable for that . . . but Cunha had given enough warnings.

Ivana Jinkings: What do you think should be done now to avoid your imprisonment?

Lula: I don't think the most important thing is to avoid my imprisonment. Just imagine the following scenario: Getúlio Vargas wouldn't have killed himself if he had had the support when he was still alive of a third of the people who went to his public wake. So I don't want to mix up commotion with political awareness. I don't want to.

After spending twelve years being beaten up, without proper space in the media, I'm happy enough to have my little caravan tours and my meetings with the people. I continue to do well in the polls and I have to be grateful to God for everything. The thing I'm most proud of is not that I was a popular president; I'm prouder of the fact that the terms I served have changed the way the state relates to society and vice versa. What I wanted as president was to make the poorest people in this country imagine themselves in my place, and that was achieved.

Juca Kfouri: Is there a reason for all this hatred against you?

Lula: I would also like to know whether there's a reason for that. My motto about the presidency has always been: first, I have always been and will always be a president for all people. But those who need it the most will have even more support from the government. And those who need it the most are the workers, those who earn the least, the dispossessed, the unemployed. They should have access to food. They should have a chance to go back to work and to attend higher education. Well, I thought that was a good thing.

I've always been told that Brazil is a "backward country" and that it "lacks schools." So Haddad and I came up with a wonderful idea: we are going to make universities accessible to poor people. And what is the miracle? Since there were universities failing to pay taxes and owing the government, we turned some of that debt into scholarships.[202] This was developed to become public policy in Brazil. Almost two million young people have attended university because of the changes we implemented. So today, when I hear businessmen say, "Oh, it's all about education," they don't really mean that. Because if they really believed in education, Brazil wouldn't have been the last country in South America to have a university, as I said before. They have never believed in education. They should be happy with initiatives that increase access to university education for low-income students.

I'm trying to find out what's the reason for all this hatred. I can't tell if it's hatred or fear.

Juca Kfouri: Do you believe that the Brazilian elite was bothered by the fact that a position that historically belonged to them started to be held by people who used to be underprivileged?

Lula: You all remember when people were saying that airports were "looking like a bus station." In other words, they were bothered by poor people flying in airplanes. If there was an American, though, they thought it was great. When the "gringos" get on the airplane wearing shorts, people who suffer from a complex of inferiority think it's cute. When black Brazilians get on a plane wearing shorts, they "don't know how to dress." That's how it is. Something similar happened at restaurants. I remember that I was in a restaurant with Jacó Bittar and Mino Carta once, on Treze de Maio Street, in São Paulo. The restaurant wasn't fancy at all. We went there to have *feijoada*. And then I went to the bathroom. When I passed by, a woman told me: "Yeah, he says he stands up for workers, but he's in our restaurant." I came back and said, "Are you going to pay my bill? No, you're not. So please . . . ." I think that's it. They don't realize that poor people like good things. The first thing that took shape in Guaribas [a city in the state of Piauí, 653 kilometers away from the capital, Teresina] when we launched the Zero Hunger program in 2003 was a beauty institute. People want to straighten their hair, to wear make-up, to wear perfume. What about quota policies? I know a black girl from Minas Gerais who has two children and enrolled in university. She told me, "President, you have no idea about the discrimination I experience in my classroom."

I still dream about seeing many black bank managers, many black dentists. But this is a process. Look at the United States. From time to time, I find myself watching racially segregated films. There are still unthinkable things happening in the United States. I once said: "We won't end discrimination against black people in Brazil because the Constitution says so. Discrimination is in people's minds. We must introduce the history of Africa to this country, or discrimination will never end." There's a lot at stake.

Juca Kfouri: Some people say that the problem with Brazil is that it never had a war, a form of disruption . . .

Lula: I see. It's funny because an agreement was reached every time Brazilian society was about to have a disruption. And then a new agreement is reached on top of it. The privileged ones aren't willing to relinquish their privilege.

Gilberto Maringoni: And what should be done now?

Lula: They know that I'll do more if I come back. After being the president and then spending four years out of the government, you have a lot of time to think.

Maria Inês Nassif: When you think about today's scenario, in late February 2018, do you really think it's possible for you to return to the presidency?

Lula: Oh, I want to go back to the presidency. It's up to God if I'll live and have a healthy life. And it's up to the members of the judiciary who are going to vote. It depends on them reading the proceedings carefully and realizing that what is being done is unfair.

Ivana Jinkings: To what extent can popular mobilization have an impact on that?

Lula: Mobilization is not enough. The Diretas Já [Direct Elections Now] movement was the most important mobilization in Brazilian history. We went to National Congress and lost the direct elections.[203] And nothing happened. After this disappointment, we waited for the Electoral College in 1985. No one is mobilizing to stop the lawsuits against me. People expect things to work properly. They expect institutions to work and make decisions. If something unusual happens, then we'll see what society looks like.

Ivana Jinkings: Don't you think you've made too many concessions during the terms you served?

Lula: No, I made the concessions that the moment asked for. I was elected president with ten senators and ninety-one congresspersons. That Congress has a total of 513. Even with this unfavorable balance, I have made upward social mobility possible for the most underprivileged people in Brazil. I helped lift 36 million people out of extreme poverty, I have settled farmer families on 47 million hectares (almost 50 percent of what was done in five hundred years of Brazilian history), I helped another 40 million Brazilians escape poverty and join a new lower middle class, I have brought electricity access to more than 15 million people, I started the São Francisco river transfer, something that even Dom Pedro tried to do when he was emperor . . . Conciliation is something that you can pursue, but choose not to. If I had had the power that the PMDB had in 1988, with twenty-three governors and 306 Constituent Assembly members, I would have made less concessions and accomplished much more than I did. In just eight years, we have improved the living standards of people in a way that many armed revolutions have not been able to achieve.

Many people ask me: "Lula, don't you think the PT needs to be more self-critical?" Do you know what I think? If we run the government and self-criticize at the same time, why would the opposition be important?

So, dammit, let the opposition be critical! I'll stand up for what I did. Let the opposition talk about what I didn't do! Otherwise, there wouldn't be opposition in this country [laughing]. Let me tell you something that people often criticize me for.

Forging a political alliance is not as trivial as some fellow leftists think. You don't make a political alliance because you like it. Why did Haddad go after Maluf's support? Because Haddad wasn't well known, and he needed a minute and a half of air time on television from Maluf![204] Listen, voting for Quércia in 1974 was the only option of any decent left-wing citizen in this country, because Carvalho Pinto was on the other side![205] Saying that Jader Barbalho is a thief now . . . Well, in 1982, he was the only left-wing candidate in the state of Pará who deserved a vote![206]

You have to consider the historical process. "Oh, Mr. So-and-so is no good now." What about yesterday, was he good? And before yesterday, was he good? Think about Ulysses Guimarães from 1974 to the 1988 Constitution. Think about how important his role was. Does it matter if he's a member of the bourgeoisie or not? Oh, he didn't want people to vote, he wanted to extend the process. But he wanted it at that moment, and then he became an amazing guy. Let's talk about Teotônio Vilela, who took up arms to kill communists in Alagoas.[207] What did he become afterwards? An icon of the struggle to free our political prisoners! We must discuss politics that way, or we'll be left with clichés such as, "Ah, Mr. So-and-so is no good" and so on . . . Look at Sérgio Cabral, who had 60 percent of the votes in the 2010 elections. This guy deceived more than 60 percent of the people of Rio de Janeiro. I doubt that any of us had any idea of what was going on. So, at that moment, was it important to make an alliance with Sérgio Cabral? Yes, it was! Because Alckmin had made an alliance with Garotinho![208] And it was important to make an alliance with Cabral. And I'll tell you one thing: I'm proud to go down in history as having introduced the largest amount of public policies in Rio de Janeiro to date. Even if they are not fully working today, this is true: I implemented them. A lot of money was invested in Rio. Now, if those in power are not doing it right today, it's not my fault. I always think about things like that. Democracy is good because you learn something new every day. It's so good that I'm going to record a video supporting Guilherme Boulos [pre-candidate to the presidency for the PSOL].[209] I'll do it! I went to the PCdoB convention to support Manuela.[210] Why shouldn't I record a video for Boulos?

Maria Inês Nassif: But this political activity is a form of exercise . . .

Lula: But this is how politics works. And I like it a lot. When I talk about mixing politics with soccer and politics with marriage, it's because it's the same thing. I always say that marriage is the best example of democracy in practice. When you get married—and I'm not talking about getting married in the church; I'm talking about living with a partner, no matter whether you're married in church or not—then you start experiencing democracy in practice. Because when you are married, you do politics by either making concessions or achieving something that you want every day. The idea that "it's in giving that we receive" applies to marriage. If you must do the dishes today, you'll do the dishes, even if you scream and shout about it. Or, for example, when your partner tells you, "I'm going out, you take care of the children . . . ." It's all about concessions. This is what makes marriage possible. When it doesn't work out, couples break up . . . Sometimes they break up two years later, even six months later. I was once best man at a wedding, and the marriage ended six months later. The same thing happens in soccer. It's fantastic. It needs left-wingers and right-wingers. The best players usually play in the center.

Ivana Jinkings: Well, this is controversial . . .

Juca Kfouri: Ivana thinks left-wingers are the best [laughing].

Lula: It depends. If it was Canhoteiro or Rivellino in the 1970 national team, then yes.[211] But then, my dear, that's it. As I said, democracy is good because you learn something new every day.

Juca Kfouri: Going back to Boulos. Do you think he's going to be a candidate?

Lula: Yes. He will. I think it's a pity that he chose to run for the PSOL. Boulos talked to me, to Dilma, to Lindberg, to Breno Altman, then he talked to me again, then he talked to Dilma again.[212] He was agitated. When he talked to me, I told him, "Boulos, let me tell you something, my dear. I'm the only guy you don't have to talk to. First, because I'm never going to tell you not to run for president. The only thing I regret is that you—since you dream about a political party—have joined the PSOL. You shouldn't have done it. You should build something new. So let me tell you something. If you want to be a candidate, be a candidate. I will never argue against that. I'm your comrade." And he has been very supportive of me. Also, I think it's good for Brazil that people start to run for office. Manuela and Boulos are honorable candidates. I can't really say the same about Marina anymore.[213] But running for office will be good for Boulos, because it's a good learning opportunity. He will realize that people don't like us as much as we think they do . . . He will realize that not everyone who waves at us votes for us . . .

Ivana Jinkings: In closing, Mr. President: why do you think running for president again is important?

Lula: Now I'll have to set my humility aside and seriously and serenely share my view on this. At this moment in the history of Brazil, and in the absence of someone better, I think it's important that I run for president again because society needs someone with credibility. Someone trustworthy. Someone capable of recovering international credibility. Someone who understands the people. Someone who talks less about economics and more about the soul of this nation. First and foremost, whoever becomes the ruler in this country must understand that the magic words are government credibility. This is something I went over at the beginning of this interview. Second, the economy needs to show signs of recovery and grow again, because we need to create jobs (and they were unable to do this). We need to create jobs to make the GDP grow and reduce public debt. This is what Brazil needs: more jobs, better wages, and money flowing internally. The way things are going, every day there is a new austerity measure, and something is cut down. And then Temer comes along and gives 30, 40 billion reals to members of Congress, while cutting social benefits. Now they want to change the Forest Code and try to put an end to small properties in the countryside. In fact, what we really need is to free this country from its constraints, so that it can grow. I would invest R$100 billion from the national reserve to make this country grow again. And why is that? Only those who believe in what they are doing can do this. If I have confidence in what I am doing, I can tell the Brazilian people: "Look, things can't continue this way. The BNDES (Brazilian Development Bank) will once again fund the economic growth of this country, Caixa Econômica will once again fund housing programs, Banco do Brasil will go back to funding small producers, and this country will grow again. "Will there be an increase in debt?" Yes, there will, but we'll pay it. And we will pay it when the GDP starts growing again. Does anyone have the courage to say these things loud and clear? I have credibility for this. So, I'm sorry to say this, but I think I'm the person with the most credibility to do this while looking into the eyes of an eighty-year-old and a twenty-year-old. That's why I want to return to the presidency. I'm convinced that I can help to solve the country's problems. Just as I am convinced that truth will prevail.

I Was Born in This Union: A Speech[214]

Lula

This speech was delivered by Lula on April 7, 2018 before thousands at the Metalworkers Union of São Bernardo do Campo, a few hours before his arrest following the issue of a warrant by Federal Judge Sérgio Moro.

My fellow comrades,

I was born in this union. It was nothing more than a shack when I got here. This building had already been built when our committee was in charge of it. I was the director of a school in Madureza here. It had 1,800 students. Do you think I'm just a mechanic? So let me tell you: I was also the director of a school that had 1,800 students. I wanted to take the opportunity to say that since 1978, we owe part of what Brazilian democracy has achieved to the Metalworkers Union of São Bernardo. This was my school. Here I learned sociology, I learned economics, I learned physics, I learned chemistry, and I learned to do politics because during the time that I was director of this union, the factories had 140,000 teachers who taught me how to do things. Every time I was in doubt, I would go to the factory gate to ask my fellow workers how to do things in this country. If you're in doubt, don't risk making mistakes. Just ask. You'll have a much better chance of making things right. This union, unlike any other, has almost 283 directors. In order to be a director here, people have to be elected to a committee by their fellow workers. It's the only way. After being elected a member of the committee, those who will be directors of the union and part of the executive board are chosen, but there are 283 directors and advisers. If this was done in every trade union in Brazil, we would certainly have fewer sell-outs in the trade union movement.

I must confess that I experienced my best political moments in this union. I never forgot my union registration number, which is 25,986, from September 1968. Since then, my relationship with this union is the strongest relationship that I think any president has ever had with it. It's so strong that I'm still treated as the president.

In 1979, this union staged one of the most extraordinary strikes. And we got a deal with the automotive industry that was perhaps the best we could get. I had a factory committee with 300 workers. The deal was good. And I decided to take the deal to a vote in a union meeting. I decided to ask the committee to get to the factory early to talk to the workers.

Since people like having a few drinks in the afternoon, I would have meetings in the morning. You know we get bolder when we have a few drinks. Well, holding meetings in the morning didn't prevent people from drinking, because they would bring their cognac bottles and I would have a "shot." It would make my throat feel better. That didn't happen today.

Well, we decided to take the deal to a vote and 100,000 people at the Vila Euclides Stadium didn't accept it. It was the best we could get. We wouldn't have vacation days taken away, we wouldn't lose our thirteenth salary, and we'd have a 15 percent pay raise. However, the workers were so radicalized they wanted 83 percent or nothing. And we didn't get it. The workers called us sell-outs for a year. I would visit factories. So, my fellow comrades, we did it . . . The workers didn't approve the deal.

We hadn't been able to approve a proposal I thought was good, and then people started to disrespect the union committee. I would go to factories and people wouldn't stop. And the press would write: "Lula speaks, but workers are deaf to his words."

We were only able to restore our prestige among our peers a year later. Somewhat motivated by a spirit of revenge, I thought: "These workers think they can have a strike for one hundred days, four hundred days. If they are determined to go all the way, let's see what they can do in 1980."

Then we had the longest strike in our history, which lasted for forty-one days. Seventeen days into the strike, I was arrested, and workers started to break the strike after a few days. [Romeu] Tuma [chief police officer], Doctor Almir [Pazzianotto, a lawyer for the union], Teotonio Vilela would come visit me in jail and say: "Hey, Lula, you should put an end to this strike; you've got to tell them to end the strike." I would answer: "I won't do it. The workers will decide on their own account."

In practice, the fact is that comrades couldn't take it for forty-one days, because they had to buy milk, to pay their electricity and gas bills, their wives started asking for money to buy bread, so they felt the pressure and couldn't take it anymore. However, it was an interesting situation because even though we didn't have financial gains, even though we lost, we won so much more. Money isn't what solves a strike's problem. It's not about 5 percent or 10 percent. It's about the political theory and political case that a strike reflects.

We are now faced with a similar situation. It's almost the same situation. I'm being prosecuted and I have been saying very clearly: "In the court case about the apartment, I'm the only human being that is being persecuted over an apartment I don't own." He [Judge Sergio Moro] knows that *O Globo* lied when it said it was mine. The Federal Police and Operation Car Wash lied in the investigation when they said it was mine. The public prosecution lied when they charged me and said it was mine. I thought Moro was going to solve this and he lied and said it was mine, and convicted and sentenced me to nine years in prison.

That's why I'm outraged. I've done so many things in my seventy-two years of life. But I don't forgive them for making society believe I'm a thief. should be: They've let criminals make *pixulecos* throughout Brazil.[215] They let the criminals call us *petralhas*.[216] They've let the criminals create an atmosphere of war that undermines politics in this country. And every day I say: none of them—absolutely none—has the courage or sleeps with the clear conscience of honesty and innocence like I do. None of them.

I'm not above the legal system. If I didn't believe in it, I wouldn't have created a political party. I would have proposed a revolution in this country. But I believe in the legal system, in a fair legal system, in a legal system that considers a case and votes on a verdict based on the records, based on the information presented by the prosecution and the defense, on concrete proof showing who is guilty.

What I find unacceptable is a justice attorney who makes a PowerPoint presentation and goes on television to say that the PT is a criminal organization that was born to rob Brazil and that Lula, being the most important figure in the party, is the boss, and thus, since Lula is the boss, the attorney says: "I don't need any evidence, I'm convinced of it." I think he should keep his convictions to his acolytes and doormats, not me. A thief certainly wouldn't be demanding any proof. People who have a skeleton in their closet keep their mouth shut and hope the media doesn't mention their name.

I have more than seventy hours of *Jornal Nacional* crushing me.[217] I have more than seventy magazine covers attacking me. I have thousands of pages of newspapers and articles attacking me. Record attacks me. Bandeirantes attacks me. Radio networks from the countryside attack me. And they don't realize that the more they attack me, the closer I get to the Brazilian people.

I'm not afraid of them. I've even said I'd like to have a debate with Moro over the accusations he has made against me. I would like him to show me concrete evidence. I've challenged the judges of the TRF-4 [Federal Court of Appeal for the Fourth Region] to have debates at whatever university they want, at whatever course they want, to prove which crime I've committed in this country. I sometimes have certain impressions—and I have certain impressions because I'm a builder of dreams. A long time ago, I dreamt it was possible to be the president of this country by including millions and millions of poor people in the economy, making universities accessible to millions of people, creating millions and millions of jobs in this country. I dreamt it was possible for a metalworker without a university degree to take more care of education than the graduates that ruled this country and its education. I dreamt it would be possible for us to reduce child mortality by making sure children could have milk, beans, and rice every day. I dreamt it was possible to have students from the outskirts by making this country's best universities accessible to them, so that our judges and attorneys were not only members of the elite. We will soon see judges and attorneys who were born in the Heliopolis favela, born in Itaquera, born in the outskirts. We are going to have a lot of people from the Landless Workers' Movement [MST], from the Homeless Workers' Movement [MTST], and from Central Workers' Union [CUT] with university degrees.

This is the crime I've committed. I've committed this crime and they don't want me to commit it again. It's because of this crime that there are about ten cases against me. And if these crimes are the reason for the charges, if I'm being condemned for making universities accessible for poor people and black people, if I'm being condemned for making it possible for poor people to eat meat, to buy cars, to travel by plane, to have a small farm, to have a small business, to have their own home—well, if that is the crime I've committed, then I'd like to say I am going to continue being a criminal in this country. Because I am going to do much more. I am going to do so much more. [People start chanting "Lula, warrior for the Brazilian people."]

My fellow comrades, I was the most popular congressman in Brazilian history in 1986. At the time, people suspected that only those who held office would have any power in the PT. Whoever didn't hold office was seen as [Lula starts greeting people] . . . So, comrades, do you know what I did when I realized people thought only members of

Congress were worthy inside the PT? I stopped being a congressman. Because I wanted to prove to the PT that I was still going to be one of its most important personalities without holding office. Because there's only one way to beat me in the PT: working harder than me and liking people more than I do, because otherwise you won't beat me.

Well, now we have sensitive work ahead of us. I may be experiencing the most outrageous thing a human being can experience. What my family is facing is not easy. What my children are facing is not easy. What Marisa had to face . . . I'd like to say that the media and the public prosecution office were mean and cruel to her when they announced Marisa's death before it happened. I'm certain of that. I think these people don't have children, that they don't have a soul, and that they have no idea of what a mother or a father feels when they see their child beaten down, when they see their child under attack.

So, I've decided to hold my head up high, comrades. But don't you think I'm against Car Wash. Car Wash does have to catch the bad guys who really stole money and lock them up. We all want that. We've been saying throughout our whole life: "Justice only arrests the poor, not the rich." All of us have said that. And I want them to keep sending the rich to prison. So, what's the problem? It's that you can't have trials subjected to the media. Because deep, deep down, you destroy people in society, you destroy their image, and afterward the judges will try them and say: "I can't go against public opinion, which is asking me to hunt them down." If you want to vote based on public opinion, then throw away your gown, choose a political party, and run for office. Being a judge is a lifelong job. Judges must vote based on court records. In fact, I think Supreme Court judges shouldn't make any statements about how they vote. In the United States, when the vote is over, you don't know how each judge cast their vote, precisely to prevent them from being under pressure.

Imagine someone being accused of murder without being the killer. What does the victim's family want? They want the accused to be dead, to be convicted. So the judge, unlike us, has to keep his nerve and be more responsible when it comes to accusing or convicting someone. The public prosecution office is a very powerful institution. That's why these kids start law school at a very young age and then dedicate three years of their lives taking public exams to get a job as judge, because their parents can afford it. In order to do the job that they do in the Brazilian society, these kids should learn more about life and learn a little bit about politics.

There's something called responsibility. And don't think I am against it when I say that. I was president and appointed four prosecutors, and I gave speeches at all ceremonies when they took office, and said: "The more powerful the institution, the more responsible its members have to be." You can't have the media condemn someone and try them afterwards. You remember when I gave a statement in Curitiba, and I said to Moro: "Globo is pushing you to find me guilty, so you can't find me not guilty. That's what you will do."

I think that the TRF-4, Moro, Car Wash, and Globo all share some dreams. The first dream that they share is to complete the coup by convincing people that Lula shouldn't run for president in 2018. Because, for them, the coup wasn't over with Dilma's impeachment. They don't want me to run because it's possible that I will be elected. They don't want Lula back because in their minds the poor can't have rights. The poor can't eat high quality meat. The poor can't travel by plane. The poor can't have access to higher education. For them, the poor were born to have only second-class food and products.

So, my fellow comrades, the second dream that they share is to take a picture of Lula in prison. Oh, I can imagine *Veja* being so turned on to publish my picture under arrest on their cover. I can imagine Globo being so turned on to show my picture in prison. They will have multiple orgasms.

They have ordered my arrest. And let me tell you something: I will comply with it. I will, because I want to hand the responsibility over to them.

They believe everything that happens in this country happens because of me. I was once convicted and sentenced to three years in prison because a judge from Manaus thought that I didn't need a gun, because I have a sharp tongue, so he needed to silence me. Otherwise I would have continued to say things like, "All right, this is it, crunch time has come." After that, peasants thought it was some kind of threat and killed a farmer.

They have tried to lock me up for obstruction of justice, but that didn't work. Now they want to catch me with preventive detention, which is worse, because it does not allow me to file a habeas corpus. Vaccari has been in prison for three years now. Marcelo Odebrecht spent over US$100 million and didn't get a habeas corpus. I won't spend a penny, but I'm going there with one belief: for the first time, they will realize what I have been saying every single day. They don't know that Brazil's problem is not called Lula. Brazil's problem is all of you, it's people's awareness, it's the PT, the PCdoB, the MST, the MTST. They know it's a lot of people.

I've been saying this in all my speeches, and our preacher has said it earlier: there is no point in trying to stop me from going around this country, because there are millions and millions of Boulos, millions and millions of Manuelas, millions and millions of Dilmas in this country to go around for me.

There's no point in trying to put an end to my ideas, because they are already hovering in the air. You can't imprison them.

There's no point in trying to stop me from dreaming, because once I stop dreaming, I'll keep dreaming through your minds and your dreams.

There's no point in thinking that everything will stop when I have a heart attack. That's silly, because my heart shall beat through your hearts, and there are millions of hearts.

There is no point in thinking that they will make me stop, I won't stop because I'm not a human being, I'm an idea, an idea that is mixed up with your ideas. I'm sure our comrades from the Landless and Homeless Workers' Movements, the comrades from the CUT and union movements know that. And this is the proof. This is the proof. I will comply with the arrest warrant and all of you will have to become someone else: your names will no longer be Chiquinho, Zezinho, Joãozinho, or Albertinho . . . From now on, all of you will become Lula and will go around this country doing what you have to do every day. Every day!

They must know that the death of a fighter can't stop the revolution.

They must know. They must know that we will definitely push for media regulation, so the people will no longer be victims of lies every single day.

They must know that you, who knows, maybe are even more intelligent than me, burning the tires that you keep on burning, organizing demonstrations, occupying land in urban and rural areas. The occupation in São Bernardo do Campo seemed so difficult, but I have faith that tomorrow you will receive the news that the land will finally be yours.

My fellow comrades, I had the chance. I was recently on the border with Uruguay, close to Livramento and Rivera, and people were saying: "Hey, Lula, pretend you are going to buy some whisky and go to Uruguay, meet Pepe Mujica, stay there and never look back. Ask for political asylum. You can go to the embassy of Bolivia, Uruguay, Russia, and from there you can keep on talking . . ." I'm too old for this. In my age I need to confront them, face to face, and I will face them by complying with the arrest warrant.

I want to know for how many days they will think that they are keeping me in prison. The longer they leave me there, the more Lulas will be born in this country, and there will be more and more people willing to fight in this country, because there is no limit in a democracy, there's no wrong time to fight. I've told my comrades: if it were up to me, I wouldn't go, but I'll go because otherwise tomorrow they'll say that I'm a fugitive, that I'm hiding. No! I'm not hiding! I'll face them so that they know I have no fear, that I'm not going to run away, and I'm going to prove my innocence.

They must know that.

Let them do what they want. Whatever they want. I'm going to tell you something a ten-year-old girl once said to me in Catanduva, a saying that has no author:

"The powerful can kill one, two, or three roses, but they will never be able to stop the whole spring from coming."

Our struggle is searching for spring.

They must know that we want more housing and that we want more schools. They must know we want a decrease in mortality rates. We don't want to see the same brutality they did to Marielle in Rio de Janeiro.

They must know that we don't accept the brutal way black youth are treated in this country. They must know that we don't want to see more child mortality caused by malnutrition in this country. They must know that we don't want to see teenagers who are hopeless about going to university, because Brazil is so foolish that it was the last country in the world to have a university. The last country! All of the poorer countries already had universities, but they didn't want Brazilian youth to have access to education.

They said it was too expensive, which makes me wonder: how much did it cost not to do this fifty years ago?

I want you all to know that I'm really proud, really, really proud, of being the only president that didn't have a university degree, but that I'm also the president who created the most universities in the history of this country, to show those people they must not confuse intelligence with the number of years you spend in school. This isn't intelligence, this is knowledge.

Intelligence has to do with choosing a side, intelligence has to do with having the courage to argue with your comrades about what truly matters, and what really matters right now is to make sure that this country restores civility. We won't let them sell Petrobras! Let's have a new Constitution! Let's revoke the oil law they're making! We won't let them sell [public development bank] BNDES, we won't let them sell [federal bank] Caixa, we won't let them ruin [public bank] Banco do Brasil. And we will make family farming, which is responsible for 70 percent of the food we eat in this country, even stronger.

It's with this belief, comrades, and with my head up high, like I'm speaking to you here, that I want to get there and tell the chief police officer: "Here I am."

In a few days, history will prove that those who committed a crime were the chief police officer who accused me, the judge who tried me, and the public prosecution office, which was ill-intentioned toward me.

For this reason, my fellow comrades, even though my heart doesn't have enough room for everyone, I want you to know that, if there's something I learned to like in this world, that's my relationship with the people.

When I hold the hand of one of you, when I hug one of you, when I kiss one of you—and now I kiss men and women the same way, without hidden intentions—I'm kissing you because when I was president, I used to say:

"I am going back to where I came from."

I know who my friends for life are and who my circumstantial friends are. The ones who were wearing suits and would come to me are now gone. The ones who are here with me are the comrades who were my friends before I became president. The comrade who used to eat oxtail stew at Zelão, the comrade who used to eat chicken and polenta at Demarchi, the comrade who used to eat calf's foot soup at Zelão. Those are still my friends. They are the ones who have the courage to occupy a land plot to build a house. They are the ones who have the courage to go on strike over social security. They are the ones occupying lands to start a productive farm. They are the ones who actually need the state.

My fellow comrades, let me tell you something: you shall see that I will get out of this greater, stronger, even more real and innocent, because I want to prove they are the ones who committed a crime, a political crime of persecuting a man who has a fifty-year political history, and for that I am very grateful.

There's no way I can repay all the gratitude, the care and the respect you have been giving me all these years. I want to tell you, Guilherme [Boulos] and Manuela [d'Ávila], both of you, that it makes me proud to belong to a generation that is almost over, and to witness the emergence of two young people competing for their right to become president of this country. Here's a big hug to celebrate that. And rest assured: this neck won't bow my head down. My mom made my neck short, so I bow my head down. And I won't bow my head down, because I will keep on holding my head up high confidently as I leave, because I will prove my innocence.

Thank you, my fellow comrades. Thank you so much for being there for me. Thank you very much, dear friends!

Lula: Notes for a Profile

Eric Nepomuceno

1.

It was November 2002, a Friday, and I was in São Paulo. Days before, Luiz Inácio Lula da Silva had been elected president of Brazil, with 52,793,364 votes, almost 20 million more than José Serra.

I still remember something I read at the time: Lula's voters had given him, in absolute numbers, the second largest vote in world history.

Ironically, he is second only to Ronald Reagan, who won the 1984 US presidential election with 54,455,472 votes, despite the complications of the American electoral system. Yes, yes, Lula was an Olympic phenomenon. And Reagan was who he was. There is no comparison.

It was a Friday afternoon, a little after 1:30, and I decided to eat at an Italian restaurant in Higienópolis, where I used to have lunch with my father whenever I went to São Paulo.

Sitting at a nearby table was a group of six or seven gentlemen in shirts and loose ties, some of them young, some not so much, who looked like successful lawyers, financial market people, or business executives.

They were all obviously outraged. "He is unfit even to be the doorman of my building," said one. "This country is lost," said the one sitting at the end of the table. "A half-illiterate *pau de arara*," he lamented, even though he apparently found it normal to eat risotto while drinking whiskey with water and ice.[218]

And first I thought that the person causing such public consternation had not even taken office as the president of my country—which was the same country of those gentlemen—and was already causing outrage.

What would it be like during his administration? How could he overcome so much resistance and rejection?

The second thing I thought was that the same country suffered (and still suffers) from a poorly disguised racism, linked to a wicked and cowardly social prejudice, and startling social racism.

No evidence could be more blatantly clear than the phrase, "He is unfit even to be the doorman of my building."

By November 2002, I was not close to Lula. I had been with him three or four times, at the most.

But I remembered the first time I heard about him in 1978, when I was not living in Brazil, and also the day we first met. I remembered that this restricted contact had enlightened me enough to understand the reasons why a significant part of well-dressed Brazilians—whose view of Brazil was so degraded—rejected him so explicitly. But I could also sense that he would neutralize this bitter rancor.

Years later, a Spanish friend, writer and journalist Pilar del Río, gave me a perfect definition of Lula's power: "He is a person of a thousand charismas."

Just as I anticipated, at the right time, precisely because he is the man of a thousand charismas, Lula effectively knew how to neutralize that resistance. But what I could not foresee was that when this resistance, this prejudice, returned, it would come with the rage of angry gods—and that he would not be the only victim of this rage, as the Brazil built by him would suffer as well. This is what we are going through in these dark days for my country.

I was not able to foresee that this fury would be provoked not only by what Lula da Silva has done in his two terms (and would certainly do in a third term), but by his own origins.

After all, a man who wasn't even fit to be a doorman became president of the republic; probably the most popular president in the history of a country that is mine, but also belongs to the gentlemen in suits, and to tens upon tens of millions of people rejected and abandoned by a perverse system; people who became invisible to the eyes of the prejudiced, to whom he was able to show that regaining dignity is something possible.

Lula was definitely fit. He was the only doorman able to open the doors of a house that could (and maybe still can) belong to everybody, and not to just a few. This was his greatest sin: to show that another reality could and should be possible.

2.

October 27, 1945 was a Sunday. And in Caetés, in the countryside of Pernambuco, Luiz Inácio was born the seventh son of a family of illiterate farmers. They all lived in a house with only two rooms, an earthen floor and no running water. They were not even poor: they were less than poor. They were part of the immense horde of Brazilians condemned to live on the outskirts of life.

Five years later, the boy would meet his father, Aristides Inácio da Silva. Until then, he and his brothers had been raised by their mother, Eurídice Ferreira de Melo. Better known as Dona Lindu, she would be forever worshipped by Lula.

His father went to Santos, in the state of São Paulo, taking another woman with him and leaving behind the pregnant Dona Lindu. He returned, stayed for a while in Caetés, but went back to Santos, taking his eldest son, Jaime, with him. He was the son who helped Dona Lindu take care of his other siblings.

Two years later, at the end of 1952, Dona Lindu received a letter from Jaime, pretending to be his father. The letter, read by one of the children who could read, instructed her to sell the house and take her family to Santos.

And there they all went, huddled together on the back of a truck, on a journey that took thirteen days. At the time, it was common for underprivileged Northeasterners to migrate south; they were the so-called "retirantes," in the back of one of the trucks known as *pau de arara*.

Yes, yes. The gentleman in the suit was right that day in the restaurant: Lula was—and deep in his soul, never ceased to be—a *pau de arara*. A boy who, together with his mother and brothers, came to a distant port—a city by the sea, where there was so much water, he would never have dreamed of in the hinterland of poverty—a boy who two years later began to work, selling trinkets on the street, next to his brother José, who later would be known as Frei Chico.

And he was a shoeshine boy, who, hidden from his father (who forbade his children from studying), went to school; he saw his mother separate from his father because she could not bear to be so mistreated; and, on the eve of his eleventh birthday, he moved with his mother and brothers to the working-class neighborhood of Ipiranga, in the city called São Paulo, which was greater than anything he could have ever imagined. He went to work as a shoemaker, then as an office boy, and then as help in a laundry, until he was thirteen. Then, he worked on-the-books for the first time, in a luminous March of 1959. He would never forget how proud he was to get his real job, no longer jumping between temporary jobs: his debut at the Armazéns Gerais Colúmbia was a step above. An achievement.

A year and a half later, in September 1960, he was hired to work at the Fábrica de Parafusos Marte—and it was like he had moved to another planet.

After all, a factory is a factory, and a warehouse is a warehouse. Or so it seemed to that anxious and curious boy.

He took a course at Senai, the National Industrial Apprenticeship Service, and his life changed course again.

3.

The first time I met Lula was a few days after the 1986 São Paulo gubernatorial elections. It was my dear friend Leonel Brizola who asked me to talk to Lula.

Why me? Because I worked as a journalist at the time and was not connected to any party. And so I went to São Paulo to interview Lula for the weekly newspaper *O Nacional*, founded and directed by Tarso de Castro.

Lula served as the federal congressman with the most popular votes from the most powerful state in the country, winning more votes than the veteran Ulysses Guimarães. The poor kid from the hinterland surprised a lot of people, but he was surprised by the surprise of others.

He knew it, and even told me that he would not only be elected but would win more popular votes than any other candidate. It was not arrogance, he explained: he simply knew how to listen to the streets, to feel the mood that hung in the air.

In the end, the interview was nothing special. Brizola wanted me to find out what Lula really thought.

I went back to Rio and told him that, at least for me, Lula was unfathomable. He was extremely intelligent and had an intuition I had rarely seen in my life—I remember mentioning the Panamanian Omar Torrijos and, most of all, Cuban Fidel Castro—who was a keen and fast strategist. I told him that every time Lula felt pressured, he reacted with incredible nonchalance and serenity, avoiding confrontation. He used the negotiation tools he learned in his days as a union leader. But, as I told Brizola, I sensed that if a confrontation were inevitable, if his power of seduction as a negotiator failed, Lula would be a ruthless adversary.

As for my personal impression, I was struck by how firmly he defended his convictions, which were as hard as stone, and by his way of looking deep into one's eyes; I was also struck by the feeling that he seemed to be always on the defensive, suspicious that he would be led into a trap, some alley from which it would be difficult to escape. I never understood why Lula acted that way that afternoon, but this is what I felt in our first meeting. He was like an enraged animal.

Brizola never said it to me, but I felt that he wanted someone from outside PDT, the party commanded by him, to find out what was the possibility of an approach with Lula in that moment of political trouble—in the always troubled Brazilian panorama. He knew that, at some point, an alliance would be more than necessary for the country. In fact, it would be inevitable.

4.

Another meeting happened years later, in April or May 1994, again in São Paulo. Brizola was a presidential candidate, and so was Lula. And, again, I was impressed by his determination.

Lula had lost the second round of the 1989 elections, thanks to the misguided maneuvers of his campaign's coordinators, to a certain sense of social inferiority—a type of class prejudice, only in reverse—in relation to Fernando Collor de Mello, the son of the oligarchy, but mainly thanks to the scandalous manipulation of the media, responding to fears among businessmen.

Journalist Ricardo Kotscho, one of Lula's closest friends, who served as a kind of adviser, and advertising director Washington Olivetto attended that meeting. In the end, late at night, I thought that it was one of the rare occasions in which Olivetto had listened more than he had talked.

Lula was excited. He said many times that he was going to win. And he insisted on one point: "This time I'm ready."

One of his opponents would be Fernando Henrique Cardoso. Election polls showed that Lula had around 40 percent of vote intentions, three times more than Cardoso.

I was struck by how self-confident he was. And I never forgot something Lula said: "Unless they come up with something, be sure that I'm going to win. I just need to keep the campaign the way it is."

Well, they came up with Plano Real, and Lula lost.

5.

He waited patiently and persistently. Once again, he lost to Fernando Henrique in the 1998 elections. But his day finally came: one month after his fifty-seventh birthday, on October 27, 2002. The poor immigrant that, as a teenager, dreamed about driving a truck around the country, would now run the entire country as president of the republic. By then his life had become something he would never even dream of in his younger years.

The boy who had fled with his family to escape misery and started to work at a young age first became a factory worker, a mechanical turner. An accident at work cost him the little finger of his left hand when he was eighteen. He spent a year unemployed until he got a job in a very important company at the time, Indústrias Villares; he became involved with the Metalworkers Union and married Maria de Lourdes, the sister of one of his best friends.

He was the happiest of the happy when she got pregnant. But he would discover the true meaning of pain when, in the seventh month of pregnancy, Maria de Lourdes and the baby died.

To get out of that abyss, Lula did what some men do: he fled to the front line. He moved ahead. He plunged deep into syndicalism. From a fleeting relationship, he had his first daughter, Lurian. He married Marisa Letícia, a beautiful and luminous-eyed widowed girl. Then, he was elected president of the Metalworkers Union and its more than 100,000 members.

He had a son with Marisa Letícia, Fábio Luís. All between May 1971, when Maria de Lourdes died, and March 1975.

Furthermore, in October 1975, he made his first trip out of Brazil and landed on the other side of the world, in Japan.

This dizzying trajectory was still hanging over his soul when, on the first day of 2003, he saw his chest being crossed by the presidential sash.

He had an endless number of projects and programs. He wanted to change the face of Brazil, his country, my country, the country of the gentlemen at the restaurant in the elegant neighborhood of São Paulo. But, most of all, he wanted to change the face of a country that belongs to tens of millions of people like him.

Perhaps without knowing its origin, he used an old quote from Darcy Ribeiro as his motto: he said that his fundamental mission was to ensure that, at the end of his term, every Brazilian would wake up in the morning knowing that they would have breakfast, lunch, and dinner each day.

Perhaps he was not able to accomplish his mission in its entire enormity. But it certainly changed the lives of at least 43 million Brazilians—the equivalent of an Argentina, almost four times Portugal, almost a Spain—who became citizens, emerging from poverty and extreme poverty, which is the bureaucratic name for misery (the same he endured as a child).

So it is: the same man who, in his days as a union leader, organized and carried out mass strikes that defied the dictatorship and helped change the country in those times of darkness, also knew how to plan and carry out actions that helped change the country in times of clarity.

Since the electoral campaign, the skillful and persistent negotiator, the intuitive seducer, "the person of a thousand charismas" made clear what he intended, by promoting a broad alliance, hitherto unthinkable, with sectors that have always demonstrated not only dislike, but a real allergic reaction to the Workers' Party and to Lula himself.

That's how the first factory worker became president of Brazil, the first president without a college degree. And so PT became the first left-wing party to elect a president in this country.

In the first weeks of his administration, a resounding display of the direction he had set forth became visible: he attended the World Social Forum in Porto Alegre and, two days later, he made his debut at the World Economic Forum in Davos, a hamlet in the Swiss Alps.

The first one struggles for a new world order, fighting against hunger and misery to promote social inclusion.

The second one fights for the defense of capital and of the privileges of the very few, to the detriment of the rights of all others. It struggles to maintain the benefits of those who have always benefited, at the cost of the abandonment of those who are eternally forsaken.

Coincidence or not, his presence in Davos served to project his image around the world and, as a consequence, to open the way that would lead Brazil to hold a consistent and unprecedented place on the world stage.

A consolidated place and a consistency that would be dissolved in an instant after the parliamentary coup that deposed President Dilma Rousseff and put an end to institutionality in my country.

6.

Any objective and balanced analysis of Lula's two presidential mandates will show, in the first place, the obvious: there were achievements and mistakes. After all, both he and his team were made of human clay, sculpted by life and doomed to imperfection.

Any minimally objective and balanced assessment of the same period will show, first and foremost, that the successes and achievements were overwhelmingly superior to the mistakes, even in the most serious cases.

There was virtually no sector or segment of society that was not targeted by a government program. From bringing electricity to the countryside to the creation of universities; from social programs benefiting millions of marginalized families to the creation of new jobs; from the redistribution of income to repaying the historic debt with the International Monetary Fund; from offering scholarships to study and train abroad to the creation of new financial incentives for arts and culture; nothing remained unscathed in those dizzying years.

And actions did not stop there. They have led to a program of accelerated growth, to the exploration of pre-salt oil, to a housing-building program, and to a series of unprecedented foreign policy actions. In short, they led to a vortex of change, which built instead of destroying.

If minimally objective and balanced, this assessment will also show that still in his first term, Lula had to use his thousand charismas to survive the first attempt of putting an end to his government.

Based on what former house representative Roberto Jefferson said during an interview, the idea of Mensalão was created, implying—and ultimately convincing the public opinion, thanks to the press—that part of the house representatives received allowances, being corrupted to vote in favor of government projects.

As a matter of fact, this money—known as a slush fund—was irregular and intended for the payment of electoral campaign debts. It always existed, it was not invented by PT, nor by the Lula administration, and it continues to exist to this date.

It did not matter then, and it still does not matter now: the goal was to ruin Lula. He survived, but key leaders of PT were ruined, starting with former house representative and former minister José Dirceu.

The most heart-wrenching thing is to note that this farce was reinforced by the members of the Supreme Court in a country that belongs to me, to Lula, and to the elegant gentlemen who saw, for the first time, a concrete opportunity to get rid once and for all of the poor migrant kid who, instead of a doorman, became president. Legal judgments were manipulated scandalously and the show prevailed: the Mensalão found a permanent place in history.

What they tried and failed to achieve against Lula was finally achieved years later against an extremely fragile link of that chain: Dilma Rousseff.

7.

It was only when Lula left the presidency, when his two terms ended, that we both had more contact.

Much has changed in him, in me, in our country and in the world, since that now distant 1986.

He is more serene, less angry. The trials of life, including the painful death of his life partner, Marisa Letícia, have left marks, which will remain forever.

I now recall a lunch in October or November 2016, in São Paulo, with him, Fernando Morais, and Paulo Vannuchi, two of his most trusted and close friends.

We talked about what could be done—not to his benefit, because he knew pretty well what to do, but to help people like Fernando and myself—in the desolate scenario in which Brazil had been transformed.

Late at night, taking advantage of this atmosphere of trust in which I did not fit very well, I ventured a confession: "I am outraged, Lula. Really! And I'm very, very sad . . ."

Lula looked at me with a glimpse of that same angry air of our first meeting: "Do you think I'm any different? I'm also very sad, but sadness does not help. You have to fight. That's what we have to do."

This is the man they have been trying to remove at all costs. It's an unprecedented persecution. Not even when we compare it to what they did to Leonel Brizola, when he was Rio's governor. And the reason for such an absurdity and for so much injustice is very simple: it is necessary to preserve at any cost a perverse, malignant, sordid system. And Lula is an Olympic danger.

After all, when he finished his second term with 87 percent popular approval—the largest in Brazilian history—the poor migrant received the first Global Statesmanship Award at the World Economic Forum, the same forum that brings together the owners of the money and is the holiest altar for the elegant men of the restaurant in São Paulo. It is against this that they are so fiercely fighting.

Against this, against the constant danger of losing the privileges of a few in favor of countless people that never had and never will have rights.

—Rio de Janeiro, March 6, 2018

Luiz Inácio Lula da Silva: A Timeline

Camilo Vannucchi, together with Thaisa Buran

October 7, 1945 – Luiz Inácio da Silva is born in Caetés (PE), at the time a district of Garanhuns. He is the seventh son of illiterate farmers Eurídice Ferreira de Melo (Dona Lindu) and Aristides Inácio da Silva. The family home, with only two rooms and a dirt floor, has no electricity or running water.

June 1950 – At the age of five, he meets his father, who had migrated to Santos, in the state of São Paulo, with another woman during his gestation. His father visits Caetés for a few days and returns to Santos, taking the eldest son Jaime with him.

December 1952 – Pretending to be his father, Jaime writes a letter instructing Dona Lindu to sell the property in Caetés and to move to Santos with her children. The family embarks on a thirteen-day trip on a flatbed truck to São Paulo, from where they head for the coast.

August 1953 – At the age of seven, Lula begins working as a street vendor on the docks of Santos alongside his brother José, who would later earn the nickname of Frei Chico. He then becomes a shoeshine boy in the city downtown.

1954–1955 – Hidden from his father, who did not allow his children to study, Lula attends the Grupo Escolar Marcílio Dias (school Group Marcílio Dias), by imposition of Dona Lindu. Tired of being abused, Dona Lindu separates from her husband at the end of 1955.

August 1956 – Dona Lindu and her children move to Vila Carioca, in São Paulo, a small working-class neighborhood on the border with São Caetano do Sul.

March 1959 – Lula gets his first registered job at Columbia General Warehouses, after working informally as a street vendor, shoeshine boy, office boy, and as an auxiliary of a laundry assistant.

September 1960 – At age fourteen, he is hired by the Marte Hardware Factory as a metalworker. Thanks to his employment, he joins the professional mechanics course at the National Industrial Learning Service (SENAI), where he completes his secondary education.

March 1962 – At the age of eighteen, he starts working at Metalúrgica Independência on the night shift. He is often required to work overtime more than allowed by law. On one of these occasions, at two o'clock in the morning, he suffers an accident that costs him his little finger. He receives 371,000 cruzeiros, equivalent to just over R$46,000 in compensation in March 2018. He continues to work normally in the factory.

1964–1967 – In the year of the civil-military coup, he gets involved in a discussion about a salary raise and is fired from Metalúrgica Independência. He is hired by Fris Moldu Car but loses his job six months later. He is unemployed for over a year. He gets a job in 1966, at Indústrias Villares, in São Bernardo do Campo. He approaches the Metalworkers Union of

São Bernardo do Campo and Diadema the following year, due to the influence of his brother Frei Chico, a unionist.

1968–1969 – Lula gets unionized and runs in the election for the situationist list. The list wins and Lula takes office as second substitute on April 24, 1969. He continues working at Villares.

May 1969 – He marries Maria de Lourdes at age twenty-three.

May 1971 – Lourdes dies in an emergency caesarean section after failed hospitalization attempts. Seven months pregnant, she was suffering from severe anemia and hepatitis. The baby does not survive the delivery.

August 1972 – Suffering from depression, Lula clings to the union activity. He moves to São Bernardo do Campo. At Villares, he begins to participate in the bargaining with the bosses and proves to be skillful. He takes part in the reelected list for the union board, now as first secretary. He runs the legal department and is responsible for the newly created social security sector.

April 1973 – He meets and falls in love with Marisa Letícia, also a widow. She has a two-year-old son, Marcos. Lula breaks up with his girlfriend, nurse Miriam Cordeiro. Shortly after, he learns about Miriam's pregnancy. He promptly assumes the paternity of the girl and the costs of prenatal care and childbirth.

1974 – Lurian, his daughter with Miriam Cordeiro, is born in March. It is Lula who goes to the notary's office to register the baby. Two months later, he makes his union with Marisa official. He later completes the process of adoption of his stepchild Marcos.

February 1975 – Lula takes office at the Union with 92 percent of the votes and the challenge to lead a category of 100,000 workers. Lula is still a terrible speaker, although a very popular and good negotiator. At his inauguration, however, he surprises everyone by reading a speech in which he criticizes both capitalism and socialism, something uncommon in the polarized times of the Cold War.

March 1975 – Fábio Luís, his first son with Marisa, is born.

October 1975 – During a Toyota congress in Japan (his first trip abroad), Lula learns his brother Frei Chico is missing and is told not to return to Brazil. Ignoring the recommendation, Lula returns and searches for his brother at the Second Army and Dops, until he finds him at DOI-Codi. The episode strengthens his opposition to the dictatorship. On October 25, journalist Vladimir Herzog is killed while being tortured at DOI-Codi.

May 1978 – Lula is reelected president of the union with 98 percent of the votes. In order to engage the workers, he transfers the assemblies to the factory doors and replaces traditional bulletins with more playful materials, with cartoons and comics. The character João Ferrador (João Blacksmith), by Laerte Coutinho, is created. The same month, three thousand Scania metalworkers, in São Bernardo do Campo, go on strike. Lula takes over the negotiations, closing a positive deal, with a 15 percent salary increase. The example spreads throughout the ABC region and other cities of São Paulo.

May 12, 1978 – His father, Aristides, dies.

July 1978 – Lula's second son, Sandro Luís, is born. While Marisa gives birth, Lula participates in a meeting of tankers in Bahia. There, in a media interview, he speaks for the first time publicly about the idea of founding a workers' party.

December 1978 – Despite the illegality, more than four hundred strikes and actions take place throughout the country.

March 13, 1979 – Organized since January, the general strike starts. The adhesion of eighty thousand metalworkers surpasses expectations, and the board transfers the assembly to the Vila Euclides Stadium in São Bernardo. Without megaphone or podium, Lula climbs onto a table in the center of the lawn and speaks in a town crier manner; the nearest workers repeat each sentence to the back row.

March 1979 – In two days, the strike has already added 170,000 metalworkers in the ABC region. The Ministry of Labor decrees an intervention, and police vehicles surround the headquarters of the union. The leaders are fired, and part of the category gets back to work. Lula proposes a truce to management, with the immediate return to work at the end of the intervention, the reopening of Vila Euclides Stadium for the assemblies, payment of days off, no dismissal, and a readjustment of 11 percent. At the meeting, he explains the terms of the truce and requests a vote of confidence from the workers. The bosses agree with the union, but they do not keep their promise. There are layoffs and retaliation in various factories. Lula is called a traitor and then proposes the dismissal of the board and the call for a new election. The gesture is acclaimed, and his leadership is strengthened.

February 1980 – The PT is founded in a ceremony at the Catholic school Colégio Sion, in São Paulo, attended by about seven hundred people, most of them unionists, students, leaders of social movements, progressive Catholics, and left-wing intellectuals.

April 1980 – One hundred and forty thousand metalworkers strike in São Bernardo and Diadema; they demand a 15 percent increase in wages and reduction of work hours from forty-eight to forty a week. Once again, the judiciary declares the strike illegal. Army helicopters fly over assemblies and conduct high-visibility patrols to try to intimidate workers. Lula withdraws his union mandate, and a new intervention is declared in the union. The protective custody of Lula and another sixteen unionists is decreed.

April 19, 1980 – On the seventeenth day of the stoppage, Lula is arrested and charged with violating the National Security Law. He is taken to Dops, where he is imprisoned for thirty-one days. He embarks on a hunger strike, which is interrupted on the seventh day after the appeal of Bishop Claudio Hummes. Assemblies take place in the Mother Church of São Bernardo after an invitation by the bishop.

May 1980 – The strike ends on the forty-first day, without an agreement. The right to strike becomes a national demand. Dona Lindu dies at age sixty-four due to uterine cancer. Lula is allowed to leave the prison under escort to attend her funeral.

February 1981 – Sentenced by the Military Court to three and a half years in prison, he appeals out of custody and, in May 1982, the case is annulled by the Superior Military Court.

June 1981 – As leader and spokesman of the PT, Lula travels throughout Brazil and to more than ten countries. In the United States, he has a meeting with Democratic senator Ted Kennedy. In Italy, he meets Pope John Paul II and Polish union leader Lech Walesa.

1982 – The TSE officially recognizes the founding of the PT and authorizes it to run for the elections. Lula is a candidate to the government of São

Paulo and incorporates his nickname, signing Luiz Inácio Lula da Silva, so that the ballots filled out with the name "Lula" can be validated. He receives 10 percent of the votes, finishing in fourth place. André Franco Montoro, of the PMDB, wins the election. Throughout the country, the PT elects eight federal congresspeople, twelve state congresspeople, two mayors, and seventy-eight city councillors.

November 1983 – Lula leads the first major direct elections rally in Charles Miller Square in São Paulo.

April 1984 – Lula organizes a supra-party committee in favor of direct elections. Rallies and demonstrations mobilize millions of Brazilians in big cities. On April 25, the Dante de Oliveira Amendment is voted on and defeated, postponing the right to vote for president.

March 1985 – Lula's youngest son, Luís Cláudio, is born.

November 1985 – With the election of Maria Luiza Fontenele in Fortaleza, the PT conquers the city hall of a capital for the first time.

November 1986 – Lula is elected constituent federal deputy. During the following two years, he participates in the drafting of the Federal Constitution of 1988 and helps to ensure the inclusion of amendments such as the right to strike, maternity leave of 120 days, and reduction of the work week to forty-four hours.

December 1987 – Olívio Dutra takes over the presidency of the PT so that Lula can dedicate himself to the 1989 campaign. (Soon after, Luiz Gushiken takes over the presidency.)

1988 – Lula is the main mobilizer of the PT's campaign for municipalities all over Brazil. The party conquers three capitals—São Paulo (Luiza

Erundina), Porto Alegre (Olívio Dutra), and Vitória (Vitor Buaiz)—and thirty-three additional cities.

1989 – In March, Lula becomes a candidate for president of the republic and heads the Frente Brasil Popular coalition, supported by the PT, the PSB, and the PCdoB. Polarizing with Leonel Brizola (PDT), Lula is appointed as a favorite until the emergence of the candidacy of Fernando Collor de Mello, senator from Alagoas for the National Reconstruction Party (PRN). Collor is supported by the banks, big industry, and the media. In December, billionaire entrepreneur Abílio Diniz is kidnapped in São Paulo. Images of the kidnapper Humberto Paz wearing a t-shirt from Lula's campaign are broadcast on TV. In testimony to the police, Paz claims to have been tortured and forced by police officers to wear the shirt.[219] In another episode, Collor's penultimate electoral program features an interview with Miriam Cordeiro, Lula's ex-girlfriend, stating that Lula had offered her money for an abortion and had never recognized the child. The testimony is broadcast by *Jornal Nacional* the next day. Finally, *Jornal Nacional*, while broadcasting the "best moments" of the last debate between Lula and Collor, overestimate the participation of the PRN candidate.[220] Lula is defeated in the run-off, with 47 percent of valid votes, against 53 percent for Collor.

June 1990 – Lula founds the Parallel Government, a nucleus inspired by an initiative of the English Labour Party, with the mission to monitor the policies adopted by Collor and create alternative proposals. Through the Parallel Government, Lula helps to organize a national movement to fight hunger—at that time, one-fifth of the Brazilian population (32 million people) lived below the poverty line. The project inspires the campaign "National Action against Hunger, Misery and for Life," released in the media by sociologist Herbert de Souza, also known as Betinho.

June 1992 – As President of the PT, Lula mobilizes members of the party at Congress and acts to install a CPI (parliamentary investigation committee) against Collor, on allegations of corruption, gang formation, misappropriation of money, and misuse of public funds. The Movement for Ethics in Politics arises, and the "painted-faces" take to the streets to demand the president's impeachment.

September 1992 –Congress approves by 441-33 the impeachment of the first president elected after the re-democratization. The vote goes to the Federal Senate. Collor is removed, and his vice president Itamar Franco takes over the government on a temporary basis.

December 29, 1992 – The Senate begins to vote on the impeachment. Collor resigns. The vote ends on the following day, and Collor is overthrown by a 73-3 vote. Itamar Franco takes office definitively as president of the republic.

March 1993 – The Parallel Government becomes Instituto Cidadania (The Citizenship Institute).

April 21, 1993 – A national plebiscite takes place to determine the regime (republican or monarchist) and the system of government (presidential or parliamentary) of the country, by determination of an amendment of the Constitution of 1988. The republican regime and the presidential system win.

1993 – In Garanhuns, Lula starts the first Caravanas da Cidadania (Caravan of Citizenship), in order to revive themes such as land conflicts, drought, and poverty. By July of the following year, Lula and his team will have carried out seven caravans, crossing the five regions of Brazil. *Newsweek* publishes an extensive report on the initiative.

1994 – A favorite for the electoral campaign, Lula tries to build an alliance with PSDB leaders, negotiating the name of Tasso Jereissati for vice president. The alliance fails with the rise of the pre-candidacy of then finance minister Fernando Henrique Cardoso, launched by Sao Paulo's Toucans (PSDB) as "the father of the Real Plan." Fernando Henrique happens to be supported by sectors that feared the victory of Lula.[221] The PT is defeated in the first round by FHC.

May 1997 – Vale do Rio Doce is privatized. In an auction challenged in court, the consortium "Brazil," led by CSN, acquires control of the company for R$3.3 billion. In the opposition, Lula condemns the measure and the amounts paid.

July 1998 – The Telebrás system is privatized by means of an auction.

October 1998 – Lula gives in to PT appeals and agrees to run for presidency of the republic for the third time, but loses again to Fernando Henrique Cardoso.

1999 – At the beginning of the second term, FHC contradicts his campaign, and the Central Bank adopts the floating exchange rate system. Brazilian currency depreciates, confirming that its parity to the dollar had been maintained thanks to high interest rates and low investment in production. Crises in Asia, Russia, and Argentina undermine the Brazilian trade balance and bring down commodity prices. FHC loses popularity, and Lula is considered a favorite for the 2002 election.

October 2000 – For the first time since its founding, the PT is the most popular party in Brazil in municipal elections. It wins in 187 cities, including São Paulo (Marta Suplicy), Recife (João Paulo), and Porto Alegre (Tarso Genro) and goes up from 1,895 to 2,485 city councillors.

January 2002 – The mayor of Santo André, Celso Daniel, is assassinated. He had been chosen to coordinate Lula's plan of government and was his personal friend. After the tragedy, he is replaced by Antonio Palocci, mayor of Ribeirão Preto.

March 2002 – Favored within the party, Lula imposes two conditions for his candidacy: a wide range of alliances, including sectors traditionally estranged from the party, and a vice president linked to the business community. José Alencar Gomes da Silva (PL), a mining and industrial entrepreneur in the textile sector, is officially elected as Lula's vice president. The duo is celebrated as a convenient capital-labor union.

June 2002 – In order to publicize his program, Lula reads the well-known "Letter to the Brazilian People," written to calm markets down. The letter shows a more moderate face of Lula, committed to the fulfilment of contracts—including the ones on foreign debt—and agreements with the IMF.

October 2002 – Following advertising recommendations, Lula shaves his beard, wears a suit to his appointments, smiles more often, and shouts less. He earns the nickname of "Lulinha Paz e Amor" (Little Lula Peace and Love). He is elected president of the republic in the runoff, on the day of his fifty-seventh birthday. About 150,000 people gather in Paulista Avenue in São Paulo to celebrate the victory. The crowd sings "Happy Birthday to you."

January 1, 2003 – For the first time, a laborer takes office as president of the republic in Brazil. Lula is also the first civilian elected president born in Pernambuco, the first without a university degree, and the first enrolled in a leftist party.

January 2003 – Lula takes half of his ministers for a trip through poor regions of the Northeast and Minas Gerais, so that they can see the misery and understand the importance of income distribution policies. Still in January, he is the first president of the republic to speak at the World Social Forum in Porto Alegre. Two days later, he addresses the World Economic Forum in Davos and proposes a global pact for peace and against hunger.[222] He launches the Fome Zero (Zero Hunger) program.

October 2003 – Lula combines social programs like Fome Zero to create the Bolsa Família (Family Allowance) program, which will become the flagship of the government. He receives the Prince of Asturias Award, in Spain.

November 2003 – The program Luz para Todos (Light for Everyone) is launched.

January 2004 – The PMDB formally joins the allied base, guaranteeing parliamentary majority for the government.

February 2004 – *Época* magazine publishes the first complaint against Lula's government. Waldomiro Diniz, adviser to the Minister of the Civil House Jose Dirceu, is accused of extorting the bookie Carlinhos Cachoeira from Rio de Janeiro.

January 2005 – The Universidade para todos (PROUNI) (University for Everyone) program is launched.

June 2005 – In an interview with *Folha de S. Paulo*, Federal Deputy Roberto Jeferson (PTB) accuses the government of paying allowances to congressmen in exchange for support for bills. This is the beginning of the "Big Monthly" scandal. Accused of coordinating the scheme, José Dirceu leaves office and Minister of Mines and Energy Dilma Rousseff takes over as chief of staff.

December 2005 – Brazil pays off its IMF debt.

March 2006 – Minister of Finances Antonio Palocci steps down after being charged with corruption. He is replaced by Guido Mantega.

October 2006 – In a race against Geraldo Alckmin, Lula is reelected with more than fifty-eight million votes (60.8 percent of the electorate). In absolute numbers, it is the largest ballot ever won by a head of state in the West. The IPCA recorded an annual inflation rate of 3.14 percent, the lowest since 1998.

2007 – Lula takes office for his second term as president of the republic. Also in January, the Growth Acceleration Program (PAC) is launched. In March, US president George W. Bush visits Brazil and announces an agreement for the production of ethanol. In May, the Bovespa closes the first half with a 22 percent appreciation, the highest since 1999. In August, the STF complies with all the complaints filed against those suspected of being involved in the Big Monthly scandal.

March 2008 – Lula inaugurates PAC (Growth Acceleration Program) works in Complexo do Alemão (RJ) alongside Minister Dilma Rousseff, who is presented as "PAC's mother" and emerges as the likely candidate of PT to the presidential succession.

September 2008 – Lula dirties his hand in oil during a symbolic extraction of the pre-salt layer, at the Petrobras platform of Campo de Jubarte (ES).

December 2008 – Lula celebrates in an announcement the fact that the country goes through the world crisis practically unscathed, and ascribes it to the triumphs of his government.

March 2009 – The Supreme Court (STF) maintains the continuous boundaries of the Raposa Serra do Sol (RO) reserve, an important victory of the indigenous population and environmentalists over the ruralists. The Minha Casa Minha Vida (My Home My Life) program is launched.

April 2009 – At the G20 meeting in London, US president Barack Obama shakes hands with Lula and says, "This is the guy! I love this guy." Lula is elected "Man of the Year" by *Le Monde*.

January 2010 – Premiere of the movie *Lula, o filho do Brazil* (Lula, the son of Brazil), by Fábio Barreto, based on Denise Paraná's eponymous book. Shortly thereafter, the candidacy of Dilma Rousseff to the presidency of the republic is confirmed.

July 2010 – Lula intensifies Brazilian presence in Africa: in eight years of government, nineteen new embassies have been opened in African countries, and trade with the continent has tripled.

August 2010 – The president inaugurates the Dona Lindu campus in Divinópolis (MG), an extension of the Federal University of São João Del Rey; the site joins the list of 126 campuses and fourteen federal universities inaugurated in the Lula government.

October 2010 – Dilma Rousseff is elected president of the republic.

December 2010 – Lula registers a balance sheet of eight years of government. The document has 310 pages and is signed by all ministers. In Ibope's latest popularity survey, Lula reaches a record 87 percent approval rate. He is elected "Global Statesman" by the World Economic Forum.

January 2011 – After passing the baton to Dilma Rousseff, Lula resumes his activities at Instituto Cidadania, taking care of its transition into the Lula Institute.

March 2011 – Lula delivers his first lecture as former president to LG executives. He earns the North-South Prize of Human Rights in Lisbon, and in Coimbra the title of doctor honoris causa by the University of Coimbra.

June-September 2011 – Lula is granted the World Food Prize in Washington, DC. He earns the title of citizen of Bogota. In Paris, he is awarded a doctor honoris causa degree by Sciences Po.

October 2011 – Lula is diagnosed with larynx cancer and begins medical treatment.

April-August 2012 – He earns the International Prize of Catalonia for the fight against poverty and inequality. In the Netherlands, Lula is awarded the Four Freedoms by the Roosevelt Institute. In São Paulo, he earns the title of Cidadão Paulistano (São Paulo citizen) and the Anchieta Medal. In Toronto, he is awarded the Nelson Mandela Human Rights Award.

October 2012 – Lula is cancer-free one year after his diagnosis. He engages in PT's municipal campaigns, especially in Fernando Haddad's campaigns for the municipality of São Paulo.

April-May 2013 – Lula receives the International Crisis Group's "Pursuit of Peace" award in New York and the doctor honoris causa degree from several universities and educational institutions in Buenos Aires, Lima, and Quito.

June 2013 – Lula is a monthly columnist in the *New York Times*. He also devotes himself to international activities to fight hunger through the Lula Institute, promoting lectures and seminars. The same month, demonstrations against the increase of bus and subway fares spread throughout the country, with violent police repression. The progressive content of the protests gives way to general, conservative, and depoliticized dissatisfaction.

March 2014 – Operation Car Wash begins. Seventeen people are arrested, including Paulo Roberto Costa, Petrobras's former supply director.

April 2014 – Lula receives doctor honoris causa degrees from the University of Salamanca and from the University Aquino Bolivia in Santa Cruz de la Sierra.

October 2014 – President Dilma Rousseff is reelected. PSDB immediately demands an audit of the presidential election, making it clear that the following months will be of tireless rejection.

December 2014 – The anti-PT rancor takes shape with the creation of the Vem Pra Rua (Take to the Streets) movement, which receives support from the PSDB. The Toucans (PSDB) request the annulment of the candidacy of Dilma Rousseff and Michel Temer in the TSE, requesting the inauguration of their candidate, Aécio Neves.

January 2015 – Dilma takes office in Brasília. Eduardo Cunha (PMDB) is elected speaker of the lower house.

February-May 2015 – The lower house starts the CPI of Petrobras. Rodrigo Janot, attorney general of the republic, files requests for investigation over politicians involved in Operation Car Wash in the Supreme Court.

Millions of Brazilians are involved in demonstrations against the government in some 160 cities in the country. Dilma's popularity plummets.

July 2015 – Eduardo Cunha splits with the government after being denounced by Júlio Camargo.

August 2015 – José Dirceu is arrested in the context of Operation Car Wash, under the responsibility of Federal Judge Sérgio Moro. Eduardo Cunha is denounced by the attorney general's office.

October 2015 – Dilma announces ministerial reform and a broader participation of the PMDB in her government. The TSE reopens the action of the PSDB to contest the list presented by Dilma and Temer. The opposition hands in the request for the impeachment of the president to Eduardo Cunha.

November 2015 – Lula and Dilma are implicated in Operation Car Wash after the plea bargain of PT senator Delcídio do Amaral.

December 2015 – PT announces its vote for the continuity of the case against Eduardo Cunha at the Ethics Board. In an act of revenge, Cunha authorizes the opening of Dilma's impeachment process. Michel Temer reveals dissatisfaction with the president through a personal letter allegedly leaked to the media. The Supreme Court initiates the impeachment process.

January 2016 – Cunha extricates Michel Temer from the impeachment request.

February 2016 – Lula is investigated by the Federal Police for traffic of influence, accused of "selling" interim measures that benefited car manufacturers. The PT marketer João Santana and his wife are arrested in the operation.

March 4, 2016 – Accused of corruption, Lula has his house searched by the police at six o'clock in the morning and is coercively driven to testify.

March 9, 2016 – The São Paulo public prosecutor denounces Lula for money laundering and concealment of assets. Specifically, the agency accuses Lula and Marisa Letícia of hiding the ownership of a three-story apartment in Guarujá (SP).

March 16, 2016 – Dilma announces Lula's appointment as chief of staff. On the same day, Judge Sérgio Moro leaks conversations recorded by the Federal Police in the context of Car Wash to the media, including the audio of a phone call between Lula and the president.

March 2016 – The next day, a lower court judge grants an injunction suspending Lula's appointment. The lower house of Congress forms the impeachment commission. In twenty-four hours, Judge Gilmar Mendes suspends Lula's appointment as chief of staff. Days later, a "super spreadsheet" containing names of members of the opposition and figures (incompatible with declared donations) is leaked. This spreadsheet was seized a year earlier at the home of the president of Odebrecht Infraestrutura. Immediately after, the spreadsheet is placed under secrecy by Sérgio Moro. The OAB files a new impeachment request against Dilma, and the PMDB officially splits from the government. In an official dispatch, Judge Sérgio Moro apologizes to the Supreme Court for leaking the recorded conversations between Lula and Dilma and denies any political motivation.

April-May 2016 – With 367 votes in favor, the lower house approves the opening of the impeachment process. The Special Committee for the

Impeachment is formed in the Senate. In May, the Senate temporarily removes President Dilma Rousseff from office.[223] Temer takes over as interim president. Politicians, artists, and intellectuals point out that the impeachment process is inconsistent and configures a coup d'état.[224] Also in May, conversations between Romero Jucá and the former president of Transpetro, Sérgio Machado, suggest the impeachment as a solution to stop Operation Car Wash.

July 29, 2016 – Lula is accused by a judge in Brasília, along with five other people, of obstruction of justice and trying to buy the silence of those involved in the corruption network of Petrobras. The Public Prosecutor's Office is suggesting a sentence of three to five years in prison.

August 31, 2016 – Dilma Rousseff is overthrown by the Senate. Temer takes office as president.

September 20, 2016 – Sérgio Moro agrees with the accusation of passive corruption and money laundering presented by the Public Ministry against Lula, considering that he had "sufficient evidence of authorship and materiality."

October 13, 2016 – The court accepts the third charge against Lula. Prosecutors request the conviction of the former president for organized crime and money laundering related to the works carried out by Odebrecht in Angola with loans from the BNDES.

December 10, 2016 – Lula is again charged by the Public Prosecutor's Office, this time for alleged traffic of influence in the purchase of thirty-six Swedish fighter jets.

December 19, 2016 – Sérgio Moro accepts the public prosecutor's fifth accusation against the former president, for passive corruption and money laundering from bribes through imprisoned former minister of finance Antonio Palocci.

January 24, 2017 – Marisa Letícia suffers a hemorrhagic stroke and is admitted to the ICU of the Sírio-Libanês Hospital in São Paulo.

February 3, 2017 – The brain death of the former first lady is confirmed. After the family's authorization, her kidneys, liver, and corneas are donated.

February 4, 2017 – The wake of Marisa Letícia takes place at the headquarters of the Metalworkers Union of ABC in São Bernardo do Campo. Very moved, Lula speaks to the crowd of twenty thousand people: "Marisa died in sadness due to the cruelty, levity, and wickedness that they did to her . . . I hope that the foolish women, who raised frivolities against her once, have the humility to apologize."

April 17, 2017 – Plea bargain agreements by seventy-eight former Odebrecht executives accuse the entire political class, regardless of party or political orientation, of the buying and selling of favors, contracts, and laws. Lula is accused with particular fury, in large part because of his reputation as a "poor working man" and "friend of the poor."

April 28, 2017 – Following a court order, Lula returns twenty-six gifts he received as head of state. In Moro's view, objects—including a sculpture by Joan Miró—should be part of the official collection of the presidency of the republic.

May 10, 2017 – In Curitiba, Lula testifies before Sérgio Moro in a five-hour interrogation. Outside, about five thousand people demonstrate in his support. The former president takes the opportunity to speak after the episode.

May 22, 2017 – Public prosecutors once again accuse Lula, this time alleging corruption and money laundering involving the renovation of a country house in Atibaia, in the state of São Paulo, paid by two contractors. The country house is owned by a friend of the former president.

July 12, 2017 – Judge Sérgio Moro sentences the former president to nine years and six months in prison for the crimes of passive corruption and money laundering. Lula is sentenced for having benefited from diverted public money to favor OAS, a construction company that, in exchange, would have renovated the Guarujá three-story apartment free of charge.

July 20, 2017 – At the request of the judiciary, BrasilPrev blocks about R$9 million from two pension plans that were under the name LILS Palestras e Eventos (LILS Lectures and Events), a company of the former president.

October 2017 – Lula's defense lawyers file a plea for acquittal of the former president, arguing that Moro "acknowledged that there are no amounts from contracts signed by Petrobras used to pay any advantage to Lula."

October 30, 2017 – A year after the 2018 election, Ibope's polling institute has placed Lula as leading the race for the first round with 35 percent of the votes, almost three times the vote intention of second-place Jair Bolsonaro (13 percent).

January 24, 2018 – In Porto Alegre, Lula is tried at the Federal Court of Appeals for the Fourth Region (TRF-4), which confirms the decision of Judge Sérgio Moro and sentences Lula to twelve years and one month in prison. There are popular demonstrations in Lula's support and disapproval of the decision. According to the Clean Record Act, Lula would be ineligible for the 2018 elections.

March 2018 – From the March 19 to the 28, Lula travels through the interior of the states of Rio Grande do Sul, Santa Catarina, and Paraná in the fourth phase of the caravan "Lula pelo Brasil." Two shots are fired at caravan buses in a trap between Quedas do Iguaçu and Laranjeiras do Sul, in Paraná.

April 5, 2018 – Judge Sérgio Moro orders the arrest of the former president and orders that he turn himself in by five p.m. the next day at the Superintendence of the Federal Police of Paraná. Lula remains at the Metalworkers Union of ABC in São Bernardo do Campo, where he stays camped for more than forty-eight hours, receiving visits from family, friends, lawyers, and politicians. Hundreds of people surround the building in support of the former president and spend the night in vigil.

April 7, 2018 – Bishop Angelico Sándalo Bernardino goes to the union and celebrates a religious ceremony in the memory of Marisa Letícia on her birthday. Lula speaks for fifty-five minutes in a truck with loudspeakers, and says he will "comply with their warrant." Visibly moved, he calls on his allies and admirers to turn into millions of Lulas. "All of you, from now on, will turn into Lula and will walk around this country doing what you have to do. They have to know that the death of a combatant will not stop the revolution." When Lula returns to the building, activists lock the gates and promise to prevent him from surrendering. After a long negotiation, the ex-president leaves the building and travels in a convoy to São Paulo. Around ten p.m., Lula arrives in Curitiba and presents himself to begin serving the sentence.

April 2018 – Supporters gather in the surroundings of the Federal Police Superintendence in a vigil for Lula's freedom. About five hundred people are camped in a lot in the same neighborhood, where more than one thousand people circulate every day. The camp has an intense schedule of debates and cultural interventions. At dawn on Saturday, April 28, two people are wounded in a gun attack on the camp. Lula receives weekly visits from relatives and lawyers, but is prohibited from receiving friends. More than fifteen thousand letters to the former president are sent to the Federal Police of Curitiba and the Lula Institute.

August 17, 2018 – The United Nations Human Rights Committee requests that Brazil's government not prevent Lula "from standing for election in the 2018 presidential elections, until his appeals before the courts have been completed in fair judicial proceedings."

August 31, 2018 – Brazil's Superior Electoral Court disqualifies Lula from running under the Clean Record Act.

September 11, 2018 – The PT replaces Lula with Fernando Haddad on the presidential ballot.

Contributors

Luiz Felipe de Alencastro is a historian and political scientist, currently professor emeritus at the University of Paris-Sorbonne and professor at the School of Economics at FGV-SP (his writings do not necessarily represent the institutional opinion of FGV). He is the author of several books, among them *The Deal of Living: Formation of Brazil in the South Atlantic*.

Ivana Jinkings is founder and director of Boitempo and the journal *Margem Esquerda*. Along with Carlos Eduardo Martins and Emir Sader, she organized the book *Latinoamericana: Contemporary Encyclopedia of Latin America and the Caribbean*, and with Kim Doria and Murilo Cleto, the book *Why Do We Shout 'Coup!'?*.

Juca Kfouri is a sports journalist, writer, and television presenter. He has been a sports radio commentator and written columns on soccer in several newspapers and magazines, such as *O Globo*, *Folha de S. Paulo*, and *Lance!*. He is the author of *I Admit My Defeat: Memories*.

Mauro Lopes is a journalist, writer, and editor of the website of shared communications and post-capitalism *Outras Palavras* and author/editor of the blog *Caminho para Casa*. He is one of the authors of the compilation *Why Do We Shout 'Coup!'?*.

Gilberto Maringoni is a journalist, university professor, and cartoonist. He holds a PhD in social history from University of São Paulo. He is professor of international relations at the Federal University of ABC and author, among other books, of *The Made Up Venezuela: Power, Oil, and Intrigue in Chávez's Time* (Fundação Perseu Abramo, 2004).

Luis Felipe Miguel holds a PhD in social sciences from State University of Campinas and is a full professor at the Institute of Political Science at the University of Brasília.

He is the author of, among other books, *Feminism and Politics: An Introduction* (with Flavia Biroli).

Maria Inês Nassif is a journalist graduated from the Cásper Líbero College and holds a master's degree in social sciences from PUC-SP. She has worked in several national newspapers, including *Valor Econômico, O Globo, Folha de S. Paulo, Estado de S. Paulo, Gazeta Mercantil*, and *GGN*. She was awarded the Press Woman Trophy for her work at the GGN in 2014.

Eric Nepomuceno is a writer, translator, and journalist. He is the author of short stories and non-fiction books. He was awarded three *Jabuti* prizes for translations and was the runner-up in the reporting category with his book *O massacre*.

Ricardo Stuckert is twenty-nine years old. He was an official photographer of the presidency of the republic between 2003 and 2011. He worked for the newspaper *O Globo* and for the *Caras, IstoÉ*, and *Veja* magazines. He is currently working on documenting the lives of indigenous groups in Brazil.

Rafael Valim holds a master's degree and a PhD in administrative law from the Pontifical Catholic University of São Paulo (PUC-SP), where he is a professor of law. Among other publications, he is author of *State of Exception: The Legal Form of Neoliberalism*.

Camilo Vannuchi is a journalist and writer. He is a doctoral student of communication sciences at the University of São Paulo and a member of the Journalism, Law, and Freedom Research Group, linked to the School of Communications and Arts (ECA) and the Institute for Advanced Studies (IEA) at the University of São Paulo.

Luis Fernando Verissimo is a journalist, writer, and screenwriter, as well as saxophonist and playwright. He worked as an advertiser, reviewer, and editor, and was a cartoonist and columnist in several newspapers and magazines.

Endnotes

1 Translator's note: *"Coxinha"* and *"mortadela"* are the derogatory nicknames given, respectively, to identify those who supported the coup and those who defended the PT. *Coxinha* is a popular fried chicken pastry served in snack bars and bakeries in Brazilian cities. The nickname's origin is controversial. However, a common explanation points to the fact that police officers frequently use vouchers (pejoratively called coxinha vouchers, due to their low value) to buy the pastry. With time, "police officer" and *"coxinha"* became synonyms in São Paulo. By extension, the derogatory term is used to identify conservative citizens, especially from the upper middle class, who are overly concerned with security. *Mortadela* [bologna] is also a popular and cheap snack. In the wake of the coup, several demonstrations were organized in support of and against Dilma. At the time, conservative websites raised questions about the legitimacy of the pro-Dilma movement, insisting that the organizers of those demonstrations offered snacks (usually bologna sandwiches) and money to convince people to participate in the protests.

2 See Rafael Valim, *Estado de exceção: a forma jurídica do neoliberalismo* (São Paulo, Contracorrente, 2017), p. 27.

3 The Federal Constitution states: "No one will be considered guilty before the issuing of the final and unappealable penal sentence."

4 Guillermo Tenorio, "La construcción del derecho en el discurso mediático: el caso de las sentencias mediáticas," *Anuario de la Facultad de Derecho*, Cidade do México, Universidad Panamericana, v.24, 2006, p. 271-2.

5 Eugênio José Guilherme de Aragão, "O risco dos castelos teóricos do Ministério Público em investigações complexas," in Cristiano Zanin Martins, Valeska Teixeira Zanin Martins, e Rafael Valim (orgs.), *O caso Lula: a luta pela afirmação dos direitos fundamentais no Brasil* (São Paulo, Contracorrente, 2017), p. 55.

6 This decision was made in response to habeas corpus n. 126.292, in clear contrast with Article 5, LVII of the Constitution.

7 According to the Organic Law of the judicial branch: "Art. 36. The judge is forbidden to: III—manifest, by any means of communication, their or another person's opinion on pending proceedings, or derogatory judgment on dispatches, votes or sentences by judicial organs, except for the criticism in the records and in technical works, or in teaching."

8 Silvio Luís Ferreira da Rocha, "A imparcialidade do juiz," in Cristiano Zanin Martins, Valeska Teixeira Zanin Martins, and Rafael Valim (orgs.), *O caso Lula*, cit., p. 159.

9 Comments on the Bangalore principles on judicial conduct (Brazilian translation, Marlon S. Maia and Ariane E. Kloth, Brasília, *Conselho da Justiça Federal*, 2008), p. 67. The so-called Bangalore principles on judicial conduct were defined by the Group of Judicial Integrity, of the United Nations. Its preparation began in 2000 in Vienna. The principles were established in April 2001 in the city of Bangalore, India, and were officially approved in November 2002 in The Hague.

10 Luigi Ferrajoli, "Existem, no Brasil, garantias do devido processo legal?", translated by Samanta Takahashi and Rafael Valim, *Carta Capital*, November 16, 2017 (accessed March 21, 2018).

11 P.A.N. 0003021-32.2016.4.04.8000/RS—Corte Especial. In this case, we must acknowledge the eminent Federal Judge Rogério Favreto, the only member of the Federal Court of Appeal for the Fourth Region who voted to open a disciplinary case against Federal Judge Sérgio Moro.

12 Corinthians 1-0 defeat against São Bento on February 14 during the 2018 Paulista Championship.

13 Eduardo Galeano's *Soccer in Sun and Shadow.*

14 The subject was Real Madrid's 3-1 victory over Paris Saint-Germain during the round of 16 of the UEFA Champions League, on February 14 in Madrid.

15 Lula spoke at Avenida Paulista in São Paulo to celebrate the election victory on October 27, 2002.

16 The Fome Zero program was created in 2001 at Instituto Cidadania, linked to the PT and renamed the Instituto Lula in 2011. The program became a public policy in 2003, in order to fight hunger and ensure food security for Brazilians.

17 Minha Casa Minha Vida was the Lula administration's popular housing program, launched in 2009. It was later degraded by the Temer administration, after the coup against President Dilma Rousseff.

18 An Ibope's survey released on December 16, 2010 showed Lula's approval rating at 87 percent, an unprecedented level. A Sensus Institute survey showed the same, qualifying Lula as the president with the highest ratings on the planet—Nelson Mandela left the South African government in 1999 with an approval rate of 82 percent. Datafolha's survey showed an approval rating of 83 percent and concluded that Lula ended his second term with more support than when he started his first term (76 percent).

19 Movimento Revolucionário 8 de Outubro (Revolutionary Movement October 8), a political organization that participated in the armed struggle against the dictatorship in Brazil, and then had a tortuous political trajectory.

20 Lawyer Airton Soares was a federal congressman for the PT in São Paulo at that time.

Luiz Eduardo Greenhalgh was the lawyer of Lula and other metallurgists arrested during the ABC strikes (1979-1980), and was president of the São Paulo section of the Brazilian Amnesty Committee in the 1970s. He was deputy mayor of São Paulo alongside Luiza Erundina (1989-1993). After several legislatures in which he was a substitute in Congress, exercising partial terms, he was elected federal congressman in 2002. His work as a lawyer is marked by the defense of human rights and of members of social movements persecuted by the system.

At the time, Olívio Dutra was the Workers' Party president in Rio Grande do Sul, and the (defeated) candidate to the state's government.

21 Lula is the youngest of the eight children of Aristides Inácio da Silva and Eurídice Ferreira de Melo, a couple of illiterate farmers who suffered hunger and misery in the poorest region of Pernambuco. He was born on October 27, 1945, in Caetés, which, at the time, was a district of the municipality of Garanhuns, Pernambuco. A couple of days before his mother gave birth, his father decided to try his life as a stevedore in Santos, taking with him Valdomira Ferreira de Góis, cousin of Euridice, with whom he would later establish a second family.

22 Marisa Letícia Lula da Silva was married to Lula from 1974 until her death, on February 3, 2017, as a result of a stroke.

23 João Santana de Cerqueira Filho was responsible for the political marketing of the Lula and Dilma electoral campaigns.

24 Fernando Henrique Cardoso was president of Brazil between 1995 and 2003, defeating Lula in the 1994 elections (in the first round, with 54 percent of valid votes) and 1998 (in the first round, with 53 percent of valid votes). His victories were mainly due to the stabilization of the economy propitiated by the Real Plan, launched when FHC was minister of finances (1993-1994), during the

Itamar Franco administration. He was senator for São Paulo from 1983 to 1992. One of the most renowned Brazilian sociologists, Fernando Henrique Cardoso had a trajectory from social democracy to neoliberalism, beginning in the 1990s, and was one of the promoters of the coup of 2015-2016 against President Dilma Rousseff.

25 The Lower House approved, on April 17, 2016, the installation of Dilma Rousseff's impeachment process by 367 votes in favor, with seven abstentions and only 167 against it; the minimum number for approval was 342.

26 The 0-0 game was held in Rosario, Argentina, on July 18, 1978.

27 Wellington Moreira Franco, one of the most active plotters of the coup against President Rousseff, was appointed by Michel Temer as chief minister of the General Secretariat of the Presidency in February 2017 and was still in office at the time this book was published. Governor of Rio de Janeiro between 1987 and 1991, for years Moreira Franco has been the target of numerous reports of corruption and is known for his ties to organized crime, especially to Comando Vermelho (Red Command). He was a close friend of physical education teacher Nazareno Barbosa Tavares, who was his personal trainer. Tavares organized and commanded one of the most spectacular kidnappings in history, that of entrepreneur Roberto Medina, owner of Rock in Rio, in June 1990.

Geddel Vieira Lima, who also plotted in the coup against Dilma, was sent to the Papuda prison, in Brasília, in September 2017, after the Federal Police found R$51 million in cash hidden in bags in an apartment used by him in Salvador. He was still in jail at the time this book was published. He was minister of National Integration during the second Lula administration, and vice president of Caixa Econômica Federal between 2011 and 2013. Geddel faces a series of accusations of corruption. He broke with Dilma and began to plot in the coup against her, having served as the as chief minister of Temer's General Secretariat of the Presidency between May and November 2016. He left office after former Minister of Culture Marcelo Calero denounced having been pressed by him to approve the construction of a building in the historic center of Salvador (a building in which Geddel owns an apartment).

Romero Jucá, one of the leaders of the MDB (Brazilian Democratic Movement), also plotted in the coup against Dilma, after being minister of Social Security during the Lula administration in 2005. He was also minister of planning for less than a month, during the Temer administration. In May 2016, he fell after a conversation with Transpetro's former president, Sérgio Machado, was leaked, in which he stated that the coup against Dilma would happen, and that an agreement had been reached with the participation of members of the Supreme Court (STF), in order to stop investigations led by Operation Car Wash—which turned out to be true. He returned to the Senate, where he assumed the leadership of the government and the presidency of the PMDB (Brazilian Democratic Movement Party). Since 1984, his entire political career has been marked by accusations of corruption.

28 Ricardo Berzoini was the chief minister of the Secretariat for Institutional Relations between April 2014 and January 2015 and later was the chief minister of the General Secretariat of the Presidency between October 2015 and May 2016, where he was responsible for the political organization of the Rousseff administration.

Jaques Wagner was chief of staff between October 2015 and March 2016 and was also responsible for the political organization of the Rousseff administration.

Aloizio Mercadante was chief of staff between February 2014 and October 2015, when Jaques Wagner replaced him. He served as minister of education from October 2015 to May 2016, but continued to participate in the organization of the Rousseff administration.

29 Marco Maciel served as a congressman, governor of Pernambuco, senator and vice president on the same ballot list as Fernando Henrique Cardoso. Connected to the military dictatorship, he was a disciple of General Golbery do Couto e Silva, breaking with the regime shortly before Paulo Maluf's defeat to Tancredo Neves in the Electoral College of 1985. He was minister of education and chief of staff during the Sarney administration.

30 As president of the lower house, Eduardo Cunha was the architect of the coup against Dilma Rousseff. He entered political life in the steps of Paulo César Farias (P. C. Farias), treasurer of the Fernando Collor campaign and pivot of his fall. With the help of P. C. Farias, he became the president of Telerj, in 1991. Since then, his political career has been marked by allegations of corruption and the organization of parliamentary groups based on the exchange of favors, positions, and money. He established the largest parliamentary caucus in the lower house with the objective of overthrowing Dilma Rousseff. His colleagues in the lower house stripped him of power in September 2016. On March 30, 2017, under Operation Car Wash, he was sentenced to fifteen years and four months in prison for crimes of passive corruption, money laundering, and money smuggling, and remained imprisoned in Curitiba at the time this book was published.

31 Journalist Rui Falcão was president of the PT from 2011 to 2017.

32 Alexandre Padilha was the chief minister of the Secretariat of Institutional Relations during the Lula administration between September 2009 and January 1, 2011. He was also minister of health during the Rousseff administration between January 2011 and February 2014.

33 Ideli Salvatti was the chief minister of the Secretariat of Institutional Relations during the Rousseff administration between January 2011 and April 2014.

34 Antonio Palocci Filho served as minister of finances during the Lula administration from January 2003 to March 2006, and as chief of staff during the Rousseff administration from January to June 2011. Arrested in Operation Car Wash, he negotiated a plea bargain in September 2017, leaving the PT.

35 Luiz Carlos Trabuco was serving as president of Bradesco at the time this book was published.

36 Henrique Meirelles was president of the Central Bank during both Lula administrations (2003-2010). After the fall of Dilma Rousseff, he became minister of finances in the Temer administration, a position he currently occupies.

37 Guido Mantega served as minister of planning during the Lula administration from January 2003 to November 2004, and minister of finances during both Lula and Rousseff administrations, between March 2006 and January 2015.

38 Long-Term Interest Rate (Taxa de Juros de Longo Prazo), defined by the Central Bank.

39 Paulo Pereira da Silva is the president of Força Sindical, serves as federal congressman and leader of the Solidariedade Party. The SELIC (Sistema Especial de Liquidação e Custodia) rate represents the premium paid to financial institutions in transactions with government securities. Its basic level serves as the basis for interest rates in Brazil.

40 Payroll deductible loan is a loan with indirect payments. Its installments are deducted directly from the payroll or from benefits received by the individual.

41 Journalist Franklin Martins was head of the Secretariat of Social Communication during the Lula administration, between March 2007 and December 2010.

42 Joaquim Levy was minister of finances during the Rousseff administration between January and December 2015. He held positions at the International Monetary Fund (IMF) and was a public official in Brazil between 1992 and 2010, when he started working for Bradesco, where he remained until 2014. He was then appointed minister of finances on November 27, taking office in January of the following year. He adopted an economic policy of austerity, with a neoliberal profile.

43 Approximately US $25 billion.

44 "Little wave" (*Marolinha*, in Portuguese) was the term used by Lula to qualify the effects of the great global crisis of 2008 in Brazil. While fighting the crisis with public investments and consumer incentives, Lula faced the recession, which lasted only one semester in Brazil. The recession was overcome in the first quarter of 2009, with a growth of the gross domestic product (GDP) of 1.9 percent.

45 Lula launched the Growth Acceleration Program (PAC) in January 2007, under the coordination of then Chief of Staff Dilma Rousseff. Its first version anticipated investments of R$500 billion by 2010, prioritizing infrastructure works to support economic growth in Brazil.

46 Paulo Okamotto was a member of the Lula Institute's management team at the time this book was published. He was a unionist alongside Lula at the ABC Metalworkers Union. During Lula's administration, he served as president of Sebrae (2003-2010).

Clara Ant was a special adviser to Lula during both terms and accompanied the former president after the founding of the Lula Institute, serving as its manager since.

Luiz Dulci was the chief minister of the General Secretariat of the Presidency during both Lula administrations. Like Clara Ant, he followed the former president after the founding of the Lula Institute, serving as its manager since.

47 Economist Walter Barelli was technical director of the Inter-Union Department of Statistics and Socio-Economic Studies [DIEESE] from 1966 to 1990.

48 Marco Aurelio Garcia was special adviser for international affairs of Lula and Dilma Rousseff's governments. He led the team that wrote Lula's government project in the elections of 1994, 1998, and 2016, and Dilma's government project in the election of 2010. He was one of the organizers and founders of the São Paulo Forum, created to bring together left-wing organizations from Latin America and the Caribbean in 1990 when he was secretary of international relations of the PT.

49 Leo Pinheiro, president of the contractor firm OAS, was convicted to twenty-six years in prison in the context of Operation Car Wash. He was detained in November and put under house arrest by the Supreme Court in April 2015. He was initially sentenced to sixteen years in prison and had his plea bargain refused because he insisted on acquitting Lula. The TRF-4 (Regional Court of Appeal) increased his sentence by ten years as retaliation. He was detained again in September 2016 and was pressured to change his testimonial and accuse Lula, to which he agreed in April 2017. Due to this change in his plea bargain, his sentence was reduced from twenty-six to three and a half years.

50 Celso Amorim was minister of international affairs during the two terms of Lula and minister of defense from August 2011 to January 2015 in Dilma Rousseff's government.

51 Former president of the United States George W. Bush was in Torto's Ranch during his visit to Brazil in March 2007. Despite major ideological differences, Lula and Bush became friends.

52 The main leader of the Cuban Revolution, Fidel Castro governed the Republic of Cuba from 1959 to 2008, first until 1976 as prime minister and then as president. He is one of the greatest personalities of the twentieth century and transformed the island into a symbol of resistance against imperialism and capitalism. He died of natural causes on November 25, 2016, at the age of ninety, after having survived hundreds of murder attempts, most of them planned by the CIA. Hugo Chávez ruled Venezuela from 1999 until his death in 2013.

53 Laura Bush is George Bush's wife since 1977.

54 Hu Jintao was general secretary of the Chinese Communist Party and president of China between 2003 and 2013. He is married to Liu Yongqing.

55 Evo Morales has been the president of Bolivia since January 2006 and was still in office at the time this book was published. He was the candidate of the peasant movement Cocaleros in his presidential campaign, a social movement with a broad social base in Bolivia. The cocaleros never branded themselves only as peasants but as indigenous farmers and protectors of a symbolic leaf to their culture: the coca leaf. The movement is comprised of several identities and objectives. It stood side-by-side along other active sectors of Bolivian society, in an agenda which comprised ethnic, social, and economic demands.

56 Gilmar Mendes was appointed minister of the Supreme Court by Fernando Henrique Cardoso in 2002, and became one of the main leaders of the right wing and plotter of the coup against President Dilma Rousseff.

57 Sérgio Moro was the first instance judge responsible for the trials of the Car Wash taskforce since March 2014 by the time this book was published. After a period of great popularity due to the construction of an image of a ruthless judge fighting corruption, it became clear that his actions had a political bias against the left wing, especially against former president Lula. Car Wash gradually became a reference on the judicial branch deviation with practices which included forging evidence, blackmailing, and threats against those targeted by the taskforce.

58 The three magistrates from TRF-4 (the Federal Court of Appeal for the Fourth Region, from Porto Alegre) sentenced Lula to twelve years and one month in

prison on January 24, 2018. This is a trial considered one of the most demoralizing to the Brazilian judiciary due to the huge amount of deviations from the most basic principles of Brazilian criminal law.

59 Cristiano Martins Zanin is an associate at Teixeira, Martins, and Lawyers. He was thirty-seven years old when he started advocating for Lula and his family in 2013.

60 Deltan Dallagnol is the attorney of the Federal Public Ministry who presented the accusation against former President Lula on September 14, 2016, in what became known as Dallagnol's PowerPoint presentation. His performance was based on a series of biased opinions of the case against Lula which were presented in a series of graphic and very rudimentary slides in a PowerPoint presentation, providing no evidence whatsoever to support the accusations.

61 The Clean Record Act was sanctioned by Lula in 2010. It makes any candidate unelectable for eight years in cases of mandate reversal, resignation of mandate in order to prevent a reversal, or conviction by decision of plenary body (with more than one judge), even if there are appeals pending.

62 The "Letter to the Brazilian People" was a document released by Lula in June 2002 during the electoral campaign. The objective of this document was to calm markets down (bankers, entrepreneurs, rentiers, and the media) as they were causing shake-ups in the economy due to Lula's odds in the presidential run.

63 A Mexican television network that can be compared to Brazil's Rede Globo.

64 Sérgio Motta took part in the foundation of the Brazilian Social Democracy Party (PSDB), becoming the main organizer in the party. He was a close friend of Fernando Henrique Cardoso and the coordinator of his campaign in 1994. He remained as the main support of FHC and led the privatization program of the Brazilian telephony system while minister of communications, in the midst of corruption accusations.

65 Antônio Ermírio de Moraes was president of the Votorantim Group, created by his father, one of the major Brazilian conglomerates with a presence in twenty-three countries in the steel, energy, cement, cellulose, orange juice, and financial sectors. He was critical of high interest rates and was obsessed with his work. He ran for governor of São Paulo during the 1986 elections but was defeated by Orestes Quércia (PMDB).

José de Alencar was a business owner and founder of the textile group Coteminas. He was Lula's vice president in both terms (from 2003 to 2011).

66 Nelson Mandela was president of South Africa from 1994 to 1999 after having been the main leader in the struggle against apartheid in his country. His life had epic highlights and he is considered one of the leading inspirers of humanity next to Mahatma Gandhi. He was imprisoned for twenty-seven years until 1990. He led the defeat of the racist regime after leaving jail.

67 *Diário da Noite* (*The Nighttime Daily*) was a newspaper which circulated in São Paulo from 1925 to 1980, part of the group of Associated Dailies of Assis Chateaubriand. Antonio Guzman was a journalist and fan of the Corinthians soccer team. He made radio history alongside Lucas Neto for broadcasting the TV show *Twenty News Stories by Antonio Guzman and Lucas Neto*, also broadcast by Tupi Radio. He worked for important newspapers in São Paulo, such as *Diário Popular*, *Diário da Noite*, and *Folha da Tarde*.

68 José Ferreira da Silva, known as Frei Chico (Friar Chico), is Lula's older brother by four years. He was an activist in the union sector of the Brazilian Communist Party (PCB) from the 1960s until the early 1990s. He was appointed in 1968 to participate in an electoral list which would run to the board of the Metalworkers Union of São Bernardo do Campo. He refused to take part in the list and appointed Lula. He is not an actual friar; that is a nickname he got from a fellow factory worker.

The *Partidão* is another name for the Brazilian Communist Party (PCB).

69 Joaquim dos Santos Andrade, known as Joaquinzão (Big Joaquim), was the president of the Metalworkers Union of São Paulo from 1965 until 1986, when he was elected to the General Trade Union Confederation (CGT). He was a supporter of the military coup of 1964. Joaquinzão symbolizes the subservience of independent unionists who flourished in the national scenario due to the strikes in the ABC region (Santo André, São Bernardo do Campo e São Caetano do Sul) from 1978 to 1980. He continuously grew apart from the military regime, and became one of the most important leaders of the general strike of 1983.

70 Emílio Bonfante was a prominent union leader in the Merchant Navy and in the strike of 1953. He was a member of the PCB and was imprisoned and barbarically tortured twice in April 1964 and in 1971 after secretly returning to the country after a two-year exile in Moscow. His wife was tortured with him in 1971. He was arrested again in 1976 and was sentenced to four years in prison. In 1978 he was given an amnesty and died in 1999.

71 Lula was elected to Congress with 650,000 votes in 1986.

72 Lech Walesa was a founder of the Solidarity free trade union of Poland. He led the shipyard workers' strike in Gdansk in 1980. Walesa was awarded the Nobel Prize in 1983 and had a decisive role in the defeat of the socialist regime in the country. He was elected president in 1990. A conservative Catholic, Walesa's leadership didn't endure for too long. He was defeated in the runoff in a reelection campaign in 1995 (by a difference of 3 percent) and when running again in 2000 received less than 1 percent of the votes.

73 Fernando Haddad was São Paulo mayor from 2013 to 2017, and at the time of this book's publication the PT candidate for President of Brazil.

74 Barack Obama served as president of the United States from 2009 to 2017. At the G20 Summit held in London in April 2009, Obama greeted Lula and said that he was "the most popular politician on Earth." He then looked at Australian prime minister Kevin Rudd, pointed at Lula and said: "That's my man right here. Love this guy."

75 In 2012, under Dilma, Brazilian ambassador Roberto Azevêdo was nominated as candidate for director-general of the World Trade Organization (WTO). He won, beating Mexico's Herminio Blanco, seen as the candidate of choice of the United States and the European Union.

76 In 2009, Rio de Janeiro won the bid to host the Olympic Games in 2016.

77 Brazilian agronomist José Graziano was elected director-general of the United Nations Food and Agriculture Organization (FAO) in 2011. His nomination was announced by President Dilma Rousseff and explicitly supported by Lula. In 2015, he was reelected with the highest number of votes on record at FAO, receiving a total of 177 out of 182 votes cast. In 2001, Graziano coordinated the creation of the Zero Hunger (Fome Zero) program, which became one of the focal points of Luiz Inácio Lula da Silva's 2002 presidential campaign. Under Lula, Graziano was appointed the special minister of food security in the fight against hunger. He later became special adviser to the presidency, and joined FAO in 2006.

78 The depth of the Brazilian pre-salt reserves ranges from one to two thousand meters under water and between four and six thousand meters underground. The deposits were discovered in 2006 by Petrobras, and Lula made their exploration a national priority. It is estimated that they contain 80 billion barrels of oil and gas, which would make Brazil the sixth largest holder of reserves in the world, after Saudi Arabia, Iran, Iraq, Kuwait, and the UAE.

79 The production-sharing bill known as "Lei da Partilha" determined that 75 percent of drilling royalties received by the Brazilian government from oilfields in

the pre-salt layer would be invested in education, and 25 percent on healthcare. The estimate was that investments in education alone would be increased by more than R$360 billion in thirty years with these measures. The resolution was practically eliminated in 2016, in the context of the coup d'état, when the lower house and the Senate removed Brazil's exclusivity on offshore oil and gas production and cancelled the allocation of royalties for education and healthcare.

80 Brazil is the second largest producer of ethanol, second only to the United States. Until 2010, it was the world's leading ethanol exporter.

81 Getúlio Vargas is one of the greatest names and a turning point in Brazilian history. He served as president during two periods: the first one was for fifteen consecutive years, from 1930–1945, a period that can be divided into three stages: from 1930–1934, as interim president; from 1934–1937, as constitutional president, after being elected by the National Constituent Assembly; and from 1937–1945, as dictator-president, following a coup d'état and the establishment of the Estado Novo (New State) regime. During the second period, when he was elected by direct vote, Getúlio was president of Brazil for three and a half years, from January 31, 1951 to August 24, 1954, when he committed suicide. His administrations were responsible for the industrialization of the country and nationalist developmental policies, with the creation of Petrobras and Companhia Siderúrgica Nacional (National Steel Company), among others. One of Vargas's achievements was the promulgation of the Consolidation of Labor Laws (CLT), which came under Decree-Law No. 5452, May 1, 1943, and was strongly opposed by businessmen. Some analysts say that it was largely inspired by Italy's fascist dictator Benito Mussolini's labor reform, Carta del Lavoro (Charter of Labor), while others consider that this is a mystification. The CLT established the payment of a minimum wage, the right to paid annual leave, and Social Security, among other measures.

82 Luiz Gushiken was a bank employee union leader, the presidential campaign coordinator for Lula in 1989 and 1998, a federal deputy for the PT (1987-1999), and Secom's chief minister during Lula's first administration until 2005. He was the head of the Strategic Affairs Center until 2006. He was found not guilty of all the accusations against him, especially those linked to the Mensalão case.

83 The University for Everyone Program (PROUNI) was created during Lula's first term, in 2005. The Student Financing Fund for Higher Education (FIES) was created in 1999 as a successor to the Educational Credit Program. It was

reformulated and expanded in 2010, during Lula's second term in office. While PROUNI grants full or partial (50 percent) scholarships in undergraduate and higher education diplomas in private institutions to Brazilian students without a university degree, FIES funds undergraduate higher education for students enrolled in paid educational establishments. PROUNI partial scholarship holders may use FIES to fund the other half of the monthly fee.

84 The Special Fund for Financial Assistance to Political Parties, better known as the Partisan Fund, consists of non-exclusive public funds distributed to Brazilian political parties. It is not restricted to election campaigns. It basically comprises union budget allocations and donations made by individuals or legal entities through bank deposits directly into the account of the Partisan Fund and other financial resources assigned to it by law. The Partisan Fund reached almost R$400 million in 2014.

85 Cristina Kirchner served as a senator for the provinces of Santa Cruz and Buenos Aires and was the president of Argentina from 2007 to 2015. She is the widow of former president Néstor Kirchner, her predecessor. She was the first lady of Argentina from 2003 to 2007. In 2017, she was once again elected a senator for the province of Buenos Aires, a position she held at the time this book was published.

86 Fernando Lugo, an emeritus Roman Catholic bishop, retired in 2005 by Pope John Paul II, was president of Paraguay from August 15, 2008 to June 22, 2012, when he was the victim of a parliamentary coup carried out by the Paraguayan right under the allegation of "poor performance." In 2013, he was elected senator, a position he held at the time of this book's publication.

87 Rafael Correa was president of Ecuador from 2007 to 2017, and appointed Lenín Moreno to run as his successor. Correa broke with Moreno when the latter took a strong rightward turn after having been elected. Correa's administration had similar characteristics to those of Lula, Chávez, and Morales.

88 The Farabundo Martí National Liberation Front (FMLN) was responsible for the guerrilla movement against the genocidal governments of El Salvador's elite. The FMLN was founded months after the murder of the Archbishop of San Salvador, Don Oscar Romero, on March 20, 1980. In 1992, the Chapultepec Peace Accords were signed, putting an end to the civil war. The Front became a political party and started to participate in the political life of the country. In 2009, it won the presidential elections with Mauricio Funes, and again in June 2014, with Salvador Sánchez Cerén.

89 Rodrigo Janot was attorney general of the republic from 2013 to 2017, having been appointed by Dilma Rousseff, and served as a partner and adviser of the Car Wash operation.

90 Rodrigo Maia was the speaker of the lower house at the time this book was published. He is the son of César Maia and the son-in-law of Wellington Moreira Franco, a congressman for Rio de Janeiro. Maia embraces a neoliberal approach to the economy. He has close relations with the Marinho family, owners of Rede Globo, Brazil's biggest media conglomerate.

91 Joesley Batista, the chairman of JBS, Brazil's largest meatpacker, recorded a conversation with Michel Temer on the night of March 7, 2017. During the conversation, Batista told Temer that JBS was paying Eduardo Cunha, the former speaker of the lower house, as well as judges, for their silence. The tape was released two months later by the newspaper *O Globo*, and all media outlets belonging to the organization combined forces to overthrow Temer, without success.

92 Cristiane Brasil is a member of the Brazilian Labor Party (PTB). She is the daughter of Roberto Jefferson, a congressman and the national president of the PTB, who was jailed for his role in the Mensalão vote-buying scandal in 2005. She was appointed by Temer as the new minister of labor in early 2018, but a court ruling banned her from the position after she was convicted of failing to pay R$60,400 to her private chauffeurs. The decision was made by the Regional Labor Court of the First Region (TRT1) and upheld in the second instance. On February 20, the PTB withdrew Cristiane Brasil's nomination.

93 Arlindo Chinaglia, a public health physician, has been a congressman since 1995. He had been reelected and was serving another term at the time this book was published. He was the speaker of the lower house in 2007.

94 Sandro Mabel, a businessman, was a congressman from 1995 to 1999 and from 2003 to 2015. He is a member of the PMDB and had close ties with Arlindo Chinaglia in 2007.

95 José Serra was serving as a senator for the state of São Paulo at the time this book was published. One of the main leaders of the PSDB, he was among the plotters of the coup against President Dilma Rousseff. He was minister of foreign affairs during Temer's administration from May 2016 to February 2017. Aligned with the United States, he adopted an anti-communist rhetoric and pushed for a shift in Brazil's international politics, isolating the country on the world stage. He left the ministry when allegations of corruption involving his name gained momentum in the news and appeared in investigations led by the Federal Police. He was a congressman, minister of planning, and minister of

health during Fernando Henrique Cardoso's administration, mayor of São Paulo (from 2005 to 2006), and governor of São Paulo (from 2007 to 2010). He ran for the presidency in 2002 (when he was defeated by Lula) and in 2010 (when he was defeated by Dilma).

96 Inheritance is taxed at the state level in Brazil. The average rate is 3.86 percent, less than one tenth of what is charged in England (40 percent). In Chile, the average rate is 13 percent. In France, the maximum rate is 67 percent. In Germany, Switzerland, and Japan, it is 50 percent.

97 A proposal to hold recall referendums in Brazil was launched in 2017. The purpose of such referendums is that the president elected in 2018 gathers popular support for revoking anti-reforms implemented during Temer's administration, especially the austerity package to freeze social spending for twenty years and the dismantling of labor legislation.

98 The Brazilian Constitution was approved by a Constitutional Congress on September 22, 1988, and promulgated shortly thereafter, on October 5. It marked the end of a cycle triggered by the military coup of 1964. It was considered one of the most advanced in the world when it came to ensuring individual and social rights.

Ulysses Guimarães was the presiding officer and one of the main organizers of the 1988 Constitutional Assembly. He was the one who dubbed Brazil's new charter the "Citizen's Constitution." He was the president of the PMDB and one of the protagonists of the fight against the military regime. He ran for the presidency as an "anti-candidate" in 1973, using his status to protest against the indirect elections established by the military. He died in a helicopter crash in Angra dos Reis, in the state of Rio de Janeiro, on October 12, 1992.

99 Housing assistance to judges, justices, prosecutors, and attorneys was established as a benefit to those appointed to work outside their city of origin, provided that they have no property of their own in that location. The aid resulted from a decision taken by the justice minister of the Supreme Federal Court, Luiz Fux, in 2013. It was extended to all categories, amounting to R$4,377 per month. When asked about the benefit, judge Sérgio Moro—who has his own apartment in the city of Curitiba, where he works—claimed that it would compensate for the lack of salary readjustments in the categories. Several legal experts see the allowances as unconstitutional.

100 National conferences, as well as state and municipal conferences, echo the spirit of the 1988 Constitution, which enshrined the principle of social participation as a means of consolidating democracy. This form of mobilization and

dialogue was fostered by the PT administrations. One hundred three national conferences were held from 2003 to 2014, covering forty sectoral areas, which mobilized about 8 million people debating proposals for public policies at the municipal, regional, state, and national levels. By 2015, a further fifteen national conferences were planned, with an estimated participation of more than two million people, from the municipal stages to the national meeting. However, the planning of the events was interrupted as the process to topple Dilma Rousseff intensified.

101 Lula was referring to the demonstrations against Temer's administration and even against Car Wash in the 2018 Carnival, which contrasted with the absence of protests against Lula, Dilma, or the PT during the event. The show put on by samba school Paraíso do Tuiuti, in Rio de Janeiro, polarized the country while parading to the theme "My God! My God! Is slavery extinct?"—a critique of the living conditions that black people experience in Brazil, and an emphatic attack on Temer's administration and its anti-reforms (Temer was depicted as a vampire in the parade).

102 On May 9, 2004, the *New York Times* correspondent in Brazil, Larry Rohter, wrote an article titled "Brazilian Leader's Tippling Becomes National Concern," implying that Lula was an alcoholic. Lula and the Brazilian government reacted strongly, and the reporter finally apologized.

103 The match took place on July 3, in Dortmund, in the second round of the tournament.

104 Raúl Castro has been the president of Cuba since 2008, having succeeded his brother, Fidel Castro.

105 Duda Mendonça was the professional responsible for the presidential campaign marketing and advertising.

106 Nilo Batista, a Brazilian criminalist, had his political trajectory linked to the Brizolism. He was deputy governor of Rio de Janeiro, on the same list as Leonel Brizola in the 1990 election. During that period, he also served as minister of justice and minister of State Civil Police, implementing a policy to combat crime while respecting human rights and social policies. In April 1994, he took office, after Brizola resigned to run for president (in the election in which Fernando Henrique Cardoso was the winner).

107 The episode happened in February–April 2016. The Federal Police searched the branch office of the Mossack Fonseca law firm in São Paulo (with headquarters in Panama), which specializes in transactions in tax havens. The operation intended to find documents that would compromise Lula in the case of

the three-story condo in Guarujá. Nothing was found. However, seized documents indicated that the offshore company owned another three-story condo in Guarujá, as well as other real estate and a helicopter used by the Marinho family, of Globo. The case did not make the headlines and disappeared from the conservative media in two days. Shortly thereafter, in May, the Panama Papers—11.5 million confidential documents from the Mossack Fonseca office, which provided detailed information on more than 214,000 offshore tax haven companies, including the identity of shareholders and managers, came to light. The documents mention the heads of state of five countries, namely Argentina, Iceland, Saudi Arabia, Ukraine, and the United Arab Emirates, as well as other government members, families, and close associates of several leaders in more than forty countries, including South Africa, Angola, Brazil, China, North Korea, France, India, Malaysia, Mexico, Pakistan, the United Kingdom, Russia, and Syria, as well as twenty-nine multimillionaires in the list of the world's 500 richest people. The documents were sent anonymously to the German newspaper *Süddeutsche Zeitung* in 2015 and, at a later date, to the International Consortium of Investigative Journalists, based in Washington, DC. To the dismay of the conservative Brazilian media, there was nothing to implicate Lula or the leaders of PT. However, the papers revealed receipts of payments made by one person from the Marinho family to the law firm for the maintenance of three offshore companies.

108 Leandro Daiello Coimbra, who served as director general of the Federal Police from January 2011 to November 2017.

At the time, José Eduardo Cardozo was minister of justice for the Rousseff administration. Cardozo, a member of PT, served as secretary during the Luiza Erundina administration in São Paulo (1989-1993), then as city councillor in the state capital and as federal congressman from January 2003 to January 1, 2011 (two terms). After leaving the Ministry of Justice, he was appointed attorney general of the union (March to May 2016). In this role, he was responsible for Dilma's defense during the impeachment process in the National Congress.

109 Engineer Paulo Roberto Costa was the Petrobras supply director between 2004 and 2012, and became known during Operation Car Wash. Engineer Renato Duque was Petrobras services director from 2003 to 2012, and also became known during Operation Car Wash.

110 PCB was banned in 1947 under General Eurico Gaspar Dutra's regime. The parliamentarians of the party were banished, and the headquarters were closed down; interventions were made in several unions, and the General Confederation of

Workers (CGT) was closed. Aligned with the United States in the context of the Cold War, Dutra severed diplomatic relations with the Soviet Union. PCB would only again become a legal political party in 1985.

111 Rede Globo de Televisão Sunday night TV show, with reports, interviews, and other entertainment, on the air since 1973.

112 Completed in January 2014, in a ceremony attended by President Dilma Rousseff and President Raúl Castro, of Cuba, the port of Mariel, in Cuba, was the object of several attacks by the Brazilian right, which considered it "ideological." However, the initiative was profitable, creating 156,000 jobs in Brazil and proving to be a strategic investment in one of the most modern and strategic ports in the world, due to its proximity to the United States market.

113 Journalist Vladimir Herzog, a member of the PCB in its clandestine years. He was arrested, tortured, and killed on October 25, 1975, at DOI-Codi's premises in São Paulo. His death triggered protests domestically and abroad, as well as the first popular mobilization to take the streets, after years of military dictatorship, in the ecumenical act celebrated in the Cathedral of Sé, São Paulo, on October 31.

114 PlayTV was a pay TV channel (it was initially called Rede 21, and was renamed again in 2008). Controlled by Rede Bandeirantes, in 2006 it made an agreement with the company Gamecorp, which took control of part of its daily schedule—from five in the evening to ten at night. Lula's son, Fábio Luís Lula da Silva, known as Lulinha, was one of the company's partners. Specializing in games, anime, and mobile content programs, Gamecorp was successful until Rede Bandeirantes broke the contract in 2008, following a campaign initiated by the conservative magazine *Veja*. Lula's reference to MTV is due to the fact that the channel is run by Grupo Abril, owner of *Veja*.

115 The Battle of Guararapes was fought in two clashes: the first on April 18 and 19, 1648 and the second on February 19, 1649. Decisive to the end of the "Dutch invasions" in Brazil, it was fought between the Dutch army and the Luso-Brazilian troops in the hill of the Guararapes, currently part of Jaboatão dos Guararapes, in the metropolitan region of Recife, Pernambuco. The signing of the capitulation took place in 1654, in Recife, from where the last Dutch ships left to return to Europe.

116 José Dirceu de Oliveira e Silva was one of the most important student leaders during the mobilizations against the Brazilian dictatorship. Arrested on October 13, 1968, with other students in the XXX Congress of the National Union of Students (UNE), in Ibiúna, São Paulo, he was one of the fifteen prisoners released and banned in exchange for US ambassador Charles Elbrick, kidnapped in

September 1969 in an action of the National Liberation Action (ALN), the MR8, and the Communist Dissidence of the University of Guanabara. Dirceu went to Cuba and returned to Brazil clandestinely in 1971, where he lived in this condition until the amnesty, in 1979. He was one of the founders of the PT. He served as state and federal congressman for São Paulo. One of the main organizers of Lula's successful electoral campaign of 2002, on January 1, 2003, he became chief of staff and the strong man of the Lula administration. He left this position in June 2005, as a result of the case known as Mensalão. In 2012, he was convicted by the Supreme Court; in 2013, he was imprisoned and released to serve house arrest the following year. He was arrested again in 2015. In 2016, he was sentenced to twenty-three years and three months in prison as a result of Operation Car Wash, and was again sentenced in 2017 to another eleven years and three months. Arrested again, he was released in May 2017.

117 Gordon Brown was the British prime minister between 2007 and 2010.

118 Gerhard Schröder was the German chancellor between 1998 and 2005.

119 In 1979, Davi de Morais served as president for the Union of Journalists of São Paulo.

120 Luiz Carlos Prestes was the most important Communist leader in Brazilian history. He led, between 1925 and 1927, the Prestes Column, a political-military movement linked to tenentism, opposed to the Old Republic, which undertook a 25,000-kilometer march through Brazil, demanding political and social reforms such as secret balloting and public education. Along the way, there were several confrontations with the army and with state troops. He grew closer to the Communists and, in 1934, under pressure from the Communist Party of the Soviet Union (CPSU), the PCB leadership accepted his membership. Ten years later, he took over the leadership of the party by being elected secretary-general. His long political career, marked by prolonged clandestine periods, and brief periods of legality (he was elected senator in 1945), ended with his death on March 7, 1990, at the age of 92.

121 As of March 2018, all names mentioned by Lula were pre-candidates for the presidential elections: Manuela d'Ávila, for the Communist Party of Brazil (PCdoB); Guilherme Boulos, for the Socialism and Freedom Party (PSOL); Ciro Gomes, for the Democratic Labor Party (PDT); Jair Bolsonaro, for the Social Liberal Party (PSL).

122 Mário Covas was the most popular senator in the Constitutional Congress. He received 7.7 million votes in the 1986 election. In the Constitutional Assembly, he was the leader of the PMDB in the Senate and one of the most important

creators of the new Constitution. In 1962, he was elected federal congressman for the Social Labor Party (PST), joining the MDB after the dictatorship extinguished all other parties. In 1968, he was the leader of the opposition in the lower house. He was removed from office in 1969 and had his political rights suspended for ten years. In 1979, he became president of the MDB and, in 1982, was elected federal congressman, with more than 300,000 votes. He went on to become mayor of São Paulo in 1983, until his candidacy to the Senate. He was founder and first president of the PSDB in 1988, being the party's presidential candidate in 1989, ending in fourth place. In 1990, he was third runner-up in the São Paulo gubernatorial election. In 1994, he was elected governor of São Paulo, and reelected four years later.

123 Airton Soares was the leader of the PT in the lower house of Congress during the vote on the amendment that would reinstate direct elections for president of the republic, after the *Diretas Já* [Direct Elections Now] campaign. The amendment obtained 289 votes in favor, but was ultimately defeated, twenty-two votes short of approval. With the defeat, Soares started to campaign in favor of Tancredo Neves in the Electoral College, resulting in his election as president in 1985, against PT's decision of boycotting the voting. Along with him, Congresswoman Bete Mendes and Congressman José Eudes were expelled from the party for the same reason.

124 Djalma Bom was director of the São Bernardo Metalworkers Union from 1975 to 1980, actively participating in the 1979-1980 strikes; he was one of the founders of the PT. First regional president of the PT in São Paulo, he was the party's most popular federal congressman in the 1982 elections, with 164,398 votes. He was the first worker to assume the presidency of the Lower House Committee on Labor and Social Legislation.

125 Sérgio Cervantes is the leader of the Communist Party of Cuba (PCC). Cervantes served as political adviser for the Cuban embassy in Brazil and has a historical connection with the PT.

126 João Amazonas was a constitutional congressman for PCB in 1946. In 1962, he was one of the leaders behind the rupture with PCB, leading to the emergence of the PCdoB. He was elected secretary general of the party, becoming its president after the party was legalized in 1985. He left office in 2001, becoming honorary president shortly before his death on May 27, 2002, of respiratory failure. He was ninety years old.

127 Guilherme Boulos is the national leader of the Homeless Workers' Movement (MTST). In February 2018 he became presidential pre-candidate for the PSOL.

128 Podemos is a Spanish left-wing political party, founded in 2014 with the intention of overcoming the paradigms of traditional politics. Its main leader is Pablo Iglesias Turrión, born in 1978, secretary general of the party since its creation.

129 Soviet troops occupied the country for ten years, between 1979 and 1989.

130 Eduardo Galeano has been a leading intellectual reference in Latin America since 1971, when he wrote the book *Open Veins of Latin America*, which became a classic. At the beginning of this interview, Lula mentioned Galeano's book on soccer.

131 Brandão Monteiro was a Brizolist leader in the 1980s. He was a federal congressman from the state of Rio de Janeiro from 1983-1984 and 1986-1991. Vivaldo Barbosa is one of the main leaders of PDT. He was also a federal congressman from the state of Rio de Janeiro for two terms and had a prominent participation in the constituency. He was minister of justice in Brizola's first government in Rio de Janeiro.

132 Lula obtained 11.6 million votes in the first round of the presidential election of 1989, Brizola had 11.1 million, Collor had 20.6 million, and Mario Covas, 7.8 million. In the runoff, Collor had 35 million and Lula, 31 million.

133 Juca Kfouri, *Confesso que perdi* (I admit my defeat). São Paulo, Companhia das letras, 2017.

134 The presidential election in which Fernando Henrique Cardoso was reelected.

135 Lula's vice-presidential candidate was Senator José Paulo Bisol, from the PSB (Brazilian Socialist Party).

136 Miguel Arraes was a socialist politician, three-time governor of Pernambuco (1963-1964, 1987-1990, and 1990-1995). He was overthrown by the military in 1964 after the coup. He was arrested on April 1 after refusing to resign as the military demanded. He was sent to Fernando de Noronha, an island where he was exiled for almost a year. He was later sent to Recife and Rio de Janeiro. In 1965, the Brazilian Supreme Court (STF) granted him habeas corpus. He was set free and exiled to Algeria. He returned to Brazil with the amnesty of 1979. His government terms where known by a decisive option to favor the poor. He was a constituent federal congressman (1983-1987) and in Congress for two other terms (1991-1994 and 2003-2005).

Eduardo Campos was Miguel de Arraes's grandson. He was a federal congressman three terms in a row (1995-2007), becoming one of the main progressive forces in Congress. He was minister of science and technology during Lula's first government (between 2004 and 2005). He was governor of Pernambuco from 2007 to 2014 (reelected in 2010). He was the main leader of PSB from 1990 on, and was a presidential candidate in the election of 2014 when he died in a plane crash in Santos (SP) on August 13 of that year.

137 Renata Campos is Eduardo Campos's widow. They had five children together. She is an economist and Ariano Suassunas's niece.

138 Sérgio Cabral (MDB) was at the time governor of Rio de Janeiro. At the time of publication of this edition, he is imprisoned in Curitiba with convictions totaling eighty-seven years of prison time in four different cases linked to Car Wash. He faces yet another thirteen different cases linked to corruption, money laundering, and criminal conspiracy among other offenses. Cabral was senator from the state of Rio de Janeiro between 2003 and 2006 when he resigned in order to become governor of the state on January 1, 2007 (he was elected with 41 percent of votes in the first round and 68 percent in the runoff); he was reelected in the first round with 66 percent of the votes in 2010. It is estimated that the misuse of public funds in Cabral's government adds up to hundreds of millions of reals. He had R$44 million worth of assets seized for auction in September 2017.

139 Ciro Gomes was PDT's pre-candidate for the presidency at the time this book was published. He ran for president in 1998 from the PPS (Socialist Popular Party), coming in third place, behind Fernando Henrique Cardoso (elected in the first round with 53 percent of the votes) and Lula (31 percent). He was candidate for the Labor Front (PDT, PTB, and PPS) in 2012, coming in fourth place in the first round with 11 percent of the votes behind Lula (46 percent), José Serra (23 percent), and Anthony Garotinho (17 percent). He supported Lula in the runoff, which Lula won with 61 percent of the votes. He was minister of national integration during Lula's first term. He was also governor of Ceará from 1991 to 1994, leaving office to be head of the Ministry of Finance during Itamar Franco's government.

140 Geraldo Alckmin was governor of São Paulo and pre-candidate of the PSDB to the presidency at the time this book was published. In 2006, he had been the PSDB candidate for the presidency, losing to Lula in the first round (48 to 41 percent) and in the runoff (60 to 39 percent). He took office as state governor for the first time on January 22, 2001 due to the illness and later death of Mario Covas (on March 6 of the same year). He was elected governor in 2002 and again in 2010. His governments in São Paulo have been marked by the dismantling of education in the state and by high investment in security and equipment for the military police to fight street demonstrations.

141 Jair Bolsonaro was the PSL's pre-candidate for presidency at the time this book was published. He started his political career in Rio de Janeiro in 1989 as a city councilor and, from September 1991 onwards, he has been a federal congressman. He is a retired military officer. He stands up for torturers and the military dictatorship. He paid homage to the torturer Coronel Carlos Alberto Brilhante Ustra—chief of the DOI-Codi (political police) from 1970 to 1974—when announcing his vote in favor of Dilma Rousseff's impeachment. He execrates homosexuals, feminism, and affirmative policies (such as racial quotas), while defending torture and the death penalty. He has adopted a neoliberal discourse as of 2017 but, from an economic perspective, he was a nationalist in the past.

142 Michel Temer enacted the military/federal intervention in Rio de Janeiro on February 16, 2018. The army took over the Ministry of Public Safety with liberty to fight criminality, reporting exclusively to Temer. At the same time, a general took over the Ministry of Defense, which was unprecedented since the constitution was proclaimed in 1988.

143 The Cruzado Plan was a program for the stabilization of the economy inaugurated during José Sarney's government (1985-1990) by Minister of Finance Dilson Funaro. The measure with the greatest impact was price control, which reduced the monthly inflation rate from 12.47 percent in February to 1.43 percent in October of the same year. Sarney's government became increasingly popular because of this measure, being considered "good" or "excellent" by 72 percent of the population.

144 The UPPs (Pacifying Police Units) were installed in several favelas in Rio de Janeiro from 2008 on.

145 Claudio Lembo was elected vice governor of São Paulo in Geraldo Alckmin's list in 2002. He took office as state governor on March 21, 2006, when Alckmin resigned to run for the presidency (being defeated later on by Lula). He faced a wave attacks from the PCC (First Commando of the Capital). At the time, he stated that the violent context was to blame on "a mean and perverse white elite," that the violence was bonded to a heritage of slavery and that the situation would only change "when the bourgeois shared the cake." Despite supporting the military coup of 1964, Lembo was always a moderate. He went so far as to be expelled from the dictatorship's official party, ARENA (National Renewal Coalition), for having visited Leonel Brizola in Uruguay during his exile in the mid-1970s. He was the president of ARENA's São Paulo state board. He was the director of legislative affairs of Itaú Bank for thirty-five years, starting in 1962. He became the most important adviser of Olavo Setubal, owner of Itaú.

146 Journalist José Luiz Datena runs a crowd-pleasing police TV show called *Brasil Urgente* ("Urgent Brazil"), which he uses to demonize criminals and defend the death penalty and violent police action. It presents Brazil's major cities as lawless and inhabited by frightening people. This TV show is broadcast by Rede Bandeirantes, one of the biggest TV networks in the country.

147 Tim Lopes was a journalist at Rede Globo. He was murdered by drug dealers in favela Vila Cruzeiro, in the Complexo do Alemão in Rio de Janeiro on June 2, 2002. He had gone to the favela with a micro camera attached to his waist to shoot scenes of a funk party. The journalist and former producer of *Jornal Nacional* from Rede Globo, Cristina Guimarães (who shared an Esso award with Lopes), produced the investigative stories of the news TV program. She had quit her job seven months prior to Tim's assassination because of the death threats she had been receiving.

148 The National Program of Public Safety with Citizenship (PRONASCI) was created in 2007 during Lula's second term, when Tarso Genro was minister of justice. It proposed ninety-four actions—involving states, municipalities, and communities–aimed at violence and crime prevention. Inaugurated in 2008, this program mixed social initiatives for women and youngsters fifteen to twenty-four years of age, police intelligence, and crime repression. The objective was to invest R$6.7 billion until the end of 2012. The program reached 150 municipalities at the time. The program was disassembled during Dilma's term, after having had a budget of R$301 million in 2010 and only R$752,000 in 2013.

149 Antônio Francisco Bomfim Lopes, also known as Nem or Rocinha's Nem (born in Rio de Janeiro on May 24, 1976), is the leader of the drug traffic in the Rocinha favela and in favelas controlled by the criminal faction Friends of Friends (ADA). From an interview given to the journalist Ruth de Aquino on November 4, 2011.

150 Mino Carta is a journalist responsible for some of the editorial projects which revolutionized the Brazilian press. *Quatro Rodas* (1994), *Jornal da Tarde (1966)*, *Veja* (1968), *IstoÉ* (1976), and *Carta Capital* (1994). He was the editor-in-chief of *Carta Capital* at the time this book was published.

151 Lula appointed eight Supreme Court judges: Eros Grau, Menezes Direito, Ayres Britto, Cármen Lúcia, Ricardo Lewandowski, Cézar Peluso, Joaquim Barbosa, and Dias Toffoli.

152 The Institute of Education, Science, and Technology of the state of São Paulo, comprised of 36 campuses throughout the state.

153 The Constitutionalist Revolution of 1932, also known as the Revolution of 1932 or the Paulista War, was an armed movement which took place in the state of São Paulo between June and October 1932 with the objective of overthrowing the provisional government of Getúlio Vargas and assembling a national constituency. The coup d'état following the revolution overthrew President Washington Luis and prevented his successor Julio Prestes from being sworn into office. The insurgents expected the adherence of other states, which did not happen, and were defeated in months by troops loyal to Getúlio.

154 The University of São Paulo (USP) was founded in January 1934.

155 A neighborhood located in the borough of Ipiranga in São Paulo, and a state school located on Silva Bueno Street in Ipiranga.

156 Ping Pong is a bubble gum brand. It was a pioneer in Brazil, first sold in 1945. The brand became synonymous with bubble gum in the country.

157 Lionel Messi, Argentinian soccer player, Barcelona's striker. He is compared to the greatest names in soccer history, such as Pelé, Tostão, Garrincha, Di Stéfano, Maradona, Puskás, and Cruyff. Messi is a five-time winner of the Ballon d'Or (2009, 2010, 2011, 2012, and 2015), which is awarded to the best player in the world.

158 Lula is referring to the 1989 dispute with Fernando Collor de Mello, in which the latter had the full support of the Brazilian elite. Collor was then affiliated with the PRN (National Reconstruction Party). He won the election in the runoff on December 17, 1989 with 53 percent of the votes against Lula's 47 percent. The campaign was marked by two facts: one, the aggressiveness of Collor's strategy, which made use of a statement by Lula's ex-girlfriend Miriam Cordeiro, who falsely accused him of encouraging her to abort Lurian, the daughter they had together in 1974. And, two, the editing by Rede Globo of the debate of December 3, 1992, making history in Brazilian political journalism as an example of unethical behavior. With time, it became clear that Collor's election would not have been feasible without Globo's interference. Collor's government only lasted from March 15, 1990 to December 29, 1992, when he resigned a few hours before being sentenced by the Senate for the crime of responsibility and having his political rights suspended for eight years. At the time this book was published, Collor was a senator for the state of Alagoas and a pre-candidate to the presidency for the PTC (Christian Labor Party).

159 Aécio Neves is the grandson of Tancredo Neves. At the time this book was published, he was a senator from the state of Minas Gerais (for the PSDB). He lost

the presidential elections of 2014 to Dilma Rousseff, who received 52 percent of the votes to his 48 percent. Aécio, the head of the PSDB and relevant sectors of the elite, was certain of victory in 2014 and began to plot the overthrow of the elected president the night the polls closed on October 26. Aécio Neves has a political career stained by controversies at a personal level and by a long list of accusations of corruption. A telephone recording was made public, in which he asked Joesley Batista (JBS's associate) for US$2 million. His sister and political mentor, Andrea, was in jail between May and June 2017, also for having solicited money from the business owner. On May 18, 2017, he was removed from his senatorial position by Federal Judge Edson Facchin, following a request by the Attorney General's Office (PGR). The PGR also requested his incarceration, but Facchin overruled it. Aécio returned to the Senate at the end of June but was once again removed by decision of the first collegiate of the Supreme Court on September 26. The plenary of the Senate authorized his return to the Senate the following month. No prosecution against Aécio has prospered in the judiciary until today.

160 The headlines of the magazine (issue no. 2397, October 23, 2014) said: "They knew about everything."

161 Olívio Dutra was one of the founders of the PT. He was a constituency federal congressman, having been elected with fifty-five thousand votes in Rio Grande do Sul. He was elected mayor of Porto Alegre in 1998. His term implemented some of the policies which marked the first phase of PT's administrations in the country, such as the participatory budget. He was elected governor of the same state in 1998. In the 2002 dispute he did not run for reelection, having been defeated in the party's caucus by Tarso Genro. After his term leading the government of Rio Grande do Sul, he was the minister of cities in the Lula administration until 2005.

Tarso Genro started his political career in 1964 in the PTB. He was a member of the Red Wing of the PCdoB in his youth, and then of the PRC (Communist Revolutionary Party). He joined the PT in 1982, being elected as federal congressman substitute (1986) and later as vice mayor of Porto Alegre in Olivio Dutra's list. He ran for the government of Rio Grande do Sul in 1990 but was not elected. In 1992, he was elected mayor of Porto Alegre, and reelected four years later. He resigned in order to dispute the caucus with Olivio Dutra. He won the dispute to be the party's candidate in the elections of 2002, but was defeated by Germano Rigotto (PMDB). He was minister in three different offices of Lula's government: Education (2004-2005), from which he stepped down to take over the presidency of the PT, replacing José Genoino after the Mensalão case; Institutional Relations (2006-2007); and Justice (2007-2019). He was elected governor of Rio Grande do Sul in 2010 in the first round with 54 percent of the votes, but lost a reelection bid to José Ivo Sartori (PMDB).

162 Dilma Rousseff's trajectory to the presidency was as follows: in her youth, she was a militant of the National Liberation Command (Colina) and then of the Palmares Armed Revolutionary Vanguard (VAR-Palmares)—organizations that defended armed struggle against the military regime. She spent almost two years in prison, from 1970 to 1972, first in the context of Operation Bandeirante (Oban), where she was tortured, and then in the Department of Political and Social Order (Dops). Rousseff joined the PDT in the 1980s, she served as secretary of the treasury of the municipality of Porto Alegre between 1985 and 1988, in the Alceu Collares administration (PDT); she served as president of the Foundation of Economy and Statistics (FEE, in Rio Grande do Sul), from 1991 to 1993, and as state minister of mines and energy from 1993-1994 and 1999-2002, during the Alceu Collares and Olívio Dutra administrations, respectively. In 2001, she joined the Workers' Party; in 2002, she participated in the team that created Lula's government plan. As part of the Lula administration, she served as minister of mines and energy (2003-2005) and, later, as chief of staff (2005-2010). In 2010, Lula chose her as his successor in the presidential elections.

163 In the Lula administration, chemical engineer Graça Foster served as the secretary of oil, natural gas, and renewable fuels in the Ministry of Mines and Energy (2003-2005), then headed by President Dilma Rousseff. In 2005, she became president of Petrobras Química and executive manager of petrochemicals and fertilizers on the Petrobras Supply Board. During this period, she also headed the National Executive Secretariat of the Program for the Mobilization of the National Oil and Gas Industry and was the interministerial coordinator of the Biodiesel Program. Between 2006 and 2007, she served as president of Petrobras Distribuidora, and was also its chief financial officer in 2007. In September 2007, she became board member of the Petrobras Gas and Energy sector. At the time, she also served as president of Petrobras Gás, of the board of directors of Transportadora Brasileira Gasoduto Bolívia-Brasil (TBG), and of Transportadora Associada de Gás (TAG). She was a member of the board of directors of Transpetro, Petrobras Biocombustível, Braskem, and the Brazilian Institute of Oil, Natural Gas, and Biofuels. In 2012, during the Dilma administration, she became the CEO of Petrobras.

Miriam Belchior served as the secretary of administration and administrative modernization of the municipality of Santo André, from 1997 to 2000, during the administration of her ex-husband, Celso Daniel. In that city, she coordinated the Administrative Modernization Program, selected as one of the one hundred best public practices in the world by the United Nations (UN) in 2000. She was then secretary of social inclusion and housing, from 2001 to 2002, coordinating the Santo André Mais Igual program, selected as one of the ten best public practices in the world by the UN in 2002. She joined the transition team of the Lula government in 2002 and became special adviser to the president (2003-2004). She was the staff's deputy chief of coordination and monitoring from June 2004, working with strategic projects. In 2007, she served as the executive secretary of the PAC. In April 2010, with the departure of Dilma Rousseff, she became general coordinator of the PAC. In the Dilma administration, she served as minister of planning (2011-2015) and president of Caixa Econômica Federal (2015-2016).

Economist Tereza Campello joined the transition team of the 2002 Lula administration. She served as deputy chief of coordination and monitoring of staff, where she coordinated projects such as the National Biodiesel Program. She also participated in the creation of Bolsa Família. In the Dilma administration, she served as minister of social development and fight against hunger (2011-2016).

164 Winner of the 2006 elections for governor in Pará, Ana Júlia Carepa was defeated by Simão Jatene (PSDB) in a 2010 reelection bid. She was a student activist linked to the Ecclesial Base Communities (CEBs) of the Catholic Church; she also served as city councillor of Belém (1993-1995) and federal representative (1995-1996). After becoming vice mayor of Pará's capital city, alongside Edmilson Rodrigues (1997-2000), she became the most popular city councillor in the history of Belém in 2000. Later, she served as senator (2003-2006), until she won the gubernatorial election. In 2017, after thirty years, she left the PT and joined PCdoB.

165 José Eduardo Dutra was president of the Miners' Union of the State of Sergipe (1989-1994) and national leader of the CUT (1988-1990). He served as senator for Sergipe (1995-2003), as Petrobras CEO (2003-2005), as the president of the Workers' Party (2010-2011), and was one of Dilma's reelection campaign coordinators.

Gilberto Carvalho is one of Lula's closest advisers. A seminarian in the 1970s, he worked as a welder and was one of the leaders of the Worker's Pastoral. He participated in the first workers' strike in Paraná, in 1979, and was fired. Founder of the Workers' Party in Paraná, he has been part of the national leadership of the party since 1984. One of the coordinators of Lula's campaign in 2002, he served as chief of staff in both Lula administrations, becoming general secretary of the presidency (2011-2015) in the first Dilma administration, and being one of the coordinators of her reelection campaign.

166 Itaboraí Martins covered the union movement for *O Estãdo de S. Paulo* newspaper in the 1970s and 1980s.

167 Tito Costa was mayor of São Bernardo do Campo (1977-1983) and a member of the lower house for the PMDB (1987-1990).

168 Law 6.339, approved on July 1976, was prepared by Armando Falcão, then minister of justice. It imposed content restrictions on the ads that candidates were allowed to broadcast.

169 Lula received thirty-three honoris causa degrees, in spite of not having a university degree; Fernando Henrique Cardoso, who was a university professor, received twenty-nine.

170 The Paris Institute of Political Studies (Institut d'Études Politiques de Paris, commonly referred to as Sciences Po) is a renowned French public higher education institution specializing in the humanities and social sciences.

171 Juscelino Kubitschek was president of Brazil between 1956 and 1961, triggering a developmentalist surge in the country. He was harshly persecuted by the military regime of 1964, ousted, and forced into exile. He returned to Brazil in 1967. He died in a car crash on August 22, 1976, on the Presidente Dutra highway. The procession with his body gathered thousands of people in Rio de Janeiro; his funeral, in Brasilia, gathered more than 300,000.

172 The National Democratic Union (UDN), the main right-wing party in Brazil from 1945 to the 1964 coup, tried to challenge the result of the 1955 election, claiming Juscelino Kubitschek had not been elected by an absolute majority of votes. Then, in 1956, a group of air force officers started the so-called Jacareacanga revolt, by diverting a plane to a military base with that name, in the state of Pará. Despite the amnesty granted to those involved, another insurrection broke out in December 1959, at the initiative of the air force and army officers. Their intention was to bomb the government palaces of Laranjeiras and Catete, in Rio de Janeiro, and to occupy the bases of Santarém and Jacareacanga, in Pará. The rebels hijacked four airplanes and diverted them to Aragarças base. After being defeated in three days, the leaders fled by plane to neighboring countries, and only returned to Brazil during Jânio Quadros's administration. Juscelino Kubitschek was removed as senator and deprived of his political rights on June 8, 1964.

173 President João Goulart was deposed in the 1964 military coup. The military had already made previous attempts to block his inauguration and implement parliamentarism. Nicknamed Jango, he was the vice president of Jânio Quadros, who resigned on August 21, 1961. Military ministers Odilio Denys (army), Gabriel Grün Moss (air force) and Sílvio Heck (navy) attempted to stop him from taking office. Since Jango was abroad, Ranieri Mazzilli, the speaker of the lower house, was sworn in instead. There was a strong reaction throughout the country. Leonel Brizola, then governor of Rio Grande do Sul, organized a national network of more than one hundred radio stations, which became known as the "chain of legality." With that, the legitimate successor was able to be sworn in. However, on September 2, 1961, a congressional action gave the nation a parliamentary regime that would deprive Jango of most presidential powers. After a referendum defeated parliamentarism, presidentialism was restored in 1963.

174 Kofi Annan served as secretary-general of the United Nations from 1997 to 2006. He received the Nobel Peace Prize in 2001. Bill Clinton was president of the United States from 1993 to 2001.

175 On October 29, 2011, doctors diagnosed a tumor in Lula's larynx, which was cured in 2016.

176 According to all the polls published between the end of 2014 and the first months of 2018, Lula was the leading candidate for the 2018 presidential election. A Datafolha poll made from January 29-30, 2018 revealed that Lula had 34 to 37 percent of the vote intentions in the first round, winning over all the other candidates in the runoff.

177 In 1989, Lula received 17 percent of the votes cast in the first round; in 1994, 27 percent ; in 1998, 31 percent ; in 2002, 46 percent ; in 2006, 48 percent.

178 A Vox Populi/CUT poll published in April 2017 showed 50 percent of the people consider Lula to be the best president in Brazilian history, while Fernando Henrique Cardoso, the runner-up, was named by 8 percent. In previous polls, before the intense smear campaign against Lula, the president was mentioned by up to 80 percent of those interviewed (2016).

179 Founded in 2005, the Millennium Institute is one of the main neo-liberal think tanks in Brazil and, as such, is dedicated to produce and disseminate information with the intention of spreading the neo-liberal mindset, swaying the media, public opinion, schools, universities, and the state. The people responsible for financing and directing it are bankers, big investors, capitalists, entrepreneurs, and the intellectuals who work for them, such as Gustavo Franco (who serves as the institute's president), Henrique Meirelles, and Jorge Gerdau Johannpeter.

Alongside with local financiers, the Millennium Institute is part of a network of right-leaning think tanks in Latin America, sponsored by the Atlas Network—supported, in turn, by the Koch brothers, Americans with a fortune estimated at almost US$100 billion and interests in gas, oil, fertilizers, and in the financial sector, among others. The Millennium Institute was one of the organizers and promoters of the 2015-2016 coup, with similar think tanks such as Instituto Liberal, Mises Brasil, and Estudantes pela Liberdade. In Brazil, two think tanks were protagonists of the military coup of 1964: the Brazilian Institute of Democratic Action (Ibad) and the Institute for Social Studies and Research (Ipes). In an interview given to *Folha de S. Paulo* in 1998, retired army general Hélio Ibiapina revealed that Ibad had ties with the CIA. The institute was later dismantled and integrated to the National Information Service (SNI).

180 TV Brasil is a public television network that went on air in 2007 and belongs to Empresa Brasil de Comunicação (EBC), the country's public media conglomerate, also created in 2007, in the first Lula administration.

181 In May 2016, Temer's team dismissed waiter José Catalão, who worked in the presidential cabinet.

182 Corinthians and Palmeiras played the semi-finals of Copa Libertadores da América in 2000. On May 30, Corinthians beat Palmeiras 4-3. In the return game, on June 6, Palmeiras won 3-2. The away goal rule was not applied at the time, so the winner was decided in a penalty shootout. Marcelinho Carioca, a Corinthians idol at the time, missed the last shot, leading to his team's elimination.

183 Léo Pinheiro changed his lawyer in April 2017; Cristiano Martins Zanin is Lula's lawyer.

184 Lula is referring to a statement given by Antonio Palocci to Judge Sérgio Moro on September 6, 2017, as part of the ex-minister's plea bargain negotiations. Lula mentions the disaffiliation letter sent to the PT on September 26, 2017.

185 Lula refers to the bench warrant filed against him on March 4, 2016, by Judge Sérgio Moro in the context of Operation Car Wash, in an action that many jurists considered illegal. In addition to the former president being coerced by a federal police team to testify without being summoned earlier, there was a search and seizure operation in his residence, as well as in the houses of family members and employees of the Lula Institute. Furthermore, the federal police intercepted his telephones, as well as the telephones of family members, collaborators, and even lawyers.

186 Carlos Arthur Nuzman, ex-president of the Brazilian Olympic Committee (COB), was arrested on October 5, 2017, accused of active corruption, money

laundering, conspiracy, and illicit enrichment, in connection to the 2016 Rio de Janeiro Summer Olympic Games. He was in jail for fifteen days. In his home, the Federal Police found sixteen gold bars, weighing one kilogram each.

187 Lula is referring to the episode of the housekeeper Francenildo Costa, who in March 2016 accused the minister of finances at the time of allegedly attending a mansion in the south lake of Brasília to participate in meetings with lobbyists to split cash and enjoy parties in the company of call girls. The case became aggravated when a bank statement from Francenildo's account at Caixa Econômica Federal with a balance of over R$38,000—which he later explained as being related to a paternity recognition litigation—was published. The suspicion of a banking secrecy breach fell upon Palocci and his staff. He resigned in March 27, 2006.

188 Paris Saint-Germain's Neymar fractured the fifth metatarsal of his right little toe in a French Ligue 1 match against Olympique de Marseille on February 26, 2018. The images of the soccer player crying his heart out were the highlight for over a week in the Brazilian media.

189 Lula lost the little finger of his left hand in a workplace accident in 1964 when he was eighteen years old. He was employed at Metalúrgica Independência in the city of São Paulo.

190 Lula is referring to the Santa Barbara cottage in Atibaia belonging to Jacó Bittar, former mayor of Campinas, founder of the PT, and a friend of his. The lot located in São Paulo and purchased by Odebrecht was offered to Lula Institute for rent or sale and was refused. The area was sold by the contractor to a third party. Although the lot never belonged to the institute, and was never used by it, the Car Wash taskforce insists on depicting it as an undue advantage granted to Lula.

191 Marisa Letícia Lula da Silva died on February 3, 2017 due to a stroke.

192 On September 7, 2015, Vice President Michel Temer sent a letter to President Rousseff, leaked on the same day to the media. In the letter, he harshly complained and announced his rupture with the government. He was outraged for being a "decorative VP" and stated: "I was always fully aware of the distrust you and your entourage had towards me and the PMDB. A distrust which is incompatible with everything we have done in order to maintain personal and partisan support to your government."

193 Sigmaringa Seixas is a lawyer in Brasília. He was affiliated to the PMDB, then PSDB, and was affiliated to the PT at the time this book was published. He was a

federal congressman for three parties, the last one being the PT, elected in 2002. He has a great political permeability and is a friend of Lula.

194 "Zé" is short for "José" in Portuguese. The businessman José Alencar, affiliated at the time to the Liberal Party (PL), was Lula's vice president during both of his terms (2003-2010). Before that, he was affiliated to the PMDB and was a senator for Minas Gerais (1999-2002).

195 Federal Congressman Marcelo Freixo ran for mayor in Rio de Janeiro for the PSOL in 2016. He was defeated in the runoff by Marcelo Crivella, candidate of the Brazilian Republican Party (PRB) and bishop of the Universal Church of the Kingdom of God.

196 After the amendment for free elections for president was defeated by twenty-two votes in the lower house on April 25, 1984, the opposition the military regime (except for PT) decided to run in the Electoral College with the Tancredo Neves/José Sarney list. They defeated the Paulo Maluf/Flávio Marcílio list by 480 to 180. Sarney temporarily took office due to the illness of the elected president on March 15, 1985, and permanently took office after Tancredo's death on April 21.

197 A Facebook fan page that had over two thousand followers at the time this book was published.

198 Free Brazil Movement (MBL) is a right-wing organization which gained national recognition after standing up in favor of the impeachment of President Dilma Rousseff. With a liberal orientation, it is the stronghold of conservative values and supports intimidation and censorship to progressive ideas in environments such as schools, universities, and museums.

199 Horst Köhler was the head of the IMF from 2000-2004. He was the president of Germany between 2004 and 2010, for the conservative party UDC (Christian Democratic Union).

200 Rodrigo Rato was the head of the IMF from 2004-2007. He had been vice president of the conservative government of Spain during the term of José Maria Aznar (1996-2004).

201 In 1980, the Metalworkers Union of São Bernardo do Campo was under military intervention and Lula was arrested for thirty-one days at the Dops facilities in São Paulo. In 1981, the military court sentenced Lula to three and a half years in prison for inciting collective disorder, but he was acquitted the following year. Romeu Tuma was Dops's general delegate from 1977 to 1982. He served as

senator for São Paulo for two consecutive terms (from 1995 to 2010), affiliated to the Liberal Party, the Liberal Front Party (PFL), and then the PTB.

202 PROUNI (University for Everyone Program).

203 The amendment was defeated by twenty-two votes in Congress on April 25, 1984.

204 Lula and Fernando Haddad sought out Paulo Maluf in 2012 to establish an alliance with his party, in support of PT's candidate for the São Paulo mayoral election.

205 Orestes Quércia was the MDB's Senate candidate for São Paulo in 1974, winning (with 73 percent of the valid votes) against Carvalho Pinto, who ran for the military regime (Arena). Quércia had served as mayor of Campinas and the 1974 elections projected him nationally. He served as vice governor alongside Franco Montoro (1983-1986) and later as São Paulo governor (1987-1991), giving rise to a movement called "quercismo" in São Paulo. He was the national president of the PMDB from 1991 to 1993, when he resigned due to accusations of corruption, which were a constant issue in his political trajectory. He was defeated in all elections he ran in after 1991.

Carvalho Pinto was governor of São Paulo (1959-1963). One of his leading secretaries was Plínio de Arruda Sampaio, who years later would become one of PT's founders. He was named minister of finances during the João Goulart administration in 1963, in an attempt by the president to appease conservative sectors. He ended up joining the coup in 1964, being elected senator by the Arena in 1966. After Quércia's defeat in 1974, he retired from public life and died in 1987.

206 Jader Barbalho (PMDB) was elected governor of Pará in 1982, serving a second term in 1991. At the time of writing, Barbalho served as senator, representing Pará since 2011. This was his second term in the Senate, as he was first elected in 1994. He served as minister of agrarian development and social security under José Sarney. A millionaire, his career is marked by accusations of corruption. In 2001, after a series of accusations, he resigned as senator to avoid a process for the breach of parliamentary decorum, which could have made him ineligible for public office for eight years. In 2002, he was arrested in Belém do Pará. Barbalho ran for office and was Pará's most-voted candidate in the 2002 and again in the 2006 elections for Congress, later returning to the Senate.

207 Teotônio Vilela had a unique political trajectory in Brazil. A mill owner from Alagoas, he supported the military coup of 1964 and joined Arena, the party of the regime. He was elected senator in 1967, being successively reelected until

1982. From 1974, during the Geisel administration, he began to distance himself from the military regime, becoming an opposition politician, although affiliated to the Arena. In 1978, he presented Projeto Brasil, with a developmental and democratic model. In 1979, he joined the MDB and became the national leader of the amnesty campaign for political prisoners. Gradually, with his libertarian positions, he became an icon of the democratic struggle in the country, but did not see the return of democracy, because he died of cancer in November 1983. Shortly before, in September, Milton Nascimento and Fernando Brant released the song "O Menestrel das Alagoas" in his honor.

208 In the 2006 presidential elections, the PSDB candidate Geraldo Alckmin was endorsed by Anthony Garotinho, affiliated to the PMDB at the time, while PMDB's candidate in the Rio de Janeiro gubernatorial elections, Sérgio Cabral, endorsed Lula. Lula registered 49 percent of valid votes in the first round, while Alckmin had 28 percent. In the second round, Lula had 69 percent of valid votes.

209 The video was recorded by Lula and released in São Paulo on March 3, 2018, during the Conferência Cidadã (Citizen Conference), an event marking Guilherme Boulos's pre-candidacy for the presidency, with indigenous leader Sonia Guajajara as candidate for the vice-presidency.

210 Manuela d'Ávila (PCdoB, Rio Grande do Sul) is a state representative. She was chosen as her party's pre-candidate for the presidential elections on November 5, 2017. Lula was at the PCdoB convention and supported her candidacy. Between 2007 and 2015, d'Ávila served as a federal representative, and was Rio Grande do Sul's most-voted candidate in the 2006 elections, with 271,000 votes.

211 Canhoteiro was a skilful left-winger in the 1950s and 1960s, considered by many to be the best in Brazilian soccer history. He played for São Paulo Futebol Clube from 1954 to 1963. He was regularly called up to the Brazilian national team, but was cut from the 1958 World Cup in Sweden for his bohemian lifestyle and a brutal fear of flying. Ferociously pursued by the opposing quarterbacks, his career was ruined after a meniscus operation. He became an employee of the Bank of the State of São Paulo, where he served coffee, always smiling. He died of a stroke on the eve of his forty-second birthday.

Roberto Rivellino, a sports commentator by the time this book was published, played in mid-left and left-wing positions from the mid-1960s to the late 1970s. He was an idol both at Corinthians (1965-1974) and Fluminense (1975-1978), and played for three years at Al-Hilal in Saudi Arabia (1979-1981).

He is considered the inventor of the "flip flap," a dribbling move used to fool a defensive player. He played in the 1970, 1974, and 1978 World Cups for the Brazilian National Team.

212 Rio de Janeiro State Senator Lindberg Farias is the leader of the PT in the Senate. He served as president of the Students' National Union (UNE) from 1992 to 1994. Journalist Breno Altman is a member of the PT. He is also the director of the Opera Mundi website.

213 Marina Silva was a city councillor, a state representative, and a senator for the state of Acre, representing the PT. She served as minister of the environment in the two Lula administrations, from 2003 to 2008, leaving the government and the party when she was not chosen as Lula's candidate for the election. After joining the Green Party, she ran in the 2010 presidential elections (finishing as the third runner-up, with 19 percent of the votes). In 2014, while affiliated to the PSB, she ran for vice president in the same list as Eduardo Campos, replacing him after the plane crash that took his life during the presidential campaign, on August 13, 2014. Once again, she was third runner-up, with 21 percent of the valid votes. In the second round, she endorsed Aécio Neves's candidacy (for the PSDB). In 2011 she founded the Rede Party. However, the group was not able to collect the 492,000 signatures needed for the party's political registration, which prevented her presidential candidacy in 2014. That same year, though, Rede was finally registered, and Marina Silva was the party's pre-candidate to the presidency (2018) at the time this book was published.

214 Transcribed by the *Brasil de Fato* newspaper and edited by Ivana Jinkings.

215 An inflatable doll that depicts Lula in a prison uniform.

216 Derogatory slang term for supporters of the PT.

217 Globo TV's widely-watched evening news program.

218 Translator's note: Literally, "macaw's perch," *pau de arara* refers to an irregular flatbed truck used in past decades to transport migrant workers fleeing periodic drought conditions in their home region. *Pau de arara* also became a derogatory slang term referring to these migrants.

219 See "Kidnapper testifies and claims political motivation," *Folha de S. Paulo*, January 6, 1990. Available at http://almanaque.folha.uol.com.br/cotidiano_06jan1990.htm. Accessed March 6, 2018.

220 After twenty-two years, José Bonifácio de Oliveira Sobrinho (a.k.a. Boni), then general director of Globo, admitted in an interview with Geneton Moraes Neto in 2011 that the station not only manipulated the edition in favor of Roberto

Marinho's favorite candidate, but also interfered in Collor's makeup and placed empty folders allegedly filled with "accusations against Lula."

221 With plenty of footage from the Caravanas da Cidadania and famous for organizing crowded rallies, Lula's campaign is surprised by a congressional bill (on the initiative of the PSDB and the PFL) that bars the exhibition of external footage in the electoral programs.

222 The first step, according to his proposal, would be the creation of an international fund to fight poverty, comprised by the G7 countries and fostered by big investors and owners of the world's greatest fortunes.

223 In a session of the impeachment commission, Senator Randolfe Rodrigues plays a prank on Janaína Paschoal and makes her acknowledge that, according to the argument used for the definition of crime, it would also be necessary to impeach Vice President Michel Temer. Shortly before, the lawyer had stated that there were no elements for Temer to be denounced.

224 Linguist and political analyst Noam Chomsky uses the term "soft coup" to denounce the coup in Brazil in an interview with Amy Goodman for *Democracy Now!* The cast and crew of the film *Aquarius*, directed by Kleber Mendonça Filho, denounce the ongoing coup in Brazil on the red carpet of the Cannes Film Festival.

CUT

Also from OR Books

A Narco History

HOW THE UNITED STATES AND MEXICO JOINTLY CREATED THE "MEXICAN DRUG WAR"

CARMEN BOULLOSA and MIKE WALLACE

Paperback ISBN 978-1-939293-79-4 • E-book 978-1-939293-80-0

"A well-written chronicle of interconnected events that blur borders and cultures—a splendid introduction to a tragic, complex and fascinating binational drama." —Sergio Aguayo, professor, El Colegio de México; visiting professor, Harvard University

How to Read Donald Duck

IMPERIALIST IDEOLOGY IN THE DISNEY COMIC

ARIEL DORFMAN and ARMAND MATTELART

Paperback ISBN 978-1-682191-53-8 • E-book 978-1-682191-54-5

"A handbook of de-colonization." —John Berger

"An unforgettable exposé of the true nature of Disney-style American 'innocence.'" —Tom Engelhardt, *TomDispatch*

A New Hope for Mexico

SAYING NO TO CORRUPTION, VIOLENCE, AND TRUMP'S WALL

ANDRÉS MANUEL LÓPEZ OBRADOR

Paperback ISBN 978-1-682191-55-2 • E-book 978-1-682191-56-9

"Andrés Manuel López Obrador pinpoints the key problems facing today's Mexico, especially corruption at the highest level of government, and sets out what must be done to put them right. This book is essential." —Greg Grandin, author of *Fordlandia*

OR Books
www.orbooks.com